In the Wake of Loss

In the Wake of Loss

SHORT STORIES

SHEILA JAMES

RONSDALE PRESS

IN THE WAKE OF LOSS
Copyright © 2009 Sheila James

RONSDALE PRESS
3350 West 21st Avenue
Vancouver, BC, Canada V6S 1G7
www.ronsdalepress.com

Typesetting: Julie Cochrane, in Granjon 11.5 pt on 15
Cover Design: Julie Cochrane
Cover Photo: Dinesh Shah
Paper: Ancient Forest Friendly "Silva" — FSC: 100% post-consumer waste, totally
    chlorine-free and acid-free

Ronsdale Press wishes to thank the following for their support of its publishing program: the Canada Council for the Arts, the Government of Canada through the Book Publishing Industry Development Program (BPIDP), and the Province of British Columbia through the Book Publishing Tax Credit program and the British Columbia Arts Council.

Library and Archives Canada Cataloguing in Publication

James, Sheila, 1962–
    In the wake of loss / Sheila James.

Short stories.
ISBN 978-1-55380-075-0

    I. Title.

PS8619.A655I6 2009   C813'.6   C2009-905469-8

At Ronsdale Press we are committed to protecting the environment. To this end we are working with Markets Initiative (www.oldgrowthfree.com) and printers to phase out our use of paper produced from ancient forests. This book is one step towards that goal.

Printed in Canada by Marquis Book Printing, Montreal

for my parents,

Kamala and Adolf James,

my favourite story tellers

ACKNOWLEDGEMENTS

Love and gratitude to my parents Drs. Adolf and Kamala James to whom this book is dedicated. You filled my childhood with compelling characters and entertaining narratives. You nurtured my own love for stories, inspiring the hard work to keep at it. Thank you for reading, commenting and continuing to correct me. And a very special thank you to my siblings: Anita, Kalpana and Michael for inspiration, example, criticism, encouragement and good humour during the writing of this book.

I deeply appreciate the support and friendship of Da Choong, Regini David, Phinder Dulai, Srividya Natarajan and Caroline White, who read drafts at various stages, offering unique perspectives and cultural contexts. My gratitude to Ashok Mathur, Larissa Lai and Ramabai Espinet for your writing and for your support of mine; to Neesha Dosanjh and Shyam Selvadurai for advice about publishers and agents; to Zara Suleman and Paul Seesequasis for feedback on selected stories; to Emmanuel Mongin for checking the science while on holiday; and to Dr. Pushpa Alexander for the help with the Malayalam.

Thank you also to Linda Svendsen, my teacher, and the short fiction class at UBC 1998–99, where some of these stories were first workshopped; to friends and colleagues in "Eat Write" with whom I share a great appetite for food and words; and to the courageous participants in *Stree* Theatre and Justice for Sri Lankan Women. I am especially grateful to Ronald B. Hatch for his exacting editorial advice and for taking a chance on these stories. Thanks to Matthew Bennett for criticism, questions and suggestions, and Erinna Gilkison, Veronica Hatch, Julie Cochrane and everyone at Ronsdale Press who contributed their talent and hard work in bringing this work to print.

My heart and thanks to Dinesh Shah for crying tears of joy and seeing me through the ups and downs of this creative process. And last but first, my little Nalin. Thank you for your patience while I did my work. I hope when you grow older, you will appreciate these stories as much as you do the tales I tell before you sleep.

CONTENTS

Ana's Mother

At first she denies it, making little jokes to herself about the impossibility of such a transgression. She even teases him, suggesting he get a substitute when he complains that their sex life is waning. But gradually it comes to her, not through the usual signs — the scent of perfume lingering on his clothes or a sudden improvement in his hygiene — but through small shifts in the world around her: a sideways look from a neighbour, the passenger seat in his car tilted back ever so slightly, the cat, restless to escape her grasp, as if any contact with her renders it vulnerable as well. She checks herself, sensing she is paranoid, creating drama where there is none. But these preoccupations unsettle her mind as listless afternoons bleed into motionless evenings, the coil glowing red on the stovetop before she can flick on the light and rescue herself from the dark. It is inevitable as the onset of winter: her husband is having an affair.

She combs her hair and waits for Ana to finish in the bathroom. Ana is her daughter. Hers. Amir has no right to lay claim to her child. It was her womb, her labour and her milk. Of course, Ana *has* to take after him. She has his droopy eyelids, his habit of jutting out his lower lip when concentrating and his stubborn insistence on doing things independently of her. Ana must get herself ready. Ana must pour the milk on her cereal. Ana must go to hockey practice. The only thing Ana cannot do is drive to the stadium. Mother or father, but mostly mother, must do this. Regardless, Ana must play hockey.

Ana tried on her first pair of skates less than two years ago, only months after they arrived in Canada. To the surprise of both her parents, she developed into a fast, able skater. The skating instructor gave her a choice to take up figure skating or hockey. Ana picked the latter, tried out and became the youngest girl on the junior hockey team. And she is dedicated. Hockey practice means up at 5 a.m. for a 6 a.m. practice. 5 a.m? Eight-year-olds shouldn't even know 5 a.m. exists. Five o'clock is a time for hard-working housewives to begin the day's chores, for devout worshippers to begin morning prayers or for cheating husbands to snore off the previous evening's excesses. Five o'clock is not for dimple-cheeked little girls.

She bangs her fist on the door. "Hurry up, Ana. You'll be late."

"It's not coming," Ana replies, through what sounds like clenched teeth.

"It will come after breakfast," her mother responds confidently.

She walks downstairs to pour milk on her daughter's cereal.

Ana's mother revs the engine. Time after time Amir has told her not to do this. It is fuel injected; it doesn't need to be pumped full of gas. She revs it again. The tail pipe exhales a grey cloud of smoke into the still, chilly morning air. Simultaneously she breathes out. She sees her breath as she sees her existence: formless, untenable, disappearing. Ana is buckled into the passenger seat beside her, her round face buried in the fake fur of her parka. Ana is a survivor, an animal captured and released into a hostile environment. She does not wait to find out whether or not the food supply is safe to consume; she gorges herself and forces her stomach to adapt, or else. Ana's mother is more reluctant. She resists this new country with every bone in her body.

The drive to the stadium takes approximately twenty minutes. They live on the edge of Bible Hill village, just outside the small town of Truro, otherwise known as the "Hub of Nova Scotia." It was Amir's idea to buy a place in the country. He promised her wide-open spaces to free her imagination. Her imagination needs no help. It works overtime, picturing her husband in every kind of compromising position. As for the country-side, its beauty suffocates her: long curvy roads cutting through expansive snow-laden fields and frosty evergreen forests. Picture perfect, it is too ex-quisite to touch. One can only observe it from a distance through window-panes and windshields. And the quiet is unnerving. She longs for the sharp calls of street vendors, the catch-in-the throat pollution caused by constant traffic, the confusion of lives shifting and colliding in the city.

He wouldn't be having an affair if we stayed in Pakistan, she thinks.

Ana lets out a sigh.

"Are you sleepy?" she asks, glancing over to her daughter.

"Coach made me goalie." And then after a pause, as if she just remem-bered. "I hate being goalie."

"Everyone has to play her part," she replies, always the sensible mother.

"Sue Knickles doesn't. Coach says she can play any position she wants. She's invaluable." Ana pauses. "Is that more valuable or less valuable?"

"Less," the protective mother says, confident of her right to change the meaning of the word to favour her child.

As she rounds a corner, the car skids to the left, as if it is punishing her for making up the truth. Steering the wheels back on course, she notes the seemingly clear road ahead. She remembers a radio announcement warn-ing drivers of black ice. Everything black in this country is bad: black ice, black lists, black markets. But in her eyes, white signals danger: white snow, white sugar, white women. Especially white women.

The stale smell of french fries and gravy greets them as they enter the stadium. The cool blue lights over the hockey rink mirror the outside sky. The effect is hard and artificial. Last week Ana excitedly explained how they could play hockey during the spring. "Fake ice, Mummy. They have fake ice."

She reminds Ana not to dilly-dally but to walk straight from hockey practice to school. Then she bends to give her daughter a kiss but instead gets a mouthful of fur. Ana has already turned her face towards her friend Mandy. She chatters while walking away, hockey bag and stick in tow.

By the time Ana's mother reaches home, the percolator is gurgling noisily. Amir is sitting at the table reading the newspaper. He looks good, morning or evening. Slim, clean-shaven with a crop of thick black wavy hair. She wants to approach him, kiss him fully on the mouth as people do in daytime television. But as usual, she walks past him to the counter and pours herself a cup of coffee. Stirring in sugar, she sorts through the mail, noticing that most of it is for Amir, except for a birthday party invitation for Ana and a nondescript envelope addressed to the occupants of the house. She opens it: a reminder about the new garbage removal schedule, starting today. She makes a mental note.

"I think we should trade in your car for a Jeep." Amir's first words of the day.

She looks up from the notice. "You do?"

"So you agree?" His eyes remain fixed on the newspaper.

"I prefer something small. Something I can park easily," she offers, knowing it will not be heard.

"It's good on the road. Lots of room for Ana's equipment."

He always brings up Ana's needs to get his way. Canada would be good for Ana, a country house would be good for Ana, a Jeep would be . . .

"So it's decided?" she asks.

"We'll take a look on Saturday."

Amir gets up and begins the ritual of adjusting his tie, straightening his jacket, searching for his keys. Usually she helps him with these things. Lately she has preferred to sip her coffee and imagine who else adjusts him.

By mid-morning, the dishes are washed, the carpets vacuumed and the counters polished. Ana's mother walks through each room like an inspector reviewing the performance of a subordinate. She wonders if this is how people develop multiple personality disorder — by playing several roles out of sheer loneliness. She opens the fridge door. It is stocked with supplies to last the whole winter. Grocery day was Monday. Laundry day is Wednesday. Today is Tuesday, her designated day off. She decides to call her husband.

"Hello?" Amir sounds rushed. "Oh, hi." Now surprised. "Is anything wrong?" A bit worried.

She apologizes for interrupting him and asks if he is free to meet her for lunch.

"No, it's okay to call. It's just that I have a back-to-back schedule." He speaks in his professional voice. "Lunch is booked. Board meeting." Then aside, in a softer voice, "Cynthia, take these in. I'll meet you there in a minute." He uses a helpful but authoritative tone. "Why don't you go into town, call a friend for lunch?"

Amir knows she does not have friends. Not close ones. Not casual lunch-meeting friends. Since they moved here, she has made valiant attempts to socialize but she is shy by nature. She is acquainted with a few of the mothers of Ana's friends, sisters from the Islamic association who post recipes on the web, and some Indian families in town, most of them older, working, raising large families. She and Amir entertain them for supper and visit them occasionally as a couple. But she feels uncomfortable at these gatherings. They always serve liquor, which Amir accepts. She disapproves of this change in him. He is indifferent to her observations.

He continues impatiently, "Look, I really have to go."

She hangs up. Her mind travels to the lunch meeting. Cynthia briefs Amir on the agenda, hands him a coffee (his secretary knows exactly how he takes it) and picks a piece of lint off his lapel.

Ana's mother needs to get out of the house to escape her own imagination. She climbs into her car. Having acquired her license only a year ago, she has grown dependent on this vehicle. It is her lifeline, her way out. She takes the long route into town, down the back roads passing farmhouses perched on snowy hills and bungalows nudging the shoulder, their driveways littered with broken equipment and rusty lawn furniture. Moving through town she considers taking the ramp onto the highway and doubling back to the safety of her home, but the welcoming sign of the Truro Mall beckons her. She decides to make a stop to pick up a few things.

After a few hours of browsing, the few things she picks up and carts to the checkout counter include winter gear for Ana (scarves, glittery purple gloves, a pair of snow pants), cotton bras and underwear (ones with high waists and elasticized fronts to keep her expanding tummy firm and tucked in). There are also extras for the house: a small turtle-shaped ashtray, though no one smokes, and a set of corn-shaped salt and pepper shakers and more hangers — these ones covered with a pink plastic coating. Silly luxuries. This is why they came to the West, for knick-knacks, underwear, winter gear. Of course Ana wouldn't be playing hockey if they had stayed in Pakistan.

Who knows, Ana could be the next Hayley Wickenheiser and bring home an Olympic gold medal for Canada, a new twist on the immigrant dream-come-true. The image of Ana racing around a rink brings a smile to her face as she places each item on the counter. The sales clerk rings them in one by one and Ana's mother watches the total increase incrementally on the cash register display. She counts the cash in her wallet.

"We do accept credit cards and debit," the sales clerk reminds her.

Reluctantly, she hands over the credit card. She still distrusts this plastic card, the ease with which one can buy things without ever having to part with the cash directly. Amir earns the money and pays the bills while she hands over her credit card and racks up their debts. Everything invisible, a clandestine operation. The sales clerk hands her the receipt to sign and glances at the card before returning it.

"Thank you Mrs. Am . . . ," she mutters, bravely trying to say the unfamiliar name.

"Never mind," Ana's mother says briskly, tired of correcting, yet again, the pronunciation of what she knows to be a simple and common name. "Have a good day," she offers, regretting her impatience.

Scattered flurries greet her as she pulls into the driveway. Remembering this morning's notice, she retrieves the garbage bag from the bin and leaves it on the edge of the road for pickup. The snow is soft on her face, ticklish, like Amir's long eyelashes dragging down her cheek. She sighs, remembering the last time they made love, several months ago. Amir encourages her to exercise, get fresh air, make friends with the weather. So she walks. First down the shoulder of the road and then through a cornfield, bearing traces of bent and broken stalks elbowing their way through layers of snow and ice. She counts the steps it takes from their home to their closest neighbour. She stops counting at 347. Wide-open spaces. She grew up in a tenement in Lahore, six families to a floor, at least seven people in a family, not counting servants and relatives who would live there for months at a time. The private business of one family would blend in with the goings-on of another. Harsh quarrels and joyous celebrations would be generously shared with neighbours, transmitted through paper-thin walls, curtained verandas, open-air windows. Here, one could forget humans existed. She turns around. Home is out of sight.

Face forward to the wind, she keeps walking. The snow leaves beads of moisture on her skin. She is withstanding the winter. It is a test of her endurance. Determined, she trudges up a hill, knee-deep in snow. Tombstones rise on the horizon, like white flags of surrender on a fallen and silent battle ridge. The Muslim cemetery. Ironically situated in Bible Hill, the cemetery has an arched gateway displaying its name, opening onto no more than thirty gravestones. She and Amir had driven by it before, and each time she noted how lonely it appeared, isolated out here in the wilderness. But Amir had assured her it was still in use. Established by Syrian Muslims in the 1940s, it is now operated by the Islamic Association of Nova Scotia.

"Really?" she had exclaimed, "We're large enough to have an association? Here?"

"We're all over the place, baby," Amir had teased her. "Shall we get a membership and reserve our plots?"

She laughed at the time, but the thought of dying amongst strangers, being buried in this cold land, was unbearable. Maybe that was why the cemetery was established in the first place, she ponders. To create a community for the dead. Or maybe it was established out of necessity. Had these new-world Muslims been kept out of other cemeteries, refused the rites of burial in Christian gravesites? She had read that this had been the experience of many black Nova Scotians some thirty years ago, discriminated in death, as they must have been in life. She shudders, pushing away the thought of what it must have been like for them. Here. Then.

Now on foot and curious to visit history, she feels compelled to explore. Her feet sink deeper and deeper into the unmarked snow. Somehow she feels like an intruder on this sacred ground. She fears being caught trespassing but there is no one around to witness her. There is a small white one-storey structure, which serves as a mosque, a place to conduct pre-burial rites. Ana's mother climbs the stairs, knocks and then tries the door. It is locked.

Visiting each gravestone, she recognizes familiar names — Khan, Hosain, Farid — but she is unacquainted with the families. The next gravestone is small. She bends to read the inscription. There is no name, no date. Old and faded, it simply reads "infant." Ana's mother is overwhelmed by a deep sadness and guilt for peering into someone else's grief. Ashamed, she straightens up and turns away. A passing truck slows down. The driver glances at her. She can't help wondering what he must think of her. What Allah thinks of her.

Picking up her pace, she steps on a patch of ice and slips, finding herself staring up at the white shroud descending upon her. One could spend hours here, just like this, cold, alone, embraced only by sky.

Suddenly she feels a sharp pain in her lower back. "Ana?" she says out loud.

Scrambling to her feet, her legs fall under her before she is able to regain her balance. The walk back is difficult. It starts raining or hailing, she is not sure. Her toes freeze. Her eyelashes turn icy. Her heart starts to race.

The house is quiet. All natural light fades as the sun drops behind the tree line. This idea of setting the clock forward is stupid; it makes the already unbearable days darken too quickly.

"Ana?" she calls out, turning on the light.

No television sounds. No parka thrown carelessly in the hallway. Ana would let herself in if she had arrived. She looks at her watch. The bus should have dropped her off fifteen minutes ago. Ana will be hungry. She starts supper. Another fifteen minutes pass. She chops onions and garlic, trying to distract herself from her growing uneasiness. Panic. She is prone to panic. Do not panic before adequate time goes by, she has been told. Fifteen, even thirty minutes is no cause for concern. Only when Ana is one hour late should she worry. Amir has told her this, some kind of reasonable argument to keep her emotions in check. His reassurances make her tense. She turns on the television to calm the spin of voices inside her. It must be the weather.

Ana does not arrive. Ana's mother checks her wristwatch several times against the oven clock, the cuckoo clock in the hall, the radio alarm in the bedroom. All indicate 4:55 p.m. She knows their bells are not ringing but she hears them, the shrill repetitive cuckoo, the buzz of the radio, the nervous ringing of the oven clock. "Wake up," they scream. She stirs the spaghetti sauce, Ana's favourite. She has been trying out western recipes after Ana complained, "we don't eat the same." She had expected the "we don't look the same" complaint, but that never came. Unable to accept that Ana prefers pasta and chicken wings to *biriyani* and *kebabs*, she resolves to cook western food only once a week. Amir could go either way. He completed his graduate studies here. His tastes widened; he acquired a Canadian accent. When he returned to Lahore for their marriage, he assured her she would love Nova Scotia. She would fit in, she would adapt, she would change, change, change. After several years of being happily married, she finally agreed to move to Canada to please him. Now she switches off the stove and slams the door as she exits. She will wait for Ana at the bus stop.

After watching the road, the trees, the sky, she returns to the house and makes a call. Her neighbour has a ten-year-old son who attends Ana's school and rides the same bus home. Of course, Donny, Bobby, Johnny, whatever his name was, would not be home either. She would not be the only worried mother.

"Hello, Mrs. Gallagher? Did your son arrive back from school? Oh, he didn't go? I'm sorry he has the flu. I hope he will recover soon. Ana is not home yet . . . No, I won't worry. That's right, I'm not used to this weather."

Two years and people still assumed she was not used to it. And they were right. Of course. She did not want to get used to it. She hung up the phone, still gripping the receiver. Tonight she will tell Amir she is unhappy. She wants to take Ana back.

It is well after five when she calls Amir. She has already called the school, Mandy's mother and others. An hour has passed. She has spent the time alternating between praying and cursing. Now she can panic. She can scream. "It's an emergency," she shouts at his secretary. He finally comes to the phone. When he says hello, she is in tears. After she puts the receiver down, she picks it up again and calls the police — against her husband's advice.

She is dressed in her coat and boots, ready to go when she hears Amir's car pull into the driveway. Cynthia is in the front seat. Suddenly she does not care anymore. Cynthia can eat her food, sleep in her bed and live in her house. She is prepared to make a deal with Cynthia and God. She will happily share or, better, trade her husband for a happy outcome. She wants her daughter.

Cynthia steps out of the car and follows Amir up the stairs to the front door.

"Any word?" Amir keeps the door ajar and shows Cynthia in, his hand on her back. Ana's mother resents Cynthia for distracting her husband, for keeping him away from his family, for turning him against his traditions. But her husband does not blame Cynthia; he blames her, and why not? It must be her fault for telling a lie, for going for a walk, for obsessing over his presumed affair.

"No. I spoke with her teacher. She left with the other children."

"Cynthia will wait here for Ana. I've given her a list of friends and neighbours to call, anyone who might . . ."

"Thank you," she says to Cynthia, suddenly obliged, grateful even. She secretly promises Cynthia that she will strip and bathe her husband, lay him naked on clean sheets and give him up for her pleasure. If only Ana would come home.

As if agreeing to these terms, Cynthia reassures her, "It's okay. I'll be right here when she arrives."

Cynthia seems so confident that Ana will arrive. Cynthia will embrace her child, help her out of her parka, feed her spaghetti.

"Maybe I should stay?"

"No." Amir responds too quickly. Maybe he wants her with him. "I've given Cynthia complete instructions on what to do. Let's go." Or maybe he does not trust her to speak with the police should they call. She would panic. A series of images races through her mind. An ambulance at a street crossing, notices for missing children posted on telephone poles, the marks of a stranger's hands upon her daughter's neck. She bites down on her lower lip and straps on her seatbelt.

Amir drives like a maniac: fast, sliding around curves, his high beams burning tracks into the road ahead. She now wishes for a Jeep. Something large and invincible, something that could trek through the bush and shine x-ray eyes into dark corners, exposing all possible predators. She looks at her watch. 6:30 p.m. Not yet officially evening. Eight-year-olds were known to be out after six. Her panic could be controlled, her imagination reined in.

Amir pulls over. He clutches the wheel. "What's that?" he gasps.

She steps out of the car. Through the open door she speaks loudly, over the wind. "A raccoon I think. No, a fox." She watches the animal scurry from the roadside into the woods then looks at her husband still clutching the wheel. "Let me drive."

Ana's mother drives steadily, watching the shoulder, her eyes scouring the countryside. They go to the school, park the car and then walk. They inquire about Ana at the gas station, the corner store; they ask pedestrians fighting the wind on their way to shelter. They search the playground, the baseball field, behind the dugouts, all the while calling her name. Ana is too short a name, she thinks. A nickname really. Neither bold nor complicated, it does not command attention. She should have named her Fatimah, Durga, Nefertiti.

When they get back to the car, Amir calls Cynthia on his cellphone.

"Cynthia, it's me." She notices his voice is shaky but intimate. "Well they say, 'no news is good news.' That's what they say, isn't it? No, I'm not sure if I believe it."

"Tell Cynthia to eat some spaghetti," she suggests before he hangs up. She knows this sounds stupid. Cynthia and Amir share something poetic. She can only think of food.

He looks at her, searching her face. She senses his shame. Looking down at her lap she says, "I'm grateful to her, that's all."

He turns his head away from her and presses it against the windowpane.

The road to the stadium is icy and deserted. Only a snow blower is spotted in front of them, heavy and ominous, creating a small clearing towards a possible discovery place for their daughter. She pictures a dusty road in Lahore, trees, traffic, people, life. She thinks about her parents, how far away they are. No family to turn to, she is forced to depend on her husband's secretary, his mistress, in their time of need.

Amir turns into the stadium parking lot. They pound on all the doors, hoping a janitor, the Zamboni driver or a dedicated skater might appear and tell them something. Something good. Of course the stadium is closed.

They walk around to the back. There is an outdoor rink. A practice spot, something the kids created by themselves, spraying water from a hose in below-zero weather. An old car park, it is now a clear sheet of ice. There is a net at one end, an abandoned stick in the middle. No one guards the net. No one plays centre. Amir runs across the ice, sliding, stumbling towards the stick.

"It's hers. It's Ana's stick." He waves it in the air.

Ana's mother moves towards him. All the kids on the team have sticks like these. Ana had pleaded with her to buy one. Mandy Davis has one. Sue Knickles has one.

She does not tell Amir this. They must keep faith. It could be Ana's stick. If he believes this, so should she. She runs to catch up with him, and he turns and holds her body against his. She feels the length of him. His quickened breath makes his already slim frame feel fragile. She senses his desperate need to believe in everything: their daughter, their choices, their future. As they embrace, each knows the other is praying, returning desperately to their neglected faith, appealing to Allah to deliver their daughter safely back to them.

There is no option of abandoning their search, so they patrol the surrounding roads for what seems like hours, before grace intervenes. A call from the police. Amir answers nervously, then exhales. Ana is safe.

When they arrive home, the first thing they see is a police car outside. Throwing open the doors, they rush in. From the hallway they can see two officers seated on the couch. In front of them on the coffee table is a pot of tea and two cups. Cynthia sits on the other side, waiting for the tea to steep. As they enter the room, there, in front of the television, is Ana.

As soon as she sees her parents, Ana runs to them, tearful and apologetic.

"Mummy, I'm sorry. I *had* to practise, coach said . . . and it got dark and started to snow and the stadium was closed. I couldn't get in to call so I started walking and then that man offered me a ride. I know you told me never to but . . ."

"Shh. *Beti*, it's all right. You're safe now." Both parents embrace Ana, but it is Amir who cries and fusses over his daughter.

"Thank you so much for your call, officer. You can't believe how relieved and grateful we are," Ana's mother exclaims, taking off her coat and gloves.

"Your little girl is very lucky. And it is a good thing you called us when you did, ma'am. A tip came in from a gas station. Someone saw a young girl in a car that was parked at the pump. She was banging her head on the side window, and luckily her actions seemed strange enough that he decided to call us. The caller described the girl as dark or foreign. The dispatcher taking the call remembered yours. He also remembered telling you not to worry, that your concerns were premature."

Ana's mother bends down and examines her daughter's head, "You are such a good girl, a smart girl. Are you hungry?"

"Famished," Ana shouts.

Ana's mother glances over to Cynthia.

"I tried to get her to . . . but she wouldn't eat until you got home. I helped myself. I hope you don't mind."

"Not at all. I am glad you did." She checks her watch. "Cynthia, you must want to get home."

Amir begins to offer, "Oh I forgot, I should drive — "

"Ana needs you," Ana's mother says firmly. "I'll call a cab."

"Thanks," Cynthia says. "But it's okay, I called one myself when the officers told me you were on your way."

Amir lifts Ana into his arms and carries her to the kitchen. "Let's go eat spaghetti."

The cab comes quickly, and after seeing Cynthia out, Ana's mother returns to the living room. Pouring black steaming tea into white mugs, she demands to know everything.

As the officers relay the details of the abduction, she listens attentively, writing down their names, the time she will be expected at the police station, the phone number of a counsellor to contact. When the officers finish their tea, they rise to leave. Ana and Amir's laughter is heard over the joyful and familiar sound of scraping plates and utensils.

"And you, officers? Have you eaten? Would you like some spaghetti?"

"Thanks Mrs . . ."

"Please, call me Ameena."

"Thanks Ameena, but we'll take a rain check. Maybe some evening when you're serving curry or something."

Ameena impulsively and awkwardly embraces the officers, these foreign men, and pulls away quickly before ushering them out into the blustery cold. Standing on the doorstep, she watches the police car drive away, its headlights lighting the dark stretch of the road, which has become so familiar to her. Stepping back into her house, she turns the key in the lock and goes to join her family in the kitchen.

Outside Paradise

The smells of pomfret, tuna and kingfish tickled her nostrils, light and fragrant, pungent and demanding. Nilika inhaled as she walked through the fish market. She squinted at the men who held their handkerchiefs to their noses, the women who breathed anxiously through their thin cotton *pallus* wrapped across their faces. For Nilika, the *chapula mundi* was the closest thing to the sea. These odours were life itself, survival.

The market was bustling with deliveries. Truckloads of fresh fish packed in ice and transported from the nearest port were pulled out of crates and thrown onto more ice, this time in full view of early morning buyers. People quickly gathered around each stall, thick as flies, but much more discerning. Restaurant owners, cooks and fastidious housewives all vied for the freshest catch of the day, demanding that the fish be laid open before their eyes, sliced expertly with the glistening slant of the knife, entrails dumped in a pail, attracting insects, rats, dogs. The once graceful then struggling creature was portioned up, efficiently wrapped in newspaper, hidden and carted off in the basket of the satisfied customer, as new buyers edged in.

Nilika prided herself on being able to distinguish the pongy odours of fish yanked up from the ocean to their airy deaths. The salty, smoky, dense and subtle smells all greeted her like old friends. She was familiar with many species of fish, how to scale and gut them, the herbs and spices in which to preserve them. Nilika was from a family of fisher folk. She had come to the city with her parents many years ago after hotel towers crowded out the small thatched huts of her community, after foreigners with skin as colourless as buffalo milk invaded the seaside where her family once fished. It had been a long time since she was near the ocean. But the market brought it all back. The only thing missing was the ocean itself, the constant chorus of waves, the mist on her skin, the feeling of renewal and the faraway gaze it evoked in her every morning. Now she could be satisfied only with the memory brought back by these familiar smells.

Nilika was on her way to Dr. Aparna's office for her *chakara soodi*. Insulin was the real name for it, but Nilika came to calling it the sugar shot because it had something to do with sugar in her body. She knew if she did not take it she could grow fat, go blind, her toes could fall off, and she could "slip into a coma and die." Dr. Aparna had shouted these last words to her on many occasions. So she went every weekday morning to the private clinic and on Sundays to Dr. Aparna's home. It was good to feel Dr. Aparna's cool able fingers dab the soft flesh on her belly with the alcohol-soaked cotton pad. Dr. Aparna always told her, "now don't forget to breathe," right before she inserted the metal needle into her skin. The doctor had spent precious time teaching Nilika to tighten her diaphragm and release her breath as the needle was inserted. When Dr. Aparna pulled out the needle, Nilika would hold a small piece of cotton to her skin, counting slowly for sixty seconds. Then she would readjust her sari, covering up the tender spot just pierced.

"Entha munchi soodi ichinaru," Nilika would say, praising Dr. Aparna for her good work.

Dr. Aparna would reply, "Tomorrow, you must try to give yourself the needle. All my other patients do. It is very easy."

But Nilika would shake her head.

"No, *Doctaru Amma*, I will hurt myself, I cannot do it. I am frightened." And Dr. Aparna would look at her disapprovingly while Nilika thanked her profusely for her kindness and care.

That was the routine. Every morning at 5 a.m. Nilika would set off on foot from her *basti* through the fish market, across the playing field, through the busy roundabout, walking nearly two miles for her insulin shot. Her seventy-year-old body was used to such physical activity. She had almost as much experience working as she did walking. At four years of age, she began carrying baskets of fish and then had to turn to washing the latrines of city dwellers. The long trek to Dr. Aparna's clinic was nothing in summer heat or monsoon rain, especially when at the end of the journey she would be greeted with the kindness of such an esteemed doctor, and be given a cool drink from the filtered water dispenser.

May was the hottest month. The sun pounded down mercilessly, skin dried and sagged on an old body like burlap bags, feet cracked and caked with dust. All of this was normal, to be expected. Nilika carried an extra pair of *chappals* in her bundle to wear inside Dr. Aparna's clinic. When she reached the courtyard of the clinic she washed her feet in the spill of water draining off the tin roof under which Dr. Aparna's car was parked. Siva, the caretaker, hosed it down during the summer heat wave. He tolerated Nilika as she stood under the awning. She would wash her hands and sometimes even turn her face towards the precious drops. Only the rich could cool their roofs, water their gardens, wash their cars. The poor were rationed to a bucket of water per household, so Nilika was grateful for whatever water was to be had. She had heard stories about Madras during a water shortage, where only salt water poured from the pumps. Train cars full of fresh water had to be sent from neighbouring states. At the station, a leak had sprung from the water tank. Hundreds of people who had crowded around waiting for the delivery pushed and shoved against each other to lick the hot metal container, desperate with thirst.

Dr. Aparna always saw Nilika at the back entrance of her private clinic, explaining that her paying patients might complain if they saw Nilika being called in before them. Nilika felt special. She did not want to stand with hundreds of others in the long queue at the government hospital. Here, she was expected and respected. Dr. Aparna would see her between patients, and even though the doctor spent less than two minutes with her, Nilika valued these visits more than anything in the world. She sat on the stoop outside the back door and waited for Dr. Aparna's helper to fetch her.

჻

Red was Vijay's favorite colour. He remembered it from his childhood, the crimson petals that burst like flames and crawled up the walls of the mansion where his mother cleaned house. He and his brother Varun used to climb the trees of neighbouring lots to sneak a peek at the garden sprawling out of control from the front steps of the house to the iron gate. The boys had begged their mother to put them to work in the house just to have a daily glimpse of the abundant and deliciously tempting oranges that hung from the trees, the berries that popped out of bushes or the tamarind pods which lay neglected on the dirt paths that cut through the foliage. But no, the mistress of the house did not want boys. She had made herself clear. "Any children entering my home will be girls. They are hard workers and are less likely to steal." So Vijay and Varun were destined to remain outside.

"Bougainvillea," Vijay said out loud, staring at his hands, "I never knew the name of the flower until I was much older."

His hands were still throbbing from having gripped the knife with such fierce intensity and purpose. Pramela, still hovering in the corner, darted her black eyes in his direction then quickly cast them down again. She was trembling and breathing rapidly, her sari had been scorched, her pock-marked face was smudged with soot.

"*Bavagaru*, what will you do?" she whispered, now gathering what was left of her sari around her.

Vijay looked at her and then to Varun, heavy and unmoving. He could have been drunk. He was always drunk, Vijay thought. The packages of arrack were still wedged in Varun's trouser pockets, the smell of liquor lifted like steam from his skin.

"We. What will *we* do?" Vijay answered bitterly.

Vijay stared at Pramela. He had never really liked her. She was nervous, finicky and, worse, totally subservient to Varun. Of Varun's three wives, he liked her the least. Maya, Varun's second wife, was his favourite, with her metallic laugh and gritty sense of humour. She was defiant even while dying; she had screamed curses at Varun and hurled a metal pot across the room. Vijay had pulled his bicycle up to the dark two-room enclave he shared with his mother, his brother and his brother's wife, in time to witness Maya's final moments.

"A kitchen fire," Varun had explained. Nothing he could do.

With Pramela, things were different, for Vijay was right there in the kitchen, sleeping on his mat when events unfurled without logic, like half-formed images of a dream. Now the morning light was urging him forward, forcing him to think about his next actions. Vijay was alone with Pramela. She was frightened, maybe more by him than his brother. Yes, of course she would be. Varun was now a lifeless corpse. Vijay held the knife and had the power to give or take. Control. He was in control.

჻

Dr. Aparna handed Nilika a package of disposable needles.

"You must use these. I'll show you again how first to remove air from the syringe, and then fill it with insulin. Then you try."

"Why not you give me five injections today, for every day you are not here?" Nilika looked mischievously at the young doctor. Sometimes she saw her as her own daughter, how her daughter might have been had she birthed one: confident, lovely, independent. But no, she thought again, no daughter of hers could be anything like this. Dr. Aparna was educated, well born. Nilika had taken care of Aparna when she was a child. She coddled her and watched her grow. Although Aparna had been an affectionate girl, Nilika knew that one day Aparna would outgrow her and see her for what she was, a simple servant.

"That's not how it works." Dr. Aparna pushed the air out of the needle before inserting it into the rubber cap of the bottle to let the liquid ooze up the length of it.

"Now try injecting it," she said calmly.

Nilika took the syringe reluctantly; a sour look pulled her face down. "Your nurse can give it to me."

"No, she's too busy as it is. Anyway, this nonsense has been going on too long. You're very capable of doing this. People younger than you give themselves their own needles."

A sharp edge crept into Dr. Aparna's voice. She roughly guided Nilika's sinewy hand towards her exposed midriff. Why was Dr. Aparna so impatient? Nilika had been the favourite servant of Aparna's grandmother. Nilika had told Aparna stories about her, bringing *Ammama* to life years after her death. And then later, when Aparna started defying her own mother, it was Nilika who opened the door for Aparna after she had snuck out at night to meet her friends; it was Nilika who accepted the blame when Aparna stole money out of her mother's purse. It was finally Nilika who was sent out of the house on account of lying on behalf of Aparna. Dr. Aparna owed Nilika some patience.

"Okay. Keep steady and — "

Nilika jabbed the needle into her belly with a great yelp.

"You forgot to breathe," Aparna exclaimed.

"You forgot to tell me, *Doctaru Amma*." Nilika looked up apologetically as Dr. Aparna guided the older woman's fingers to the next task at hand. She withdrew the needle and Aparna dabbed the sore with a cotton pad.

"See, it's much better when you do it," Nilika said.

"Yes, I know. But you must remember, you cannot come for a week. I am taking my cousin on a small trip. Go to the government hospital if you need help."

Nilika wrapped the box of needles, some cotton pads and the small bottle of insulin in her bundle and waited.

Dr. Aparna disappeared through a curtain into the next room. Nilika could feel the salty mix of anger and sadness well up inside her. Dr. Aparna had forgotten to offer her water. Nilika looked around the room. Without taking her eyes off the curtained entry, she moved quietly to the water dispenser and helped herself. She did not wash her glass but left it on the table, beside the plastic gloves and antiseptic.

_ೞ_

Vijay waited at the train station. The train to Mumbai was late. Always late when time was scarce. Pramela had not arrived. He had asked her to meet him here rather than risk the suspicion of the two of them being seen travelling together on the street. He had started to cycle part of the way then decided to leave his beloved bicycle behind the Kalpana Cinema, walking the final distance to the station. That way if the bike was found, the police would assume he was at the pictures. They would waste time directing the eye of a flashlight into the riveted faces of the audience, or they would evacuate the hall and demand that everyone present identification. That would take hours. He would gain some time. Now he regretted allowing Pramela to come along. She was usually a quiet woman, but all women talk, he surmised, even the quiet ones. How many people had she told and how many would she tell when they reached Mumbai? Fear darted through his body. Why did he have to meddle in his brother's affairs, the brother whom he loved and hated? He rubbed the tickets nervously between his thumb and forefinger. He had two, his own and one for Pramela. A waste of money, he thought.

Suddenly a wave of energy rippled through the crowd. Children craned their necks to see the train pull into track three. He turned around once more to look for Pramela. No. She had not come. He started to move.

"_Bavagaru?_"

Vijay turned back. He saw only the mass of passengers, strangers now pushing him to board the train. A woman, clad in a black *burka*, stood defiantly in his way. He looked past her.

"I am Pramela."

He recognized her voice first and then the black eyes, seemingly larger and more luminous. It was the only part of her visible.

"It is my friend Malika's. I used it as a disguise," Pramela explained.

Vijay paused to breathe, to take her in and gather his thoughts. He could tell she was smiling behind the veil.

"Did you tell anyone?"

"No one."

Humbled by his error in judgment, Vijay nodded in approval.

"Come. I'll take you to your seat." He wanted to hold her arm and lead her through the crowd but he was unsure how his actions would be read. Then he thought, no, he would simply be seen as her husband, as long as she did not throw off his arm. He cupped his palm below her elbow. It felt small and weightless. Her body was like a sail, he imagined, easily steered by him. When they reached the ladies' car, he released her and whispered, "When we arrive in Mumbai, wait for me near the ticket windows off the west platform. And don't talk to anyone. I'll come and find you."

"I will wait, *Bavagaru*."

"And please don't call me brother-in-law anymore. We must change our relationship. It is safer that way."

Pramela looked at him now, her eyes filled with tears. He wanted to explain more, but people were crowding around. Pramela put her hand on his forearm. It was a claim of sorts. The village Pramela came from had a custom, whereby a man's widow became the property of his brother. Maybe things will work out, he thought. Maybe he will learn to tolerate her, like her even.

"Just wait. I'll come," Vijay said gently.

He watched her climb into the train with mothers clutching small children, groups of college girls, with neat braids and pleated skirts, fashionable career women clutching handbags from the West. These were not their people. He and Pramela were expected to ride in the third-class compartments. They were expected to have no money. Before he had left, Vijay had emptied his safe box and the tin where his mother kept her savings, gathered from her allowance from Dr. Aparna. The amount would be enough to pay for shelter for himself and Pramela until he could get work fixing bicycles or, if lucky, hire one to run errands. His mother would recover and forgive him in time.

ॐ

By the time Nilika walked back to her *basti*, the sun was pounding down like that insistent *Amrikan* music the *auto wallahs* had taken to playing in their rickshaws. Boom, boom, not a moment's rest — an unrelenting bombardment of rhythmic heat.

Nilika stopped at the doorway and removed her *chapals* before entering. Mrudula, her neighbour, was passing by, carrying a bundle of washing on her head.

"Did your daughter-in-law burn the chapattis this morning? So much smoke. Watch her. I tell you, she is a useless girl," Mrudula advised.

Nilika waved away Mrudula's comments and entered her home. The first room was the sitting area where Varun and Pramela had installed a mattress. This luxury item, part of Pramela's dowry, was a sitting couch during the day and, at night, the couple's bed. A television set, part of the dowry collected through Varun's second wife, occupied the corner. When it was not in use, it served as a *mandir*; a small icon of the blue-skinned Krishna, surrounded by divas and incense sticks, rested on its flat surface. A wooden door led to the kitchen consisting of a portable gas stove, a cold box, a brass pot for water and various pans, bowls and utensils. Here Nilika and Vijay laid their mats every evening. For years Nilika had maintained her two rooms in an orderly and impeccable fashion. Cleaner than the houses she used to scrub and polish.

She had often complained to her neighbours, "You should see how these rich people live. Clothes everywhere, dust piling up on books, and the latrine! What is the use of a flush toilet if the master is urinating on either side of it?" She shook her head in disgust as one by one the other women brought forward the secret household habits of their employers. But that was time past. Now she had no work but the few chores in her own home. Her older son had a wife to keep house for him and the younger was clean and quiet. Vijay never left a trace of a footstep on the floor or his shadow lingering on a wall. She was lucky that way.

Nilika was looking forward to a cup of *chai* but was disturbed by the smell of smoke. What could Pramela have burned? The smoke seemed to hang between the walls, confined, desperate to push its way through the door. All the windows were shuttered.

In a louder than necessary voice, Nilika called through the closed kitchen door, "Hey, Varun, Pramela? What are you cooking in there?"

Nilika opened the shutters and allowed the sun to pour into the otherwise dark room. Children gathered right outside the window staring up at her, curious about her yelling. She rudely closed the shutters in their faces, returning the room to darkness. Then she entered the kitchen.

૪

The train from Hyderabad to Mumbai was an overnight journey with several stops on the way. The afternoon peeled back a series of images: lush paddy fields, dusty villages and squatting children by the tracks. Vijay sat near the window, allowing the wind to blow off his face, carrying with it the recent memory that was so vivid and stark in his mind.

When the train pulled into Salapur, Vijay decided to stretch his legs. This stop would be slightly longer than usual. Several more cars would be added to the train to accommodate the eager population on their way to the great coastal city. The platform was crowded with passengers, railway officials and workers balancing suitcases, trunks and cloth-sacks upon their heads. Vendors scurried about with their canteens of coffee and tea, singing a chorus of *"chai, chai, garam chai."*

Vijay found himself walking towards the ladies' compartment. When he reached the car, he looked through the windows trying to spot Pramela. He found a group of women, dressed in *burkas*. He stared at them trying to discern Pramela's eyes within the group. Finally, one of the larger and he presumed older women pulled the shutter down over the window. He turned away and bought two cups of *chai* from a vendor. Jumping into the car, he walked down the aisle. There were a few men in the compartment settling their women down for the journey; others, boys as old as sixteen, young men themselves, were still travelling under the guidance of some female family member.

He walked purposefully though not hurriedly, trying to locate a pair of black eyes.

"There he is."

Pramela's voice caught him. He turned. She was still wearing the *burka* but sitting beside an English or American woman, who wore a *kurta pyjama* with a *chunni* draped carelessly over her shoulder, exposing the curve of her breasts.

"Please meet my . . . ," Pramela started.

"*Baagunnaara?* Madam," said Vijay, breaking in tenderly. "I am P. Vijay. And your good name?"

The woman gave her name and greeted Vijay in flawless Telugu.

"Mrs. Lambert speaks Telugu. The very good kind. She studies in an American college in . . . ," Pramela began.

"Wisconsin. But I am Canadian. It is amazing the different reception I receive when I tell people that. Almost everywhere I travel, people prefer Canadians. And it is *Ms.* Lambert, Marion emphasized, and started to speak Telugu. "The university has a department where I've been studying Telugu for several years now. I'm here to do research."

"She gave me so many clothes. Look." Pramela held up some blouses and a pair of jeans. Suddenly she blushed and glanced away from Vijay. Then she folded the garments and placed them back in her cloth bag.

"I've brought you some *chai*. Excuse us," Vijay said addressing the foreigner. He guided Pramela out of the train.

"Try not to be too friendly with her," Vijay said passing her the tea.

"Do you think I'm stupid?" Pramela said, her eyes darting back and forth. She looked down at the tea then pulled the veil away and drank greedily. "I haven't even had water. I was so frightened and then that lady spoke to me. It was such a relief. After all, I didn't do anything. I — "

"Shh. You want to go back? I'll send you back." His voice was low but steady.

"Fine, I'll go back to my village. That's where I should have gone."

Vijay realized how little they knew each other. Pramela had been married to his brother for only three months before Varun began to torment her. She had come from a village where her family farmed a small plot of land. They were considered wealthy by his own family's standards. Her father offered a substantial dowry for Pramela because she was so dark and her face had been deeply scarred by acne or some childhood disease. But looking at her sharp eyes, Vijay began to see her charm, her strength. Of course, she too was suffering. She did not know him or what happened before she came to their cramped home. And she had no reason to trust him. He *had* killed her husband, after all, right in front of her eyes.

"Pramela, I need to tell you . . . there were other accidents. Varun's wives, before you, both died in kitchen fires. He collected nice dowries, then put an end to them. I am not lying. I wished it wasn't so. You can believe me or go back and tell everyone what I've done."

She looked down. The swarm of people now crowding around the passage pressed against her.

"I'd better return to my seat." She moved towards the train entrance.

"Wait." He spoke quietly and as gently as he could. "We can be married if you like, in Mumbai. It will be easier."

Pramela covered her face and lowered her eyes. "Yes. May I keep the clothes?"

He smiled as he realized she had addressed him intimately and respectfully. "Yes," he said, and ran back down the platform, jumping into his car as the train pulled out of the station.

ॐ

Heat and death were ghastly combinations. The corpse had begun to smell. Still, the police insisted it remain in the room while they took photographs, quarantined the area, and finished their questions.

Nilika weeping over her son, kept repeating, *"Aiyo, Aiyo. Naku yemi chasavu.* Rama, Rama, how have I deserved this? Murdered in cold blood in his home."

The policemen kept asking questions.

"Where is his wife?"

"I don't know."

"Where is his brother?"

"Working. He works hard, he delivers fish from the market every morning. He has a cold box. Varun is his only brother. Oh Rama."

Then they questioned the neighbours and led Nilika to the police station. She wanted to speak with Dr. Aparna, but she did not have her phone number, and even if she had, Dr. Aparna was not at home.

ॐ

Vijay had begun to relax, having passed half the journey in the heat of the day. The sun guided the train west, its large eye blinking in and out of view as they rounded the bend. It would soon sink into the horizon and only cool breezes would accompany the darkened sky awaiting him now. He sat between a *sadhu* dressed in ochre robes and a businessman who was irate at not being able to secure a seat in the first-class compartment. The businessman kept glancing at his gold watch, as much to keep an eye on it as to look at the time. The *sadhu* was still. His face and arms were smeared with ash. He stared ahead into the distance, or perhaps the future. The only movement he made was to snort phlegm into his handkerchief. Vijay took the time to plan his next step. By morning they would arrive at Victoria Station. First he would find Pramela, then they would take a bus deep into the city. Where, he was unsure. He had never been to Mumbai. But he had heard it was large enough to get lost in. Once there, no policeman could track you down, even if they had a pack of dogs on your trail. He and

Pramela would be well hidden. They would be safe.

Vijay focused on his plan as he hoisted himself onto the upper bunk. Soon the rhythmic rocking of the train and the click clack of the wheels on the rails lulled him to sleep. He enjoyed the cocoon-like feeling, being sandwiched between the low ceiling and the upper bunk in the small compartment. It was confining and comforting. He pulled off his vest and used it as a pillow. The cool air created by the train's motion in the still night flowed in through the window like mother's fingers lightly caressing his skin.

When the train pulled into a station at night, there was none of the insistent chatter heard in the daytime. Sellers did not clamber aboard peddling their wares, announcing in their singsong voices their particular commodity. Foreign travellers did not have to put up their guard against the horde of beggars congregating around them, their white skin attracting pathetic pleas for money. None of the daytime activity would ensue. Instead, there was the rustling of bags being gathered together, whispers and assurances, the irritable cry of a child being woken for the next stop. It was an almost clandestine leaving. Then, as secretly as people left, others boarded and filled the vacated spots. Vijay experienced these comings and goings through the haze of half sleep. Then the engine started up and sluggishly rolled out of the station resuming its pace and rhythmic motion, lulling new passengers into dreams of faraway places.

Set against this background, Vijay found himself pulled into a field full of blossoms. Varun was ahead of him running and calling for him to keep up. But he could not. He was dizzy from making circles faster and faster. The flowers were blurring around him, colours were exploding, the smell intoxicating. He was twirling, spinning, falling . . .

"Pune? Is this Pune?" The voice was hoarse and anxious. It yanked Vijay into consciousness.

"*Evaru?* Who . . ." He opened his eyes to see the businessman still prostrate in the lower bunk across from his, staring wide-eyed, red-eyed at a man in khaki.

"What stop is this?"

"Calm down, sir." It was a policeman speaking. "The train hasn't stopped. This is a routine check. I want to see your identification and your train ticket." The businessman, groggy and confused, sat up, cursed quietly and tried to fidget with the lock on his briefcase chained to his own wrist, his gold watch glistening amongst a nest of wiry black hairs.

Panic rose within Vijay like smoke. He would be reported missing in Hyderabad by now. Maybe there was a warrant out for his arrest. But how could they be so fast? At any rate he could not stay to find out who or what they were searching for. He wished he had slept with his head near the aisle. Then he could have checked for policemen on the train ducking in and out of compartments asking for identification and tickets. He knew he had to get out.

The businessman was now cursing loudly as the policeman crouched over him, trying to help unlock the sleek leather case. Vijay, slender and graceful as a cat, slipped into the aisle and headed towards the door.

"*Hallo*, you, where are you going?"

Vijay ran down the aisle and pushed into the latrine. Inside, as he stood against the door, he could hear voices, a series of footsteps. He was not sure how many were heading towards him. Someone had vomited a yellowish liquid just inside the doorway, inches away from his feet. He swallowed and wiped the sweat from his upper lip. The stench and the sight of it evoked a similar response in him. He bent over the hole to see the blurred images of railroad sleepers underneath, welcoming piss, shit and vomit from passengers travelling from all over India. He stood up feeling both dizzy and alert. The pounding on the door pushed him forward. Opening the window to its fullest extent, he stretched his arms outside and hoisted himself up. The rush of dark sky and a steep decline greeted him. Clutching the side railing, he clambered out and up. A policeman's head darted out of a window, looked forward and back before disappearing inside the train. The dark green scenery washed by, the wind was exhilarating. Vijay, on the roof of a moving train, lay down under the stars.

Pramela could not sleep. She felt suffocated in the *burka* and wished she could remove it. But she would not take the risk. Then she wondered about Vijay. Why didn't he wear a disguise? Hadn't he watched the films? Fugitives always don a mustache and dark sunglasses, turbans or hats. She propped herself up on her elbow and looked outside the window. The train had stopped. Pramela could make out the shadowy outline of huts in the distance, a moon-lit rice paddy field just beyond the tracks. Some women continued sleeping while others lethargically sat up in the lower bunks, passed around snacks and came up with theories about the delay.

"Maybe it was a cow on the tracks."

"Or the engine. I've heard of this. An engine can fail and we'll be sitting here until daybreak."

"Yes, until another train will come and smash into us," someone said sarcastically.

Then a little girl who had craned her neck out of the window shouted. "*Amma*, lights."

Her mother moved her aside and looked out. "There are sparks, about four cars away."

Passengers took turns leaning out of the windows to glimpse the back cars, which were standing this side of a tunnel. There was a commotion happening farther down the tracks, but no one could make it out. For two hours they sat, talked and wondered. No conductor had made his way through the compartment, and none of the ladies ventured outside their own car. Restlessness and boredom spread throughout. Marion Lambert awoke and tried to sit up but bumped her head on the bunk above her. She cursed and brought out a book from her purse. Opening it, she fastened a tiny light on the top of the page. She began to read as Pramela watched, curious about the gadget and the private world Marion seemed to have disappeared into. Pramela wanted to enter that world and learn to see what Marion saw on the white page peppered with letters. It seemed an eternity before Marion finally closed the book.

"Why doesn't anyone tell us what's happening?" Marion repeated to an unresponsive and exhausted car full of women.

The other passengers seemed used to such delays. Many had fallen asleep; others opened their tiffins and indulged in a midnight snack. Mothers comforted their peevish children, fanning their outstretched bodies with magazines, keeping the dense heat and rising stench of sweat at bay with an arm's wave.

Soon a group of college girls came into the compartment. They were excited about the news they had to report.

"It was a thief on the roof. He was burned going under the tunnel, electrocuted, that's what they are saying."

"Serves him right. A thief!"

"How do you know he was a thief? It could have been some poor fellow who couldn't pay the fare."

"Serves him right. Why should he get a free ride?"

"Nobody deserves such a fate for not paying a fare."

Pramela was dying to rip the *burka* from her body. But she remained still and listened partially to the conversations bubbling around her while her mind wandered to the place that would be her future. The next day she would be married. The next day she would start her new life.

Suddenly the train engine started up. Pramela lifted her veil. The wind blew cool kisses on her hot and expectant face.

৵

Nilika was spending the night with her neighbour Mrudula, leaving her home to Varun's ghost. She imagined it there, trapped and restless, evoking the presence of his two former wives. Perhaps they were hurling pots and chiding him or maybe he again was free to torment them. She berated herself for not raising Varun better, asking herself over and over, "What have I done?"

A metallic rapping at the door interrupted Nilika's early morning thoughts. Two policemen bullied their way into the small room. Mrudula's children awoke and sat up, turning their black saucer eyes towards the gruff voices now commanding the household.

"We have found your son. At least we think . . ."

"Vijay, my Vijay. Oh thank god, I knew he couldn't be far."

"He has been killed escaping the police."

Nilika stared at the policemen for a moment. Then she burst out, almost pleading, "What no! What are you talking? Vijay is a mouse, quiet and kind. Varun, he is the other way, angry and . . ." Nilika stopped herself.

"Your son, Madam, he was on a train to Mumbai. The police found him trying to escape; he was accidentally killed."

"Accident? He would not have an accident. He is careful, not once in his life did he fall down, even as a baby, quiet and careful. You have made a mistake, a terrible mistake."

"If you want the details you can come to the station."

"His body?"

"A charred kebab," the policeman responded. "He is practically cremated as it is. Not a good situation, but think of it this way, there are no expenses for a funeral pyre. The body is in Pune. You can go identify it if you want."

"Yes." She thought about the tin canister, her money for emergencies.

The policemen left, swinging their batons. They looked like a vaudeville act, a tap-dancing duo, a cane-carrying team that Nilika watched in *Amrikan* movies. It was a comedy perhaps. But she did not understand the humour.

Nilika returned to her home and went straight to the tin where she kept her savings bound in an elastic band. She had saved 4,000 rupees. She was hoping it would go towards Vijay's wedding, not to pay for his or Varun's funeral pyre. She opened the tin. Empty.

Nilika scrubbed the floors, the walls, every pot and stick of furniture in her house. She continuously mopped the spot where Varun had been slain. The blood had been washed away yesterday. Still, she ground ash into all surfaces, emptied the last pail of her rationed water and released pools onto the cement floors only to sop it up with rags and cloths and finally the shirts of her sons. Still it was not enough. She opened the cardboard box where Pramela's few possessions were stored, and dumped her bright red wedding sari on the floor. For the first time she asked herself, "Where is she? Did she murder my son, then lure the other off on the train?" But even Nilika could not convince herself of this story. Nilika tore the sari and scattered the rags like the petals of wild roses all over the floor.

༄

The sun baked the platform. Passengers were swept through the station as if by a wave of the sea. Pramela clutched Marion's hand and negotiated her way off the train through the oncoming crowd of passengers waiting to board. It was at least twenty minutes before Marion and Pramela found their way to the ticket windows. Marion hoisted a large knapsack on her back and strapped its belt around her waist. She looked taller and bigger and whiter now, against the backdrop of the smaller, thinner, browner faces crowding Victoria Station.

"Are you sure you don't want me to wait with you?" Marion asked Pramela.

"No. My husband will come." Pramela liked calling Vijay her husband.

Marion glanced at her watch, so did Pramela. She wondered what so many saw in that circle of glass. Marion looked towards the direction of the train. The platform was crowded.

"You know, they say the entire population of Australia passes through Victoria Station everyday," Marion said.

"What is Australya?" Pramela asked.

"A continent," Marion replied. Noticing the blank look on Pramela's face, she continued, "A country, an island."

There was so much Pramela did not understand. She bid farewell to Marion and watched her walk away, tall, odd, but knowing, into a vast sea of people. Pramela's eyes searched for the familiar figure of Vijay. She repeated the new word over and over, like a mantra. Australya. She wanted to remember this special thing she would ask her new husband.

༄

In the late afternoon, the fish market was the complete opposite of what it was at dawn. Stalls were closed. The bustle of activity disappeared leaving only the stench of old fish and rotting garbage. The only people on the road were those whose misfortune it was to live near the fish market making their way home. And of course those who lived in it, lying in the make-do shelter of old boxes and abandoned crates. Today, she saw the fish market differently, realizing how far it was from any trace of the ocean. Empty now.

When Nilika reached Dr. Aparna's clinic, she jiggled the gate and summoned the caretaker towards her. At first Siva shooed her off, but her persistent banging brought him near. "What do you want?"

"Open the gate."

"No one is here. Doctor is away and the clinic is closed."

"I know." Still she remained standing, clutching the bars of the iron gate. Then after a pause. "I want to sit and rest."

Siva opened the gate and Nilika followed him into the yard of the clinic. It was peaceful and cool. The sun was spreading red and gold tentacles of light on the roof, but there were enough trees in the courtyard to create a corridor of shade between the clinic and gate. There were no patients moving in or out the door, only old Siva pouring pails of water on the thirsty flowers lining the interior walls of the yard. He continued his chores as Nilika slowly made her way to the back entrance of the clinic.

She sat on the stoop and opened her pouch tied to the waist of her petticoat, retrieving a package of needles and the insulin bottle that Dr. Aparna had given her. She studied the needle and tried to remember Dr. Aparna's instructions. Then she inserted the needle into the insulin bottle and pulled the plastic top up, allowing the liquid to climb the length of the syringe. It was lovely, foreign, a delicate thing. How could she possibly be afraid of this? Hadn't she outlived both her sons? What was left to be feared?

Nilika sighed and brought the needle close to her skin. Dr. Aparna had told her to take it once every morning. But what difference did it make? Morning or evening, time was time. Something she had to spare, plentiful as the air or the ocean, extending far beyond her.

In the Wake of Loss

Two weeks after Liam's death, I awake to the sound of traffic building up on the street below my window. This surprises me, given my sister Suraya has had to rouse me from sleep and urge me out of bed. The noise does not bother me but simply serves as a reminder of the moving and engaging world outside. Inside, the air feels dense. Static. Dust, dead skin, millions of invisible molecules surround me. Suffocating me. Yet I need it. All of it. Air.

I miss Liam. Every night I pull the covers over my head and in the morning find them tangled at my feet, my skin prickled with goosebumps. I pull the covers back up over my head, block out the light and try to sleep again. But it doesn't come. Instead, a series of images slips between my conscious thoughts.

I see his feet. A brown mole raised on the right foot. Close to the big toe.

Just that. Then there's a flash of his shoulders, broad but not bulky, with a sprinkle of tan freckles on each side. I laughed when I first saw this surprising display of colour. It contrasted his smooth face, spotless and white. There's the image of his childlike smile, the sudden dimples on his cheeks, the tilt of his head as he rests it on his hand, whenever he's taken aback by something that I've said. I try to recall the sound of his voice.

I breathe. Years of voice training have taught me to breathe properly. Deep slow breaths drawn from deep in the lungs to sing through the phrase and allow the notes to spin. It's been a long time since I've dared to release the sound of my own voice. I peek above the covers.

The day arrives, pulls into the station, right on time. Grey cloudy skies with short clearings of sun signal more of the same. After years of living in England, I am still unused to the gloomy overcast skies. In one swift movement, I throw off the covers and swing my legs to the side of the bed, placing my feet on the cold floor. There is a square of sunlight on the wood. I step into it and for a moment feel warmth. It disappears.

My first class is a clarinet tutorial. It is a special day for the students. They will demonstrate their ability to play on a size-two reed. It's the first step of a maturing clarinetist and the kids have been practising an étude, using the new reed, for weeks now.

I can hear Suraya downstairs making breakfast. She actually whistles while she works. Except for her coffee-coloured complexion she is a real-life Snow White. A living example of what we all should be: caring, helpful, hardworking. I am her older sister but it is she who takes care of me. She arrived days after Liam died. Now she whistles an aria from *La Traviata*, articulating sixteenth note runs and flourishes with perfect pitch. I want to ask her to stop but will not.

The clock strikes seven. I wonder if Suraya will offer to iron my blouse. I've been taking advantage of her kindness. I allow her to prepare breakfast, run errands and make up excuses for why I am unavailable to speak with friends and colleagues. In turn, she allows me to be. She is the only person who believes I deserve to grieve. After all, I shoved him out of my life. We had a five-year relationship. The past year was spent negotiating between a friendly peace and a permanent separation. This was the stage we were at. Still entangled but not together. I haul myself up and go to the bathroom. My reflection stares back at me from the full-length mirror. My light brown skin appears pale, revealing a network of blue veins just below the surface. I examine my pubic hair. I tug at a grey strand jutting out of the black, curly bush. Yanking it out, I look for others. I want it to hurt, but it doesn't. The grey is gone but the triangle is still thick. I could bald myself one hair at a time, a preoccupation that would fill weeks, ending with a patch of virgin territory on an aged map. I turn my eyes to my eyes. The circles under them are dark, the lines deeper. I am forty-two years old and remind myself that these changes are natural.

The tub is green with verdigris. It has built up over the weeks. Suraya pushes me to let her clean up. I resist. The tub is a marker reminding me how far things have gone. Maybe my noticing it is a sign of how far I've come.

I let the water run. As the bath fills, I look outside and into the neighbour's flat. They have new windows, large, modern ones, which extend to the floor. I have a good view of their living room. In the corner is a squishy beanbag chair, the kind people sit in and can't get out of. They are never home, the Gordons. They have a life somewhere beyond here. The chair sits patiently, waiting to envelop someone. I think it's lonely.

The bath is too hot. I can't blame anyone for the temperature of my bath water.

"Rhea?" Suraya calls out in her sing-song voice.

Suraya learned about Liam's death from our mother, whom I told during our monthly telephone call.

"Liam's gone."

"Who?" she had asked.

"You know who he is," I barked.

Mother replied sarcastically, "Oh. The Irishman. The potential father of the possible children you could have had." Emphasis on the word *could*.

My mother is British, my father Pakistani, which makes Suraya and me mixed blood and mixed up. Suraya and I were both born here. We are bi-racial with dual citizenship. All round advantages. When we were kids, my parents decided to leave England for Canada to escape "the bloody IRA." My mother hates micks more than pakis.

I finally said, "He's dead, Mother."

She asked, "How did he die?"

I hung up.

I love putting my head under water. When I was a kid I couldn't stand it. I was terrified of not being able to surface. I became an expert at the dog paddle. Now, I have no fear. I puff out my cheeks, hold the air for ten seconds and release it under the water. I practise this more than I do the clarinet. I wonder if they know I'm a fraud? My students? That I only know a little more than they do. Many of them, within ten years, will outplay me. That's the problem with music education. You are made to be familiar with all instruments and it steals you away from mastering that which you love. Or maybe it is meant to test how deeply you love.

"Rhea, are you up?" Suraya calls out again.

She has such a sweet voice, the sweetest in the family. She should have been the musician. Instead, she has worked for twenty years as a dental hygienist. Always practical, she chose a career in medicine and kept music as a hobby, heeding my father's advice. I suppose it's not such a waste, her voice. It could be soothing for those patients dreading the dentist's drill. She could calm them by merely talking about the weather.

"Rhea?"

On the side of the tub is a vase full of bath beads. A present from Liam, a token of his affection during one of our more romantic periods. He loved buying me little gifts and I loved accepting them. I picture him in a small boutique trying to make up his mind. Surrounded by expensive perfume bottles, he chooses something inexpensive but intimate. I drop a bead into the bathwater, imagining it dissolving and seeping into my skin. Something from him being absorbed by me. I reach for another and lift it up to my eye contemplating its extraordinary colour, between cerulean and aquamarine. The bead admits light but cannot register the image imprinted within.

"Rhea, are you okay?" Suraya calls again.

I knock over the vase. It tumbles and makes a clanking noise loud enough to indicate to Suraya that I'm awake. Alive. The vase doesn't break. It merely scatters hundreds of eyes, staring accusingly up from the floor.

I don't know why I thought the noise would reassure Suraya. Instead it has had the opposite effect and she comes upstairs and pokes her head into the bathroom.

"Oh. Look what you've done," she says, picking up the bath beads and returning them to the vase. She places the vase up on a shelf, out of my reach. Then she sits on the side of the tub and combs my hair. Her gesture reminds me of another time in my life when I had been comforted by her. I was in my late twenties, post-abortion and already regretting my decision, not from any particular ethical perspective, but because I was certain I had squandered my only chance to have a child. Suraya had listened to me, reassuring me that I was young, and that although I was feeling lousy, my body would bounce back. Of course it did, and I vowed to take precautions to avoid another unexpected pregnancy. Suraya and I never spoke about the matter again.

Except for that one incident, we had never been particularly close. We were not confidantes but private individuals, even as children. In fact, normally I would have covered up as soon as she entered. Normally she would not have entered. But what the hell, what is there to hide? She is a few years my junior. We have the same genes, the same skin tone, almost the exact body except that hers has been stretched and re-shaped slightly after bearing two sons: Anand and Arron, two fine boys, just shy of being men. I realize that for the past twenty years we have occupied a completely different universe.

Suraya brings me a clean towel and runs downstairs to rescue the whistling kettle from the stove.

My armoire is an antique. It was the first of many collectibles to furnish "our" house. There are two newspaper clippings taped to the door. The report of the accident and the funeral notice. His. I move from one to the other, re-reading his name, his age, the date, the event, as if to confirm that they are referring to Liam, my Liam. It's the only proof I have. Still, I need more: a film clip, a line of witnesses, his first-hand account. I have stopped picturing the accident. Now I picture the funeral, his family dressed in black, gathered in a green field in County Galway. His mother whom I recognize from photographs, the sister I met during her occasional visit to London, the host of faceless relatives and friends who populated his hilarious anecdotes.

"I don't keep in touch with my old life," he once said when I asked to meet his family. I suspect there were other reasons for why he didn't invite me back home, but I didn't press the matter and he offered nothing. I assume they know little if anything about me, yet these strangers occupy my thoughts daily. Though virtually absent from his life, they are the ones who carried through the rites of his death and claimed whatever he achieved. I glance at a shelf of compact discs. His music. He dedicated the last one to me. I read the inscription. *For Rhea. Only you.* I did exist for him. I do exist.

I dress conservatively these days: white blouse, blue skirt, brown stockings, black shoes. Always moving to the next thing. One task at a time: brushing teeth, watering plants, staring out the window, turning on the television. That is how I kept from attending the funeral. My menial tasks filled unscheduled time in tandem with poignant moments of the service: the hymns, the prayers, the eulogy, the tears. The lowering of the casket must have been around 11 a.m. "Coronation Street."

I make my way downstairs to the kitchen table where Suraya sets a cup of tea in front of me. I sip it, cautious not to burn my tongue, yet welcoming its heat on my hands. Moving around my kitchen as if it were hers, she juggles two or three tasks at once. I watch her as a guest would: waiting for a signal to jump in and help. She doesn't signal. I decide it's better to stay out of the way.

"Listen Rhea, a friend of mine from Ottawa is visiting London, I may meet her for lunch or bring her around. I hope that's all right with you?"

Even nodding feels like an effort but I do my best. Suraya has been away from her husband Jack and her sons for almost two weeks now. She must miss them. She may even miss Ottawa. That is where Suraya was before coming here to be with me. That is where I was before coming here to be with Liam.

I met him while he was on tour with his band for three weeks in eastern Canada and the U.S. before returning to England. I was out with friends on a Saturday night. Along with a handful of fans and a couple of drunks, we sang and clapped right through the final set until last call. Liam plunked himself down on a bar stool, bought me a drink and asked me where I was from. I asked him to come home with me and find out. I was in search of a life partner. He fancied a one-night stand. I made him breakfast and he made my bed. I opted for an affair and he invited me to London.

It is my seventh year in London. Five years with Liam. Two years without. Of course, I could re-count the number of years and consider our many separations. Perhaps it is more like two years with Liam, five years without. Now, given the recent events, I will have to recheck my logic. Seven years of knowing Liam; the rest of my life, not knowing.

I kiss Suraya on the cheek as she hurries me out the door. The autumn air is damp and cool and I am greeted by the familiar sounds and sights of the neighbourhood. It used to be very working class, but now there are enough renovations of older buildings to make things attractive to new residents. Fashionable boutiques and ethnic restaurants threaten to push out the corner shops and the chippies. Still, the area has its share of council flats, although many of them were sold off to private buyers, compliments of Maggie Thatcher. She was before my time, before I arrived. But Liam remembered her well and could curse her better than anyone I know.

I walk five blocks to the train station, take the stairs two steps at a time and rest on the landing. My body feels heavier this morning. I pant as I climb the final stairs to the platform. I must be peri-menopausal. That's the word for it, irregular periods for the last six months. They always come when least expected, like a tease. "You thought we were gone. Fooled ya!" Maybe it's threatening me now. My uterus will start shedding itself during the singing of "God Save the Queen." I hope not. I look forward to the perks that come with menopause: no bloody mess, of course, no expense for tampons, no extra panty days, no cramps, no contraceptives. Oh yes, and no pregnancy.

I've had sex with three men since I met Liam. Two were the kind that I regretted (even in the middle of the act), whose faces I had forgotten as soon as they rolled over and fell asleep. Whose names were mumbled once and then lost amongst the ambient noise of the coffee shop or pub where we met. Men I took in order to spite Liam. Angry sex. I dated the third man during one of our breakups. He was too sweet. He wanted to marry me. He wanted to spoil me. He wanted to have children. But I kept on wanting Liam. His hands spread flat on my back. His sudden burst of energy.

"Shall I come over?" Liam wanted an answer from me. After a year's hiatus from our romantic life, a successful "trying to break up" period, he had telephoned. Now, I had to make the decision. "I'm coming over," he announced.

I wonder now if he knew he would be dying soon and planned to say goodbye. Or maybe he wanted one last fuck for old time's sake. At any rate, he arrived, sat across from me drinking tea, his lovely Irish lilt threading the morning into a net of stories. We talked for a while about the recent Booker Prize winner and argued about whether it was the Irish or the Indians who had succeeded in writing English better than the English. Then there were the silences filled with his "can't help smiling" smiles. The "I know I'm bad, but love me anyway," smiles. But he was never bad. Not in the way men are bad to women. No lies, no affairs, no temper. He simply didn't want home, spouse and children. He didn't want what I did. So I looked elsewhere. Then I'd return to him after a week, a month, a year. The situation got so ridiculous that friends stopped inquiring how "we" were. Our on-again, off-again relationship became an inside joke, predictable, even boring. After finishing tea, I lit into him about how he should take our separation seriously. Liam pulled out his tin whistle and started playing. I grabbed it from him and he grabbed me. As usual, we wound up in bed. I joked about my addiction to him, the heaviness of his body, his chin and nose burying into my neck. When we made love, I asked him to pull my hair when he came so that I could feel more. He did. And I did.

The train is crowded. I'm wedged between a large man and a group of uniformed schoolboys. There is nothing to hold on to. I could rest my elbows on the shoulders of one of the taller boys, or lay my cheek against the wool-covered chest of the man. I balance between these thoughts, holding the newspaper in front of me, folded into a square. I read nothing.

I teach music in a private school for boys, everything from strings to singing. My favourite class is the clarinet tutorial. An unpopular instrument in this particular school. I practically had to bribe the boys to take it up in order to fill the needed chairs in the orchestra. I have to groom one student to play the oboe. I foresee bigger bribes in the future. The boys are between the ages of eight and eleven. They dress in the school uniform. White shirts, blue blazers, grey shorts.

Philip calls them half pants. He loves that.

"They're not quite the full thing, are they?" he once said. "They're like half price or half past, not quite there."

Philip speaks with open vowels, an upper-class accent, full of potential and privilege. He is my best student, only nine years old. He will develop into a fine musician. Michael is another story. He is the oldest in the class and has been playing the longest. He can barely play a scale without squeaking several notes in succession. I have encouraged him to try other instruments but he is determined. He has a keen ear and a good sense of rhythm. I often let him conduct when I've had enough of his squeaks, and

I sense the other students are becoming annoyed. I have a soft spot for Michael. He is pale with big blue eyes. He is quiet. He is sad. I feel like hugging him and saying, *It doesn't matter if you can't play. We all forget our childhood lessons. We move on to other things; we even stop listening to music altogether. Don't worry, love*. But I don't. I'm his teacher. I am paid to encourage him.

I haven't said a word for the past week, but I need the money so I make the effort, arriving punctually to teach the first class. Taking a deep breath, I enter the classroom and write SORE THROAT in big white chalky letters. Ghost words spelling lies to little children. My not speaking has an interesting effect on the class. The students become quiet and whisper to each other, as if they have empathetic sore throats. I hold up the exercise book, write the page number on the board, and continue holding up sheets of music until we make it through the warm-up. The tapping of the baton on the music stand and the woody and sometimes strained sound of clarinets are all we hear.

Philip is not in class this morning. I make a note to remind myself to go to the office and inquire about his absence. Things will be a little off this morning. The boys are at that age when their cheeks are still rosy. This reassures me — of what, I am uncertain.

Michael walks in with his instrument case. He is late. The other children twist their heads and horns around to witness his entrance. Michael is tall and gawky. Moving through a stage between child and pre-teen, he inadvertently draws attention to himself. Finding the safety of his chair, he opens his case and fits the barrel onto the body of the horn. He remembers the details of putting things together. Other children slam the instrument together mouthpiece first, "because that's the top." I've told them numerous times that it is delicate, the most delicate part. It should be the last section to add, like the icing on a cake. My analogy doesn't work. They know the reed is the icing.

Michael gets out his reed. He licks it. All the boys love licking their reeds. They lap them up like lollipops. Tasteless but fun.

We cannot continue until Michael tunes his instrument. I buzz out a sound on my pitch pipe and write out the instructions on the blackboard. IMAGINE THE NOTE. WHAT IT LOOKS LIKE. HOW IT SOUNDS. THEN BREATHE IT IN AND RELEASE IT. I don't explain. It works for some, not others.

I stand in front of the class and raise my baton. Suddenly a violent up-surge through my body causes me to shake. I drop the baton to the floor and bring my hand to my mouth. I keep it there as I walk, not run, out of the room.

The walls of the cubicle are green. There is black mould around the base of the toilet. I kneel on the floor and gag but nothing comes out. My insides are empty. My body is rebelling. I want to go home. Leaving the cubicle, I stop to look at myself in the mirror, realizing for the first time that I am furious with Liam. Angry, enraged, bitter, sick. A stale taste lingers in my mouth. Water is not enough. I dispense some soap into my hands, bring it to my lips and swirl it around my teeth. I do not spit but swallow.

By the time I make my way back to class, my students have fled. They must have sensed it in me. Something not quite there. I walk to my desk and pack up my things. If I quit my job now, I could leave. Just leave. Go back to Canada. Admit failure. Leave Liam before he finally leaves me.

"Miss?" I turn around. Michael is standing at the door with his clarinet in hand. "I played a note with my new reed."

I want to shoo him off and tell him to go play with the other boys. Please don't ask anything of me, I want to say.

He enters and sits down, balancing the horn between his mouth and his right thumb. He blows. I hear nothing. He looks at me, expecting a re-sponse. I shake my head, no. Again. Nothing. He smiles apologetically. I sit down in the chair beside him and motion for him to try again, cupping my chin in my hand. I haven't the energy to urge him on. I don't demand much. I expect less. As I wait for Michael to produce a sound, my eyes wan-der to the row of empty chairs. I see Liam, seated in the back row, waiting for me, his arms folded, legs crossed. A smile passes across his face, then a wink. How can I remain angry with him? He is my audience, watching me as I had watched him so many times. He will leave after my perform-ance and I too will pack up my things and go. I bury my head in my hands. When I look up he is gone, leaving behind an earnest child adjusting his fingering, filling his lungs. Michael brings the horn to his mouth and, after another unsuccessful try, his large blue eyes well up with tears.

Gently I brush his bangs from his forehead and he tries to keep from sobbing, gulping air, shoulders trembling. I wonder why this means so much to him, what makes him persevere. I realize that I have not spent much time with this student, writing him off in favour of those with more recognizable talent. But who am I to question his desire, his love of this instrument. I look at his body, a bit slumped, and his embouchure, biting a bit too much of the mouthpiece.

"I did play a note," he coughs out through a phlegm-filled throat. He reaches for tissues in his pocket to blow his nose.

"Do you believe me?" he asks as if his word is in question.

"Yes," I say decidedly.

And as I watch this wide-eyed boy, struggling to recover and forget the moment, his face suddenly breaks into a smile.

"You can speak," he says surprised and elated.

I pause.

"Yes." My hand instinctively covers my mouth as if I had let a secret slip. I speak again, "It seems so."

"Excellent," he offers, pleased with himself as much as me. He waits for me to continue.

I look at the clock. Michael does not move.

"No one else really cares about it, Miss . . . ," Michael starts. "The sound. It's funny and wise, like a nerdy cousin or an old man." Then he looks straight at me. "I suck."

I can't help smiling.

"You have talent, but maybe not here," I respond, lightly touching the bell of his horn.

Michael does not appear uncomfortable or hurt. Just still, as if swallowing this thought, contemplating its sour flavour.

"And," I continue, "there are a lot of other worthy instruments: brass, percussion, strings."

He nods but I know what he is feeling. They would all be replacements, second choice. He does not give up easily.

"All right," I say. "If you played a note once, you can play it again."

I tell him to straighten up and place my fist gently on his diaphragm. I ask him to breathe. He takes a shallow breath from his chest.

"Now breathe again and fill up this part of your stomach as if you are pumping up a swimming tube. Your air should push my fist away from your body."

Michael listens and learns, repeating the breathing and then uses his own fist to check his diaphragm. Then I adjust his embouchure, reminding him that less is more in this case. He withdraws the mouthpiece incrementally from his mouth so that his upper teeth are sitting almost perfectly in the middle of it.

But the sound does not come. I encourage Michael to continue his breathing and practise a little longer on the smaller-sized reed.

"Thanks, Miss," he says laying the horn in his lap and he gives me an awkward embrace. I return it, happy to feel his soft arms around my shoulders and the faint smell of sweat in his hair. I am a teacher and he, a student, who is struggling to learn.

"Now, we have fifteen minutes before the next class. Shall we listen to some music?" I offer.

He nods and we decide on Bach's cello suites.

For the rest of the day, I speak sparingly and pace myself as if I am running a marathon. Breathing. The breathing helps. I go through the motions of recovery, faking it — but this is what we are taught, aren't we? To practise living, day by day, whether we feel like it or not. As I leave my classroom, I pick up a text message from Suraya. She knows better than to call. Suraya has suggested we meet for a drink and dinner at a nearby pub. We had gone out for dinner once during her visit. She talked, I listened. I expect her to be full of news from her friend.

"I was stood up," Suraya explains as we settle into a cozy corner table. "Actually to be fair, she cancelled at the last possible moment. But it's just as well. Jack called. It seems Anand was drinking last night, got into some brawl. He spent the night in jail. Jack says Anand is okay, though. But what a surprise; you know he's always been the quiet one compared to Arron."

We stare at the menus a bit before Suraya orders us some beer. Then she starts again.

"Jack reassures me that everything is okay, but I can tell . . . well from Anand actually, I spoke with him. His voice seemed so distant as if I were a stranger. And I guess it may feel that way to him, given whatever happened last night."

"You want to be with him."

Suraya stares at me.

"Oh this," I say of my voice. "I got it back with the help of a student."

As I speak I am intensely conscious of the process. This is how I talk. This is what I sound like.

"Of course you should be with him," I continue. "Fly home tomorrow, Suraya. I'll be fine."

She looks at me steadily.

"I am fine," I say.

"We'll see, tomorrow. I'll call Jack tonight. We'll see," Suraya says again.

As the barmaid sets our drinks on the table, Suraya studies my face, as if assessing how I am doing. Then she gives me a fond smile and raises her glass.

"To Liam," she says softly.

I cannot raise my glass. Not because I do not want to, but because I am trying desperately to hold myself together. In the time it takes her to say those two words, tears stream from my eyes, snot runs from my nose and strange gulping sounds emerge from my throat. It is overwhelming, disgusting, such a relief. I reach for a napkin and feel Suraya's hand on my shoulder, then caressing my arm. I am crying for the first time since Liam's death. I go to the loo and bring myself back to normal, or whatever close-to-normal looks like. When I sit back down, we clink our glasses together, silently this time before drinking.

After a few minutes, Suraya attempts conversation again.

"So, how did your student help bring back your voice?"

I tell her the story about Michael and his clarinet. His stubborn perseverance and the note that refused to sing. My initial reluctance to help and then my sudden belief in him. But what I do not tell her is the ending. Suraya's cellphone rings and she steps outside the pub for privacy and quiet. And it is just as well. The ending is ours. So I sit alone for a time and look out the window to a busy London street and the grey clouds struggling to part as I recall . . . *Michael, taking apart his horn, carefully resting its body in the case while tender and sorrowful tones of a cello fill the room. I bid farewell to Liam and dreams I once held dear, watching Michael conduct imaginary musicians, waving his hands elegantly in the air.*

On Ruby's Birthday

The sky blue Ventura sits gleaming on the black asphalt driveway. It looks like a prize on a platter. Rajan climbs the slight incline from the sidewalk and approaches the car. He stoops to find his reflection in the side mirror and sweeps his hair back. He is lucky with his looks and appears much younger than his age. The dark circles and shadows on his face will surface later in the day. He will ask Haran *Maama* for the use of his car. The last time he had asked his uncle to borrow it was at least a month ago. Rajan had washed and waxed the car before returning it and Haran had been impressed. Perhaps today Rajan will ask if he can keep it overnight.

Rajan looks towards the large white mansion surrounded by foliage. The sunlight reflecting off the walls and the warm breeze playing with the leaves carries with it a memory of Sri Lanka: Revathi hanging the clothes out to dry, fragrant frangipani petals falling from the trees into her beautiful, luxurious hair; his children, their laughter high-pitched and vibrant, playing and running, circling a palm tree then racing through the clothes on the line, chased by their mother's warnings to behave. Rajan strides up the stairs to the double doors and rings the doorbell.

"Rajan, hello. Come in." Haran's wife, Mona, escorts him into the suburban palace. Mona is sixty-four years old, tall and elegant. Rajan hands her a package of frozen baklava, adding, "It's from my workplace." Mona smiles at Rajan. He hears, "Are things any better for you, dear?"

The living room is three times the size of his apartment. There are seven bedrooms and two sitting rooms, four baths and three doors to exit and enter the house. One could move through the house and never know someone else is present. Rajan has waited six years for Haran to invite him to stay. When he first arrived in Canada, Haran had explained, "It's my wife's family home so I cannot extend an invitation unless it comes from her." That same day, Mona had whispered to him that she had convinced Haran to sponsor Rajan. Rajan had not bothered informing her that the United Church sponsored him; Haran simply paid for his ticket and met him at the airport. These particulars could be corrected later when Rajan was on his feet.

"It will take a year or two," Haran had explained, while driving from the airport. "Put your past behind you and seize this opportunity."

Rajan could only respond, "Thank you, thank you."

"Canada is good that way," Haran had continued. "You are young and educated, but even the uneducated class can move up in this country."

Haran had lived in Canada for forty years. He had escaped the bloody riots in Jaffna, the emergence of the LTTE, the Liberation Tigers of Tamil Eelam, and the full-on civil war. Haran still refers to Sri Lanka as Ceylon. Rajan does not correct him.

Haran sits in the easy chair and Rajan on the couch. It is large, made for a family, certainly not this couple. The vastness of the couch makes Rajan uneasy. There is a ghostly aura about it, wrapped in plastic, unsoiled. Rajan thinks of the pristine and distanced view of death in the west, so contrary to his experience in Sri Lanka where bodies burst open with bullets and lie for days rotting in the sun.

"How's the job, any new prospects?" Haran inquires.

"It's difficult to find prospects. I get up before the sun rises and return home after it sets. I work every other Saturday and — "

"Lunch breaks. That's the time to make phone calls, scan the dailies and create new contacts."

Rajan thinks about his lunch, the frozen spanakopita sliced and nuked in the crowded lunchroom he shares with other workers, the same product laid out in plastic containers, boxed and wrapped every day, six days a week. The lot of them had half an hour to eat, smoke, and stand in line for the toilet before the supervisor rounded them up for their next shift.

"That's a good idea," Rajan nods.

Mona enters carrying a tray with a pot of tea, cups and a plate of small white puff pastries. She places the tray on a glass coffee table in front of Rajan. He notices she does not serve the baklava. He tries the sweet. It has jelly inside which sticks to his gums and the roof of his mouth. His tongue works hard redirecting it down his throat. What he craves is a savoury breakfast, a morning in Jaffna. Rajan sips his tea, swirling it around in his mouth before swallowing. Mona smiles and stares, as if watching a child.

After the tea and small talk, Rajan hands Haran an envelope. Inside, three 50-dollar bills and two 20-dollar bills are organized according to value and laid out face up. It is the last payment Rajan owes for the plane ticket and other small loans.

"No rush for this," Haran mentions. Still, he takes the envelope from Rajan's hand and unlocks the top drawer of an antique desk in front of the window. Rajan watches the desk drawer carefully. It is a well, a black hole where things are deposited and transformed into something else. This is the drawer into which Rajan's only photographs of his family had disappeared. His children: Vinay, Suda, Nalani, Shyam, Sarath, Aya and Moni. Names he recites each night because he cannot remember the details of their faces. Only his wife Revathi's face is clear. Her eyes, her voice. In particular, he remembers her words.

"Your uncle lives in Canada. He can help us get away from here."

"Cowards leave. How will things change with everyone leaving? We'll be there thinking of our parents, our family, our friends," he had shouted back.

"Consider our children. How can they grow up here? Everyone who can is leaving."

But he had ignored her pleas and, instead, instructed her to take the children by bus to a government safe zone while he set off to join the Tigers in combat. Just before he parted, he embraced his children one by one, toy soldiers lining the veranda, straight backs and brave spirits. Then he said goodbye to Revathi. She laid her hand on his heart and whispered, "Don't go." She was calm, seemingly resigned, but she still made this final attempt to alter his course and their fate. His last recollection of Revathi's face was one of quiet desperation, and the last photograph of her, taken during happier times, lay buried under bills and stationery, in a dark desk drawer.

That first day Rajan arrived in Canada, Haran had studied the photographs and with a look of regret put them unceremoniously into the drawer. "The more you look at them, the more difficult it is to recover." He then handed Rajan a photograph of his home. "Something to aspire to," Haran had said, clutching Rajan briskly around the shoulder. Unable to ask for his own photos back, Rajan had left with the one of the house: large, square, concrete. Today, from the same drawer, Haran retrieves his car keys and drops them into Rajan's palm. Closing his fist around them, Rajan promises to return the car no later than eleven. Haran does not extend the offer until the morning. Rajan does not ask.

Never mind, Rajan thinks to himself, we will have plenty of time. He has already picked out his daughter's birthday present, a red silk *kurta pyjama* with mirrors patterned on the front. He imagines Ruby twirling around, light reflecting off the glass. A smile leaks out. Now with the remainder of his pay in his pocket he will venture down to Little India to buy his baby this gift.

"Well then." Haran moves to the door. Rajan follows.

"You need a wife to press your clothes," Mona says sliding her hands down the length of his back, smoothing down his jacket. Rajan turns to her, not quite understanding her meaning. He shakes her hand.

"No need to be so formal. We're family." She drapes her arms around his shoulders and gives him a hug, then breaks away from him and steps back. Rajan realizes he is sweating profusely. He puts his shoes on in the foyer and takes a moment to study himself in the large brass-framed mirror. The back of his jacket is badly wrinkled and the dark lines around his eyes have emerged much earlier than usual. He steps out of the house to catch a glimpse of a trampled garden and seven small shirts hanging from the clothesline, twitching and trembling in the warm breeze. The sky turns overcast above him.

ᴔ

Ruby crawls into the cardboard house her father made for her. The edge of the cardboard scrapes against her skin. *Kkkeerr*. It is not a bad feeling . . . not a serious scratch which starts raw and red then hardens into black itchy scabs. No. It is more like the cool sensation of Daddy's nails sliding down her back. Ducking her head into the doorway, she angles her shoulders so that they fit. Then she pulls her long legs under her, one at a time.

This is her place. Ruby looks through the cut-out cardboard window at Mummy's place: the heavy blue drapes guarding the living room against sun, the dust circling in a shaft of light fighting its way through the small tear in the curtain, the green vinyl couch, littered with magazines and an ashtray full with the shells of pistachio nuts. Mummy's place is dirty, she thinks. Ruby's place is clean.

Ruby turns her attention to the right side of her house. The brown wall in front of her is a shade darker than her skin, many shades lighter than Daddy's. Daddy's hands are very brown. He has black wiry hairs that jump out of the spaces on his fingers on either side of the knuckles. He can cut really fast . . . through the cardboard *kerrrrkkkk* . . . into her house. He promised her a window that faces the kitchen. He promised he would finish it on her birthday. Then she will watch Mummy at the sink, elbows deep in the water, washing the dishes, pulling at the plug . . . *gurgle gurgle*.

Mummy tugs at Ruby's ankles. "Come out of there."

Ruby resists, clinging to the slippery cardboard floor. Nothing to grasp. Mummy wins.

"What are you doing? We have to get ready for your birthday." Mummy's hands are rough. They are dishwater hands. Only her nails are nice. Mummy has long fingernails painted red that scratch red lines on Daddy's back. Ruby saw them. Ruby wants a big house so she can hide from Mummy. One with an upstairs and downstairs and seven bedrooms just like Daddy's.

Mummy strips Ruby in the living room, yanking her pyjama bottoms down and making her step into her undies.

"Soon you'll be too big for me to do this." Ruby tries to balance on one foot by holding Mummy's bun, a thick plait coiled like a snake on her head. Mummy slaps Ruby's hands away playfully. "You'll mess my hair."

Mummy fits a dress over Ruby's shoulders. It is tight. "One arm at a time," Mummy demands. Ruby is outgrowing her dress, the waistband fits too snuggly around her rib cage, her legs look long and spidery under the short flounce of the skirt.

"Daddy's buying you something new for your birthday."

"Daddy's making me a kitchen window."

"Daddy's treating us to supper. Let's go out and get a bottle of wine. We can really celebrate." Mummy gives Ruby a big hug. "You're five years old today."

Ruby grabs her yellow raincoat and drags her stringed mittens along the floor. Mummy grabs Ruby's wrist and drags her through the door, *fraaapppp* . . . it slams, trapping the dust, the shells and a stack of sticky dishes inside.

༄

Grey clouds do not get Selvi down. Birthdays are a time for resolutions, change and good luck. Selvi can sense Ruby's excitement through the damp mittened hand held tight in her own palm. Excited about gifts, excited about seeing her father. It has been three weeks since Rajan's last visit, with many excuses in between. But Selvi has forgiven him. Everything today will be sugar-coated with the anticipation of his coming through the door, lifting Ruby in his arms and then turning to her. He will hold her in his gaze before touching her hair, then her cheek.

"Are you hungry, baby?" Selvi turns to her daughter.

"I want a *dosa*. Nooo . . . two." Ruby lags behind. She has long legs for her age, all knobby knees and turned-in ankles. She walks unsure of her direction, twisting and turning her head, looking for something she has missed. Usually this irritates Selvi. Today it is endearing.

"You can have anything you want." Selvi grips Ruby's hand tighter. A love clasp, a stay-don't-run-away clasp.

"Are *you* hungry, baby?" Ruby plays her favourite role.

"I want five *dosas*, Mama," Selvi responds on cue.

"Baby." Mama voice.

"Mama." Baby voice.

"Baby." Giggles.

"Mama." Joy.

Selvi scoops Ruby up before pushing against the glass door to enter the Arani Café.

"Put me down, baby. You're tooooo small." Ruby is not finished with the game. Once inside the restaurant, Selvi lets Ruby slide down the length of her body to the floor.

"*Aiyo*, the rain. My hair is all ruined." Selvi feigns dismay.

Sudarshan approaches them. "Hello, beautiful. What are you doing here on your day off?"

Selvi whispers, "Someone's birthday," and points to Ruby who plops to the ground, sitting cross-legged in the restaurant entrance. She plays with her stringed mittens, twirling them like rotor blades lifting into the air.

Sudarshan acknowledges the conspiracy. "Honoured guests should not sit on the floor. Come with me, I have a special place for you, madam." He speaks directly to Ruby while guiding them both to a table by the window. Winking at Selvi, he pulls out the chairs for them. First the baby, then the mama.

"Now, order anything you want. It is my pleasure and my treat."

Sudarshan owns the restaurant, which offers a mixture of South Indian and Sri Lankan food. He hired Selvi as a waitress seven years ago and Arani became her home away from home. When she left her parents soon after high school, the restaurant became a surrogate mother, feeding her all her favourite Sri Lankan dishes. Sudarshan became her father figure. He encouraged her to learn more about her culture, forced her to speak her long-neglected mother tongue. Things her parents wanted her to do. Things she could never do for them.

With Sudarshan's gentle nudging, Selvi inched herself back to her roots. She found herself spending evenings browsing the stacks at the Metropolitan Library in search of clues as to what was happening in the land of her birth. Sri Lanka, that teardrop island flung off the sharp nose of India that continued to eject her relatives like ping-pong balls across the ocean, through the Canadian immigration maze, landing noisy and needy in her parents' two-bedroom apartment. She read about the Sinhalese government that refused to recognize the rights of Tamil civilians, meeting their passive resistance with violence and contempt. She read about hopeful petitions, peaceful demonstrations, frustration and riots. She read and read until she found it. Something she had unwittingly been searching for. So shocking in its simplicity, so beautiful and barbaric that she had to look away from the page, close the book, open it and read it. Again and again.

1981, the burning of the Jaffna Library, the treasure chest of ancient history and contemporary Tamil thought. It was such a passive target, full of broken-spined novels and palm-leaf manuscripts, armed only with the certainty of numbers and the economy of poetry. Indefensible against its ignorant and bloodthirsty assailants, it shot up in flames, deliberately torched by Sinhalese police. Then it disappeared — black smoke into a black future. It was an event that foreshadowed horrendous violence: pogroms led by

Sinhalese government thugs, self-righteous and entitled; the birth of Tamil militants, sprouting like weeds through cracks in the pavement, spreading first their ideology then their brutality like pestilence. It triggered a long drawn-out civil war, a war that still continued and therefore could not be neatly placed in the annals of history. A war that had to be pieced together by rare newspaper articles, testimonials and childhood memories of over-heard adult conversations. A war which, when studied from afar, took on the plot of a Shakespearian tragedy unfolding in an ancient language, investing each protagonist with immeasurable strength and inconsolable suffering. It was in the depth of this research and discovery that Selvi looked up and fell in love with Rajan Shantaram: the slight upward slant of his deep and piercing eyes, his rich dark complexion, the muscles of his arms clearly defined under his shirt. He had sat down across from her at a long study table. Although she noticed him immediately, he seemed oblivious to her existence, transfixed instead by the articles spread out in front of her, reading their titles upside down. Finally, she made her move, knowing full well the answer to her question. "Are you Tamil?"

Ruby digs into her *dosa* with two hands. *Sambar* and coconut chutney fringe her lower lip and chin and splatter the tabletop. Ordinarily, Selvi would have corrected Ruby's eating habits, directing her to keep her left hand off the table and roughly wiping her face clean. But today is today.

Although the café is filling up quickly with the Saturday mid-morning crowd, Sudarshan calmly pulls up a chair beside Selvi. She notices his paunch, sagging sloppily over the waistband of his trousers. He has aged over the seven years she has known him, but in a nice way. His features have a slight effeminate softness about them and his balding head is bold and shiny, like a trophy boasting hard work and tenacity. Unattractive features in other men, they suit him. They are comforting and forgiving.

"I think I met your lover-man last night," Sudarshan says jovially.

"Rajan? Rajan Shantaram?" Selvi's voice rises in pitch.

"We supplied some food for the Tamil Justice and Liberation Group. Some special fundraising event."

"What are you doing getting involved with politics?" Selvi asks, attempting to cut Ruby's *dosa* neatly into pieces.

"Spying on you. Does he belong to that group?"

"Of course. I told you he's practically the founder." Selvi's eyes narrow as she quotes Rajan. "Our cause is to fight the grave injustice, degradation and violence against the Tamil minority. Freedom for our people can only be achieved through a separate and independent Tamil Eelam." Then she lifts her head and waves her hand in front of her face as if clearing away cobwebs. "He once told me that if I served him, I served Sri Lanka."

"He told you that?" Sudarshan inquires.

Selvi flashes her smile at Sudarshan. "I told him he was dreaming."

Sudarshan laughs and after a moment he releases a sigh. "Yes," he mutters.

"What?" she asks.

"Well, while he and his Tigers dream about an independent homeland, our people are being slaughtered in their sleep. You know their rebellion just gives the government more justification for ethnic cleansing. Soon there will be no Tamils left to live there."

"Come on, Sudarshan, you are Tamil. Thirty years of peaceful protest and the government kicks them in the teeth. What would you do?" she asks emphatically.

Sudarshan leans closer to Selvi and lowers his voice. "I know what I would not do. I wouldn't recruit children to join the rebels, or hold civilians hostage in the war zone, denying them the rights they themselves claim they are fighting for. Or, God forgive them, kill fellow Tamils for criticizing the actions of the LTTE."

Selvi looks down at the soggy *dosa*, untouched on her plate. Ruby continues eating hers happily.

"Listen Selvi, we Tamils demand our dignity. We want our rights, as do the Tigers, but is an independent state worth the cost?"

"I don't know. How should I know?"

Then Sudarshan adds gently, "Instead of playing rebel by proxy, Mr.

Shantaram should be marrying you and raising his child. Ruby deserves that. You deserve that. I hope he's not waiting for someone better to come along. You tell him that you are the best."

"Oh, I tell him every time I can," Selvi assures him. "But what can I do? He's rich, tall, handsome and . . . ," Selvi whispers into Sudarshan's ear, "Married. Rajan is married."

"Oh," Sudarshan starts then pauses. "All these years and you — "

"Now don't become moralistic. There are worse people I could love."

"Perhaps," Sudarshan mumbles. "Shantaram. Yes I am sure that was his name. Show me his picture again."

Selvi reaches into her bag for her wallet, flipping it open in front of Sudarshan. He takes it from her. A dimpled Ruby and a brooding Rajan look out at him.

"So what do you think? Is he worth the wait?"

Sudarshan stares at Rajan's image, searching and questioning it. "I suppose he is as good looking as the next dashing hero."

Then, decidedly, he closes the wallet and hands it back.

"Perhaps I have the wrong fellow after all. You see, this Shantaram, he works in a factory, some Greek food company. I was told that the poor fellow lost his entire family in the war. A sad creature, really. Not your playboy at all."

"Oh." Selvi pauses, stuffing the wallet back into her purse. "Too bad. Someday I'll introduce you."

Sudarshan smiles quietly. A smile that is unsettling to Selvi. He gets up and moves into the kitchen to manage the rush of orders. Selvi resists following him. Part of her wants to join the wait staff and bus tables until the clanking and chattering die down and the restaurant empties out, allowing the servers to count their tips. She reminds herself that today is *her* day off and remains seated, eating her *dosa* and sipping her *chai*. She will spend the day with her daughter and the night with her daughter's father.

Selvi shifts her attention to the rain. The tingly expectant feeling is wearing off. The *sambar* leaves a bitter taste in her mouth and Ruby is whining about something, dipping her sleeves into the spill of liquid food surrounding her. Selvi closes her ears and eyes to her child, something she is becoming better and better at doing. She wants Rajan. She wants him to pick up Ruby and her and drive them somewhere. Anywhere. She wants them to be together in their own world with no direction, no time constraints and no goodbye foreshadowing every meeting.

Selvi stands up. She passes a dollar coin to Ruby who leaves the tip wedged between the teacup and saucer.

Sudarshan comes out of the kitchen, clutching a lollipop for Ruby. He helps them with their coats.

"You know, if you ever get tired of your playboy, there is an old man who would love to have your company."

"What old man?" Selvi flirts.

"You are a charmer." Sudarshan holds the door open for Selvi and Ruby to pass.

As they push into the rain towards the liquor store, Selvi looks back, unsure of her direction. She holds onto the image of Sudarshan, standing dry and warm on the other side of the glass door.

ॐ

Three o'clock on Gerard Street, a stream of bumper-to-bumper traffic follows a streetcar, a slow-moving elephant. Rajan knows the art of overtaking an elephant. Watch for a space then slide quickly around it and slip in front of the creature before you hit a tree. Rajan is a good driver. He has sharp eyes and quick reflexes. He wishes he had been driving that day. The day the army had infiltrated their region. But he was a new recruit, an extra body for combat hiding in the back of the lorry with others, old men and young, some just boys. If he had been driving that day, he would have smashed through the checkpoint and headed up to the hills where he would have stayed to fight.

Rajan sighs and checks the side mirror, sees a space and signals into the right lane. He steps on the gas only to be blocked by parked cars ahead.

He brakes and waits to let the cars on the left pass before he merges back in line. No driver is generous today. In fact they are especially aggressive on this rainy Saturday afternoon. It is his day off and he is stuck between cars. Selvi expects him at five o'clock. At this rate he will be lucky if he can place his order by then. Ruby wants to eat string hoppers. He'll pick up the food after he buys the *kurta pyjama*. One hundred and thirty dollars create a reassuring padding in his back pocket. Half of his paycheque turned into paper gold. He likes the feeling, light and debt-free.

From now on, everything he earns will be his to spend at will. Maybe he will buy Selvi something too. A sari. She does not even know how to wear one properly, but it will be fun to show her. When Ruby is asleep, he will unfold the six yards of material, tucking the corner into her petticoat and wrapping it around her slender hips. He will show her the demure way of wearing it, high on the waist, the *pallu* folded neatly over her breasts, fixed in place with a silver pin. Or the sexy way, pleated under her soft belly, the *pallu* draped over the slope of her shining shoulder hanging freely to reveal her deep cleavage. He pictures her standing in front of him, looking awkward but expectant. He will move her gently onto the bed and work his way through the layers of cloth, to her smooth skin, her warm flesh enveloping him, allowing him momentarily to forget.

Rajan swerves out of the left lane and into the right. Pressing on the gas, he is determined to pass the streetcar. Suddenly it stops. Two kids riding double on a bike, maybe eight years old, the same age as his sons, Sarath and Shyam, pedalling quickly, calling out . . . then Rajan hears the screams of the children directly in front of him. The yellow signal of the crosswalk flashes furiously. The streetcar bells ring in succession. The sidewalk on his right is packed with pedestrians. Where to turn? He slams on his brakes and smashes the Ventura into the tram.

His head comes down hard on the steering wheel. When he raises it, the angry face of the streetcar driver fills his left window.

"You could have killed those kids. We got rules here, buddy. You better learn'em before you start driving like a hotshot."

We got rules HERE. Rajan knows the rules. He keeps quiet. Any infraction could send him back. He recalls the questions he had to answer to prove his story, calling up again and again the past events. Reworking them in his head so as not to betray his loyalties or reveal himself to be a rebel. Reinventing them so that the Canadian official would empathize rather than despise him.

There were bombs falling all around. I was driving northward on business. I had instructed my family to leave for a safe zone but the roads were clogged with people fleeing the sudden attacks. No buses were running. There was no possibility they could make it out. I had to abandon my vehicle and walk over a mile in the pitch black night, back to my home. When I arrived, the garden was trampled, the house quiet and my family . . .

"Are you okay?" Troubled onlookers ask the children.

The two boys nod and brush off the well-intentioned inquiries. They are more interested in the car, the dent, the crushed metal.

"Wow."

"Cool. D'ya see it smash into the streetcar?"

Rajan steps out of the car to assess the damage. The streetcar is fine. The left side and bumper of the Ventura are badly dented. The traffic remains at a standstill. He is trapped: an immigrant in an alien country, an immigrant with someone else's car, an immigrant who caused a crash that could have killed two kids. Canadian kids.

Again Rajan hears the passersby ask the children, "Are you sure you're okay?"

Rajan wants to scream, *I didn't hit them. They're okay, OKAY?* He feels as if any scratch on any knee, no matter how old, would be blamed on him.

"Sorry," he offers.

A police officer arrives and asks Rajan for his license, ownership and insurance papers. Rajan's hands start to shake as they do each time he comes face to face with an official. Any official. He opens his wallet and expects that he will have to hand over cash, but the familiar nod and gesturing which indicate that bribes are expected and accepted do not occur. The license is easy to produce. Rajan looks for the other papers in the glove compartment, unsure if they even exist. He thinks through lies. Should he say it is his car, pretend he had forgotten the papers at home. He finds them. Thank God he remained silent . . . anything you say will be used against you . . . anything you do will be held against you.

The cop gives the papers a cursory glance, jots down some information and asks Rajan a few questions. "You'll have to get the owner to drop by the station and file a claim." Then he adds accusingly, "No-fault insurance, as you know."

After scribbling down some details, the cop hands a ticket and the papers back. Rajan thanks him and apologizes profusely. He is unsure what he expected — to be ushered to the station in handcuffs, a gun pointed at his head?

The streetcar driver is miffed. "Now, let's see if you can get out of this spot."

Rajan steps back into the car. The cop directs him. The sidewalk is filled with a curious audience who watch him slip away. Driving slowly, he is unsure about this no-fault thing. He is certain it was his fault; he had been thinking of Selvi. Then again, maybe he is innocent. After all, it was Selvi's fault.

✣

The chanting grows louder as Selvi and Ruby approach Queen's Park. She had heard that a demonstration was planned and had even considered participating but today was Ruby's birthday. Today she would see Rajan. She recalls that he had never been present to celebrate any of Ruby's birthdays, including the day she was born. For the first time, Ruby's birthday has fallen on a weekend so neither his work nor his wife can keep him away. Rajan promised her he would spend the night. Maybe this will mark the first day of Rajan's long awaited change that would bring him full-time into her life. As she and Ruby negotiate their way through the crowd, Selvi's spirit lifts and she shouts out in solidarity, "Liberation for Tamil Eelam!"

Ruby echoes her mother's sentiment but calls out, "Libers for Tamilela."

A young man rushes up to them. "Excuse me. But that is not the message we are trying to communicate today. This demonstration is to demand a ceasefire. Could you sign this, please?"

The young man thrusts a clipboard and pen in front of Selvi.

"Petitions like this are being circulated worldwide and going to the United Nations. We're demanding that the U.N. recognize this genocide against Tamil people."

Taken aback by this forceful young man, Selvi stops and puts her plastic bags on the ground. They carry two wine bottles, a few groceries and birthday paraphernalia: balloons, streamers, a birthday cake in a flimsy white cardboard box. Selvi balances her umbrella over her shoulder and dutifully signs the paper. Handing the petition back, she smiles, trying to bridge some understanding between them. The young man, a boy really, looks about seventeen, thin with a gaunt but determined face. Just off the boat, Selvi thinks. Probably straight from Vanni or another Tamil area equally besieged.

"I too am against the war," Selvi reassures him. "But we still have to fight for our rights."

"That's exactly what we are doing. We are here for the Tamil people, not the rebels, not the politicians, but the children, the women, the men."

Selvi wonders if Rajan is here, lost in the crowd or scheming with the organizers and wrestling for the megaphone. As she bends to pick up her bags, she notices Ruby running ahead chasing a big black banner streaked with red paint, its material billowing like a sail headed down University Avenue.

"Ruby!" she commands in a loud voice. "You stop this instant. Right now," she screams.

Ruby freezes on the spot. Selvi hurries up to her daughter, huffing with her quickened pace and the weight of the bags. She grabs Ruby's shoulders roughly, knocking a bag accidentally against the child's back, releasing a high-pitched yelp.

"Don't you ever run away from me. Do you understand? Look at this crowd. You'd be lost in a moment."

Ruby turns away from her mother and extends her arms towards a woman approaching them.

"*Ammachi!*"

"Rubina, happy birthday!"

The woman lifts Ruby into her arms.

Selvi looks up to see her mother and father. The banner floats by, carried by chanting teens.

"*Amma, Appaa*, hello," Selvi says, surprised.

"Selvi, it is good you are here. We were calling your house all morning. We want to bring Ruby her presents."

"Presents?" Ruby shrieks with delight.

"Maybe tomorrow, *Amma*. We have plans today."

"What plans could be more important than your child's birthday. We would like to spend some time . . ."

"I know, *Amma*. I should have called but — "

"Fine, we can come over now. I was just telling your father, it is too much for me standing here. We have done our part. Now we can all leave together."

"No, *Amma*. Rajan's coming over," Selvi says curtly.

"Oh," her mother responds.

Selvi's father turns away, his disappointment in her suddenly manifested on his face. She knows he cannot bear to hear Rajan's name, but instead of expressing his disapproval or anger he becomes sad and pathetic. Selvi hates this weakness in her father. She had first become aware of it years ago.

Selvi was nine years old and had been awakened by the ringing of the telephone. It was like an alarm. Selvi jumped up and rushed to the living room to pick it up before it woke her parents. But she was too late. They were already up, huddled near the phone, her father grasping the receiver. She listened as he spoke in Tamil, mostly asking questions and nodding. Then her father passed the phone to her mother, and Selvi glimpsed his red, teary eyes and hunched, trembling shoulders. He was weeping. When her mother finally hung up, she noticed Selvi and whisked her back to bed, a firm hand on her back, scolding her for not sleeping.

The next day over breakfast, Selvi's father hid behind a newspaper. Selvi knew something had happened the night before. Something back home. *Back home*, the place where she was born but could never return. When she asked her mother why her father was crying, the answer was simple, "The library in Jaffna burned down." Selvi responded, "Huh?" And then her mother added, "Your father's favourite books were there. He spent every Saturday of his youth at that library. Now don't worry."

His books? Is this what drove her father to tears, left him silent and distant, unable to value what was in front of him? Unable to see her? No matter how she teased or cajoled him, served or comforted him, his love and attention towards her was shadowed by something more important. When her father disengaged, Selvi began her retreat. First into her world of make-believe, then into books, television, shopping malls and video arcades. The world outside of their apartment drew her far away from her family's turmoil. Far away from the stream of relatives who arrived in small batches and spread out on the couch, her bed and then any unoccupied space on the floor. This *maami*, that *maama*: aunties and uncles like trees, took root in the living room and grew horizontally, swallowing the light until there was no space for Selvi. So Selvi went out for air and caught her breath in the arms of teenage boys and in the beds of reckless men. Her rebellion had remained invisible to her parents until eight years after the Jaffna Library burned down and Selvi finished high school, found a job waiting tables and left home.

"So we will never meet this man?" Selvi's mother demands. "Not even on Rubina's birthday? How long will you carry on with such secrecy? It is about time you settled down with someone responsible. Someone who can take care of you. You remember Rani Selvaratnam? She has a nephew. He just arrived from Colombo and came home. He saw your photo sitting on our coffee table, and just like that he says, 'I like that girl's face.' And I had to tell him, of course, about Ruby, otherwise his mother would tell him in some bad way, and what does he reply? 'I don't mind that she has a daughter. I would like to meet her.'"

"What?" Selvi is startled out of her memory, unsure how long her mother has been badgering her with the same topic. "Don't start, *Amma*," Selvi says quietly.

"Come," Selvi's father says to his wife, glancing adoringly at his only grandchild. "We should be on our way."

"Ruby?" Selvi's mother lowers her granddaughter down to the sidewalk. "You must come to *Ammachi's* house tomorrow and open your presents."

Ruby nods her head and Selvi watches her parents as they disappear into the throng of Tamil Canadians. Selvi organizes her bags, angry for the delay, annoyed with her parents for constantly reminding her of her bad decisions. Lifting the cake box, she instructs Ruby, "Here, carry this. It will slow you down. And no running away from me."

Ruby holds her arms out stiffly and obediently while Selvi warns her, "Now don't drop it."

As they walk on, Selvi monitors Ruby's movements, aware that her daughter is on her best behaviour, making up for her past folly. Ruby reminds Selvi of herself, always trying to be the good girl, but inevitably missing the mark. Selvi regrets speaking harshly to Ruby and retrieves the cake from the child as they begin their descent towards the subway platform.

ॐ

"It's too small." Mummy kneels on the living room floor and forces Ruby's right arm into the sleeve. "What were you thinking, Rajan?" Mummy forces Daddy away.

Daddy shrugs and walks into the kitchen plopping the paper bags on the counter beside the slightly damp cake box. A pink balloon falls from the wall and bounces lazily down the hall.

"You'll have to exchange it for a bigger size."

"I can't. It was on sale," Rajan replies.

"It's pretty. I like it. I want it."

"But it's too small, baby."

"You're the baby." Ruby squirms out of Mummy's reach and rushes to Daddy in the kitchen, one red sleeve dangling from her shoulder.

"Daddy, make my window." Ruby opens the drawer and draws out a knife, sliding it dangerously close to her open palm. Ruby feels Mummy's rough hand on her wrist.

"Put that away. I told you that drawer is off limits. Rajan, can't you watch her for a minute."

"I want to cut my cake," Ruby shouts.

"We need to eat supper first," Mummy shouts louder.

Rajan escapes into the living room. Ruby follows Daddy, carrying her cake box. She leaves behind the knife and the *karump dum* of Mummy closing the drawer.

"Bring that cake back here," Mummy shouts.

"No," Ruby exclaims, "I want the cake in *my* house."

"Ruby, no," Mummy yells, but Ruby has already pushed it inside the cardboard house. Ruby wins, Mummy loses.

"Fine, have it your way. But don't blame me if your cake gets squashed."

Daddy crouches in front of the cardboard house and pulls the cap off a black marker. Ruby likes the smell.

"Before we cut out your window, you have to tell me where you want it. Here or here?" Rajan speaks in his gentle but responsible Daddy voice.

"Make it to the kitchen."

"Then you have to decide how many windows. One or twenty-one?"

"Seven." Ruby squirms. "Like your house."

Daddy squeaks the outline of a window on Ruby's house with his black marker, caps it and puts it into his pocket.

"Selvi, I need a knife," Daddy tells Mummy.

"Why are you asking me? You know where it is."

Daddy ignores Mummy and lifts Ruby up above his head.

"I'm flying. Mummy, I'm flying."

Daddy dumps Ruby on the couch and sits down. Ruby grabs at Daddy's wallet tucked into his back pocket.

"Show me," Ruby demands. Daddy pulls papers from his wallet, until he finds it, the photograph of his big beautiful house. Ruby crawls onto Daddy's lap. "Tell me again about the bedrooms." Daddy describes Vinay's room lit with stars, Suda's room full of sweets, Nalini's room noisy with animals, the round room where one gets dizzy walking in circles for Shyam and Sarath, the energetic twins, Aya's room with a flower-bed floor and the sunshine room for baby Moni.

"But Ruby's room is the best. It is full of toys and chocolate cake."

Then Daddy takes the cap off the marker and slides the soft tip of the marker up Ruby's finger, singing, "This is the way to Ruby's house."

"When can I move in?"

"Soon, baby. Soon. Daddy has to paint the walls."

"And make windows."

Ruby picks up the remote control and points it towards her cardboard house. Then Daddy puts his hand on Ruby's and repositions it towards the TV. Ruby pushes the buttons. The screen flashes bright colours and loud voices in front of her. She glances back and forth from the black line travelling up the length of her arm to the *pakkowww* of bombs exploding on the screen. Ruby bounces up and down on Daddy's lap. "Again," she demands. Daddy has long legs. He keeps them close together and then opens them, letting Ruby fall halfway to the floor before bringing her up again. Ruby laughs gleefully. Each time he lets her fall, the pitch of her laughter rises higher. It blocks out the crinkling and clanking of Mummy in the kitchen.

There are more bombs on the TV . . . buildings crash . . . *pakkowww*.

"The food is cold," Mummy shouts.

Daddy picks up the marker and draws a longer line up Ruby's arm.

"Honestly, Rajan, three hours late."

Ruby presses the volume button. Up. Up. Up. Daddy's marker goes up her shoulder.

"We've waited all day . . ."

Lots of red lines appear on the TV. The marker tickles her neck.

"You knew it was her birthday."

Ruby can make the TV really loud. The smell of the marker is getting stinky.

Mummy walks in with a plate and hands it to Ruby.

Mummy glances at Daddy. "You can help yourself."

Mummy walks away. Daddy feeds Ruby with a spoon, one mouthful for Ruby, one for Daddy. They continue to eat while watching TV.

"Well, do you want your food?" Mummy calls to Daddy.

Mummy forces Daddy back to the kitchen. The marker falls out of his hand. Ruby's bare arm falls under the cover of the *kurta*.

Ruby eats string hoppers with her right hand. She brings her plate up to her tongue so she can lick it clean. She can do this because Mummy and Daddy are not here. She clicks off the TV. All the bombs, *pakkowwws* and red lines disappear. Quiet. Everything.

Ruby creeps around the corner with her empty plate. Mummy and Daddy are in the hallway with their string hoppers. Streamers and balloons line the walls, Mummy and Daddy look like they are in a circus. Daddy's hands are around Mummy's waist. Mummy feeds Daddy with her fingers, from her plate. They are whispering.

"Stay overnight."

"I've got to be back by eleven."

"You promised, Rajan," Mummy whines to Daddy. "Did she put a curfew on you?"

"I want to go back."

Mummy pushes. "I don't know why you even bother to come here?"

Daddy pulls. "Because I want to come here."

"Ruby means nothing to you. You show up late on her birthday." Mummy moves away.

"She's my daughter." Daddy brings Mummy close to him.

"Well maybe you should start treating her that way."

Daddy holds Mummy's face and kisses her. "Shh. You're getting to be a nag."

"Just like your wife?" Mummy laughs.

"What?"

"Like-your-nagging-old-wife." Mummy speaks softly and slowly, going in for another kiss.

Daddy's hand covers Mummy's mouth. "Don't speak about her."

Mummy's fingers pull his away. "What? Is she a saint or something?"

"SHUT YOUR MOUTH." Daddy pushes Mummy away.

"If you're so in love with her, go home and fuck *her*."

Thuuuddd. Daddy punches Mummy. Mummy's head hits the wall. She slides to the floor, pulling down the streamers and balloons . . . string hoppers splatter everywhere . . . breaking glass . . . *krssssshhh*.

Daddy is shouting, "She's dead for God's sake. Don't you realize that. They're all dead. Because of me, they're . . ."

Mummy's eyes get bigger.

"Baby, baby," Ruby screams and runs to Mummy, wrapping her arms around her.

Mummy clasps Ruby to her, a tight clasp, a never-let-go clasp. Daddy pulls at Ruby's empty sleeve.

"Selvi . . ." he begins.

The sleeve slips out of his hand. Ruby clings harder to Mummy and screams and screams. Daddy slams the door.

Then quiet.

Ruby looks at shattered glass and a broken Mummy.

"Baby?"

~

It is past midnight when Rajan finally returns home after a long and rambling drive through downtown Toronto to the high-rise off the 401 where he lives. Entering his bachelor apartment, he is finally alone. He undresses and hangs up his clothes to avoid wrinkles, meticulously taking apart the image so carefully constructed in the morning. The tap in the kitchen sink is dripping. Rajan turns it on and runs cold water over his hands and splashes his face. His stomach growls. He opens the freezer, stacked with boxes of spanakopita. They are as good for breakfast as they are for lunch and supper. Taking out a row of pastry, he lays it on a cutting board. He finds the knife in the drawer and slices the layers, which flake off: particles of skin, old and dead, brown layers protecting frozen filling. He pauses and considers writing a letter to Selvi.

Then he lies down naked on his foam mattress and turns his eyes to the ceiling. The paint is chipping off, accented by the flickering lights of passing cars, accompanied by the rushing sounds from the freeway. Rajan tries to conjure up fond memories of his family: his wife hanging the laundry, his children racing through the clothes on the line. Every night for the past six years Rajan has re-created the events of the most horrific day of his life. But now? After what has just happened? He cannot. Images of Selvi flood his mind. She will demand an explanation. He owes her an explanation.

But what can he tell her? The truth? The truth is he tried but never fought with the Tigers, fleeing instead from soldiers who shot their lorry driver in cold blood. The truth is he did have a wife, but the last time he saw her she was lying motionless on the ground, her sari blood-soaked between her legs. The truth is he fathered seven children before Ruby, only to witness their broken bodies tied with their own shirts to a sagging clothesline.

The truth is . . . he'll never know the complete truth, for he did not crouch down to check whether his wife's cheek was cold with death, nor did he run to his children to listen for a lingering heartbeat. The truth is he thought only of himself. If the soldiers had done this in their search for him, they could still be on their hunt. Lurking behind the door, ready to ambush and torture him for information.

The only thing Rajan can write Selvi, with any certainty, is that he ran, hid and escaped to Canada where he had an uncle who could help him. An uncle who charged interest on every penny Rajan borrowed. An uncle who lives in a mansion with seven bedrooms and who lent him a sky blue Ventura on his day off.

Suddenly Rajan jolts up. He forgot to return the car.

ॐ

Selvi cannot remember how she got here, how she negotiated the distance from the hallway floor to the safety of her bed. She does not care. What she wants is release. It does not come. She shifts her hand from between her legs to the side of her face. Pressing the tender bruise as if to test her threshold of pain. She tries to make sense of Rajan's words, his sudden confession and the string of lies he has told her over the years. How could she have been so blind, so stupid? So she resolves to leave him, visit her parents and see Sudarshan. Birthdays are a time for resolutions, changes and good luck. Then she remembers Ruby. Where is Ruby? Selvi attempts to rise. Using the corner of the bedside table to support herself, she tries again, knocks over the lamp and falls back. She surrenders her head to the pillow, allowing her mind to swim, float and sink deeper into oblivion, heavy with the events of Ruby's birthday.

⌇

The sunlight streams through the tear in the blue curtain. Ruby tiptoes across the fallen streamers and burst balloons, careful not to walk on the pieces of broken glass in the hallway. She makes it safely to the living room and crawls into the cardboard house her father made for her. Daddy promised he would finish it on her birthday. Daddy drew a big square on the outside with a black marker where a new window would be. Ruby liked the smell and the squeaky sound of the marker against the cardboard. She liked the way Daddy could make straight lines without using a ruler. Daddy traced a black line on Ruby's skin, starting on her middle finger, all the way up her arm ending with an arrow on the tip of her chin. Ruby examines the line, scared her own touch will make it disappear.

If Ruby sits still long enough, maybe Daddy will walk through the door, cut through the black lines and open her window into Mummy's kitchen. Then she can watch Mummy at the sink, elbows deep in the water, washing dishes, pulling at the plug. She longs to see Mummy but she doesn't want Mummy to see her. There is no better place to hide, yet this is the first place Mummy will look to find Ruby. Ruby snuggles into the corner of her cardboard house where her birthday cake still sits untouched. She opens the box to see a number five sunken into the chocolate surface but still smiling up at her. Hungry and alone, she picks at the icing and waits.

On a Mountain on an Island

It was an in-between time in the relationship. Their two lives were entangled by invisible threads, simultaneously constraining and comforting. Each night Miriam and Lynne would collapse onto the same mattress, breathe the same night air and awaken to a common sun, only to part ways during the day. Then, when they finished leading their separate lives, they would meet again in bed.

Miriam once suggested they sleep in one of the upstairs bedrooms during slow periods, which meant most of the winter. That way they could access light and have a view of the mountains first thing in the morning. But Lynne was insistent that they maintain decorum. Some kind of self-imposed rule about keeping the guest rooms ready for the guests, should they arrive unannounced. The guests, as Lynne called them, were paying customers at the bed and breakfast the two women had owned and operated for close to five years. The main floor bedrooms were reserved for the guests. The basement was the couple's private suite.

Miriam stretched her arm across the bed, sensing Lynne's earlier-than-usual departure. Lynne's body left no impression on the mattress; there was no lingering scent of sweat or stray hairs on the pillow. Miriam turned away and wrapped her long brown legs around the bolster, the oblong cushion she had started sleeping with. Her doctor had recommended it to help keep her spine aligned, but it did more than that. It comforted her when she was lonely and occasionally provided a soft form on which she took out her anger.

Miriam looked up from her pillow to see the smooth white plane of Lynne's back. She was standing still, facing the window. There was no inspiring view; the window opened onto a gravel driveway that sloped up to the gate where their welcome sign hung proudly, slightly dulled by weather and time: *L&M's Bed & Breakfast*.

"Is it snowing?"

"Drizzling," Lynne replied.

Beads of moisture created an intricate, transparent pattern trailing down the pane. Lynne followed their individual journeys from the top to the bottom until each disappeared and was upstaged by another. This was her ritual before showering, to meditate on the weather. She appreciated this quiet time before the world awoke.

"Did you call the terminal?" Miriam propped herself up and started clipping her toenails, littering the clear blue landscape of the cotton sheet with white flecks.

"Yes. There were no delays. Perhaps they decided to stay in town last night to look around."

"Or they changed their plans. It wouldn't be the first time," Miriam added.

Lynne turned around. Once again, the first moments of the day were corrupted.

"Could you refrain from doing that in bed?"

Miriam clipped off another nail as Lynne left the room.

Lynne had a system for waking up her body. It required discipline and determination. Hot then cold, then hot and finish with cold. It got her blood circulating, her senses tingling. She could work fast and efficiently. Today there was chopping and piling wood, the roof of the shed needed re-shingling — a job she had postponed far too long — and she had to salt the drive. The temperature was expected to drop. She would do that first, before the guests arrived. The outdoor work could never be put off in case the snow came down. This winter was unpredictable, regardless of the many weather channels that proclaimed differently. Later on, she thought she would whip up some banana bread, a warm welcome for the travel-weary visitors.

By the time she stepped out of the shower she had her tasks set out and timed. They lay before her like a row of jewels ready to be picked up one by one. At night she would sleep with the pleasure of knowing she had put in a full day's work. The satisfaction would be as weighty as diamonds sagging in her pocket.

"Another boatload from China," Miriam said aloud to herself with a voice devoid of emotion. The TV newscaster was more expressive.

Miriam was lying on the couch in the living room. She had spent a good deal of the year in this very position, following specific news stories: Pinochet's impending trials, NATO troops in Bosnia and now the boatloads of Fujian people seeking refuge in British Columbia. Never before had the news appeared so dramatic, even the events on this very shore could have been scenes in a movie. Why not? Fiction seemed to hold more truth in its telling than any so-called objective journalism. Perhaps some very clever producer, Orson Welles–like, had devised the news to spark some excitement and sense of urgency into her complacent life. After all, how would she and Lynne know the difference? They had not travelled in five years, participated in a community or even bothered to vote in elections. Still, life went on.

Maintaining the house and running the business consumed most of their savings. So Miriam, who had once been allergic to stock markets, had agreed to invest the little that was left into something called "ethical" stock, made for the capitalist with a conscience. This was what she had become. With her teacher's salary, a mortgage-free house and income-generating investments, she maintained an arms-length distance from the unstable world. It could keep on confessing its cruelty and compassion. She lived on a mountain on an island. There was little that could touch her.

Miriam flipped through some channels and returned to the local island news. Images of more Fujian refugees filing out of industrial containers flooded the screen. Local people from Victoria were interviewed: "Canada is tired of footing the bill for illegal aliens." Years ago Miriam would have reacted to such a statement with rage and frustration. Today she was simply curious. She marvelled at the spirit people had. Those, like her parents, who had the will to cross an ocean to a foreign land and an unknown future, and those with the audacity to make public announcements without any trace of empathy or embarrassment. She considered offering her home to the refugees. This was not a moral act, but a practical one. Why should two people occupy a large house on a beautiful mountain? Let life invade their home with its poverty, contradiction, pain, but most of all passion. Let them feel the tangible effects of being connected to something bigger than each other.

Having salted the drive, Lynne entered the living room carrying wood for the fireplace. She glanced at Miriam, lying on her stomach, remote control secure in her palm like a weapon, her legs extending beyond a white shirt. She looked like summer displaced.

"Why don't you put some clothes on?"

"You've seen it all."

"Not for my sake," Lynne said, neatly stacking the wood by the fireplace.

"You still think they're going to show?" Miriam reached for her cup. Her shirt rode up, exposing the half moon of her buttocks and blue polka dot panties. Lynne rested her eyes on the familiar flesh that appeared young and vulnerable. She felt the lift of desire.

"I'll start a fire."

"Good idea. It's chilly in here," Miriam muttered before turning away to sip her coffee.

Lynne went out to fetch more wood.

The red light on the answering machine flashed insistently like a help signal, quick and bright, requiring immediate attention. Lynne, bringing in the last load of wood, noticed it and glanced with annoyance at Miriam, talking on the phone and oblivious to the message light. Miriam was speaking to her mother. After years of overhearing Miriam's conversations, Lynne had learned the obvious differences between Kutchi, Gujarati and Hindi. Kutchi was the familiar mother tongue Miriam spoke often and intimately with her mother, while Gujarati was the common language reserved for her father, *Bapu Ji*, her sister *ben* and brothers *bhais*. Hindi was the language for distant relatives and, what the hell, Miriam would throw in some Swahili for old family friends. "Jambo" instead of hello. Once in a while Lynne would happen upon Miriam reminiscing in Spanish over the phone to former colleagues who had travelled to Nicaragua with her, demonstrating international solidarity in the hopeful days of the Sandinista government. Miriam even spoke French occasionally to old political science grads from her alma mater, McGill University, reminding Lynne of her own frustration at not being able to learn French even though she studied it in grade school and was Canadian born and bred.

It was as if Miriam's tongue still bore the traces of succulent sweets savoured in faraway lands. The taste freshly rising in her mouth each time she spoke to someone who shared the experience. When Lynne heard her partner speak these languages, it suggested Miriam's past life. Her habit of crossing borders, her ease at taking lovers, with language, nationality and, at times, gender, no obstacle. Lynne alternated between marvelling at and envying Miriam's free and globe-trotting existence. When once she expressed this early in their relationship, Miriam had replied, "I feel anything but free. It's just in the blood, I guess. We Ismailis migrated halfway around the world from Persia to India, Kenya to Britain and now here. Even if I wanted to, I wouldn't know how to stop moving." And a year into their relationship Lynne thought that perhaps Miriam's inherited wanderlust had wearied in her bones and she was in search of a resting place. Why else would Miriam have chosen her, a white Protestant, an unremarkable working class lesbian barely passing for butch. Loyalty and hard work was all she had to offer. And Miriam had accepted. All Miriam's once-travelled roads converged and led up a narrow one-lane path to their home.

Lynne unloaded the stack of logs near the fireplace and moved into the kitchen. She pointed to the answering machine, motioning Miriam to wrap it up. Instead, Miriam winked and handed the receiver to Lynne. Lynne rolled her eyes before accepting it.

"Khem cho?" Lynne said as Miriam disappeared down the hall. Then switching to English, she spoke in turn to Miriam's father, mother, sister and aunt, filling them in on the latest news on the island. Miriam's family called every Sunday like clockwork and Lynne, respectfully and politely, did the rounds. But today, the conversations were strained. She was impatient. Other people were trying to communicate with her, sending her soundless signals. Red and urgent. She finally put the phone down and set the tape in motion.

A voice on the speakerphone said, "Hi. Is this Lynne? I hope, well if it is . . ."

"Yes, it's their number," an irritated voice said in the background.

"Listen, we had to check out that Da Vinci exhibit at the museum. Hey, did you know he was gay?" Lynne heard laughter and giggling.

"Cut to the chase," said another voice.

"I had no idea. Talk about green. Oh yeah, anyway, we're gonna be late . . ."

"Tell them about Teri and me," a quieter voice added.

"Oh yeah, and we ran into some friends on the ferry so we're thinking of bringing them with us. Four of us . . . that's fine, right? You said you weren't full and . . ."

Then a long tone clipped off the excited voices mid-sentence. Lynne rewound the tape and listened again as if to pick up a secret code. It sounded as though they were laughing at her, a mother excluded from her children's antics.

The flush of the toilet brought her back to the moment.

"When did this message come in?" Lynne yelled out.

"I don't know," Miriam replied from behind the bathroom door.

"Why didn't —" Lynne stopped herself. "They could be here any minute."

The phone was her responsibility. The B&B was her responsibility. All she could expect of Miriam was to be presentable and polite.

Lynne started tidying up the kitchen. She whispered curses at Miriam who had left the papers she was grading the night before in several piles on the table. She glanced at the title, "Questioning Culture and Civilization in *The Lord of the Flies*" by William Golden, written by Mark Hanley, Grade 11 English Lit. The subject sounded important and complex. Lynne knew there must be some internal logic to the mess of papers, but she did not care. They were in her way. She had asked Miriam endless times to mark her papers at the desk, her requests constantly ignored. After stacking the papers into one grand pile — red-marked or not — she carried them downstairs to their bedroom.

When Lynne returned to the kitchen, Miriam was seated at the table leafing through the newspaper.

"Mir, I'm running behind. A couple of rooms need to be prepped and I want to do some baking," Lynne said steadily, trying to hide her exasperation.

"Banana bread?" Miriam replied without missing a beat.

Lynne leaned against the counter, tall and tense, her arms crossed over her flat stomach. She turned her lips in, a habit she had whenever she needed to make several decisions at once.

"Maybe I should make something else, a fruit cake? It's seasonal," Lynne offered.

"Of course they probably don't celebrate Christmas," Miriam said. She reached over her head and swatted the Christmas mobile that hung above the table, setting off a crescendo of tinkling bells. "I really don't know why you bother with this."

Lynne shot a resentful glance at Miriam.

"I bother with it because it makes this place feel homey and Christmassy," Lynne responded stiffly.

"Isn't it a bit childish?" Miriam asked lightly.

"Fine. I'll move it."

"Oh sweetie, don't move it. It's cute. I just think it's funny that you make the effort," Miriam continued, still playing with the bells.

"Have I ever stopped you from your fasts, taking off to the mainland to celebrate Eid or whatever? Do I ever . . ."

"Someone's sensitive today," Miriam teased.

"Well it's true," Lynne responded, pulling out a cookbook from the shelf. "There's a difference."

"Yeah, the difference is you. You used to lecture me about how religion was a . . . what did you call it? A patriarchal breeding ground."

"It is. Most religious life is defined by men, constructed around male deities and prophets and, well, you know the rest."

"So why do *you* bother?"

"I don't have to explain my spirituality to you."

"Neither do I."

"I'd hardly call 'jingle bells' spiritual."

Lynne slapped the cookbook down on the table.

"I just want to make banana bread," she said and, unhooking the mobile, she walked down the hall, jingling all the way.

As Lynne hung the mobile in a guest room, a list started popping up in her head. First the beds. There were four guests, or that was what it sounded like. She was unsure if that meant two couples, or one couple and two friends, or four friends who wanted their own single rooms. She would prepare two more rooms anyway. That meant they would be full up. No vacancy. Lynne smiled to herself as she gathered toiletries and clean towels for each room. She was not going to let Miriam's negativity spoil her mood. They were expecting guests during the slowest season of the year.

It had been two months since L&M's had a guest. October 24 — Lynne could neither forget the date nor Eileen. She was a writer escaping Vancouver, craving distance and time to heal from a severed relationship. When she arrived, Lynne assumed she sought time alone. But Eileen was neither quiet nor reclusive. She kept inviting Lynne out. "Let's drive down the coast," or "Maybe if you had time, you wouldn't mind showing me around town."

Lynne, always enthusiastic to be a perfect hostess, offered to oblige her one and only guest. Eileen was a large Métis woman, standing almost six feet tall with plenty of flesh padding her bones. She was fifty-four years old with impossibly high cheek bones — the Dene side — and fiery red hair — from the Celts. Lynne smiled and confessed her own Scottish roots. Playing hostess to Eileen would be comparable to entertaining an eccentric aunt. While Miriam taught class, Eileen and Lynne set out, hiking up mountains, exploring and commenting on the Indian handicraft stores in the tourist enclaves, walking the beach. Beachcombing, as Eileen put it, was an undeveloped science. "You have to be willing to see everything and look for nothing."

As they explored the sand and surf, skin tingling with salt, cold fingers, red noses, the two women gathered beach wood and built a fire. They drank coffee and watched the sea turn purple with storm clouds overhead. Eileen turned to Lynne, speaking in the softest voice.

"You know, I don't enjoy writing anymore. It's just a safety net. A way to justify my life, give me an occupation. I'd rather spend my days out here, searching." Then she broke out into a huge grin. "I'm simple, I guess. Just looking for love, like everyone else. And if that doesn't pan out, a bit of money would be nice."

Lynne was intrigued. She wanted to take Eileen's hand in that moment. Instead, she gripped her knees and smiled, appreciating Eileen's honesty, her intimate confessions, her flaws and quiet humour. Eileen seemed to have a kind of self-acceptance that neither Miriam nor she possessed. The night before Eileen was scheduled to leave, Lynne awoke, restless and anxious. She could not stop thinking about Eileen, picturing her upstairs sleeping, folded into herself under the duvet. Finally Lynne walked upstairs and stood outside Eileen's room. She imagined crawling into bed with her, feeling her warm, large body embracing her, cupping the weight of her breasts in her hands before opening her mouth to receive one and then the other. She stood there for fifteen minutes arguing with herself. Should I? Shouldn't I? She created possible excuses just in case Eileen's feelings were not returned.

Then her sensible side kicked in. Miriam was downstairs. They were running a business. She was a professional. Returning to the basement, she tucked herself into bed and nuzzled her face into the nape of Miriam's neck. Then, for the first time in months, she made love to her: a quiet, aching, deceitful love.

By the time Lynne finished the rooms, the smell of zucchini bread was wafting through the air. The snow had also started, soft flakes but thick, the kind that belonged in the east, not in the balmy Vancouver Island winter climes. Miriam had slipped into a pair of jeans and her dark hair was pulled back in a clip. She had tuned into an oldies radio station and her body was curved over a mixing bowl, spooning out the last of the chocolate-walnut batter into a baking pan. Lynne rested her hand on Miriam's shoulder. The gesture was too formal. She had forgotten how to be casual and affectionate. She withdrew her hand.

"You're baking two loaves?"

"Don't worry, I didn't stray from the recipes."

"Smells great. Thank you."

Static was starting to interfere with the station.

"Hey, can you adjust that? My hands are . . ." Miriam withdrew her hands from the bowl and wiggled her chocolate-covered fingers. Lynne nodded and played with the dial until Frank Sinatra's rendition of "Fly Me to the Moon" came through loud and clear. Miriam started crooning along with it.

"You sound good."

"I taste better," Miriam responded, sliding two fingers around the sides of the mixing bowl, gathering the last remnants of batter and offering it up for Lynne to sample.

Lynne opened her mouth.

"Hmm. Delicious."

"Surprised?"

Lynne laughed, "Yes, actually."

Miriam clasped Lynne's face and kissed her firmly on the lips. Taken aback by the sudden show of affection, Lynne blushed.

"Oh my God. You're red," Miriam exclaimed. "You look just like you did the first night we met."

"You mean before you took advantage of me."

"You poor innocent!" Miriam chuckled and gave Lynne's face a squeeze, leaving chocolate smeared on her cheeks.

The two women had met when an activist group that Miriam belonged to was raising funds for Iraq's casualties of the Gulf War. They had organized a sing-a-thon. Miriam had noticed Lynne, a tall, fair-haired woman changing CDs, setting the sound levels and directing eager singers to mind the cables as they made their way to the stage. Wearing a red evening gown, stiletto heels, a feather boa slung around her neck, and a rhinestone tiara perched in her black hair, Miriam took the stage. During her performance, she flipped the boa out into the audience and inadvertently knocked over the microphone stand. The stand could not be counted on to remain upright. Miriam constantly fumbled with it, unable to concentrate. Then Lynne appeared, held the microphone, ducking in front of her, trying to be as invisible as possible. Miriam was free to ham up her version of "I want to live in America, Everyone give to America, No desert storm in America, Oh to be born in America," complete with castanets, choreography and caustic asides. When the performance was over — thunderous applause, calls for encores, bows — she wrapped her boa around Lynne's neck and planted her full crimson lips on Lynne's sweet pink ones: their first kiss, before an enthusiastic audience. A blush swept across Lynne's face. Miriam was smitten.

That was the beginning of their lust and love, in that order. Then came the details. When would they move in together, where would they live, how to arrange the furniture? After searching for decent and affordable apartments in Vancouver's east end, the women decided to buy. But prices were soaring and they were reluctant to take on a large mortgage that would keep Miriam locked behind a desk at some community organization and Lynne on the road with another wanna-make-it-big rock band.

Then Lynne inherited the house. It was no less than an act of God. Aunt Kate, who had never married, died and left a sprawling bungalow on Vancouver Island to her only single niece. A solidarity gesture, Miriam surmised. When Lynne and she drove to see the house, they were not sure what to do. Although it was set in paradise, perched high on the mountain with a view of the sea, inside was a mess. It needed major renovations: rewiring, repainting, reworking. Miriam suggested they turn it into a bed and breakfast. She was ready to flee the city, the feminist movement, her old life.

"It's away from traffic and endless meetings, close to the big surf and fresh mountain air. We can look down on all of creation," she had exclaimed.

"But you'll be bored. There's nothing to do out there, none of our friends . . ."

"We'll cater it to women. Eager explorers and burnt-out activists will come out for weekends. We'll live vicariously. We'll plan retreat weekends and advertise specials for groups."

Miriam had clasped Lynne's hand. She was optimistic, ready to take a chance and pour her future into the curve of her lover's palm. Lynne kissed the delicate flesh at the bend of Miriam's wrist as if to accept the offering and the responsibility.

"Don't ever let me say I told you so."

The sun tucked under the peaks and the flurries grew stronger. The chocolate-walnut and zucchini loafs were cooling on the counter. Miriam was sweeping the kitchen floor.

"Lynne, where did you put my stuff?" Miriam called out.

"What stuff?" Lynne replied as she stuffed scrap paper under the logs in the fireplace, ready for lighting.

"My school essays. What did you do with them?" She emptied the dustpan and returned the broom to the closet. "You better not be using them for scrap."

"They're downstairs on your desk where they belong."

"Thank you, mother."

"The kitchen table is no place . . ."

Miriam covered her ears with her hands and started humming. She went downstairs to grade her long-overdue papers. Seated at her desk, she leafed through the essays and corrected spelling mistakes. She wrote comments with exclamation marks to emphasize the weight of her teacherly response, and berated herself for not completing the task earlier. She had developed the bad habit of procrastinating and falling behind in her grading. Essays assigned in early November were not handed back until January. The students did not seem to mind, but she had already been taken aside by the principal. And although she appreciated her job — it took her away from Lynne's brooding silences and forced her to engage with people — she was beginning to resent the long days, the insolent tone of teenage resistance, and the fact that her salary was necessary.

She also resented Lynne for not living up to her end of the bargain, their tacit understanding that identified Lynne as the breadwinner allowing Miriam the freedom to explore interesting projects and pursue intellectual yearnings. She wanted to recline in Lynne's steady and stable love. Relax, knowing she could stop taking care of the world and allow someone else to care for her. Someone who could fix things, move things and demonstrate tangible results. But neither of them had done enough research; they had not realized just how slow business would be for much of the year. And because Lynne was better at maintaining the property, repairing, cooking, taking care of business, Miriam agreed to take a job to bring in the extra income. Every weekday morning she would drive forty-five minutes from their home to the school and make the same drive back up the mountain. Lynne would have something on the stove, and Miriam would enter and seat herself at the dining room table. She simply lived there: room and board, like any other guest, except without the special treatment.

After grading half the essays, Miriam abandoned the others and flopped on the mattress drawing the bolster between her legs. She fell into a restless sleep, dreaming she was skinny-dipping in the middle of the ocean, floating on her back, her face offered up to the sun. Suddenly she heard horns and saw ships surrounding her. She needed to get to shore, and though her arms and legs were moving through the waves, she could not swim out of the same spot. While she was treading water, the ships closed in on her. Maybe they could rescue her. But then she spotted men on the decks, sailors, leering at her nakedness. She looked to the shore and there was Lynne, oblivious to her danger. Lynne was having fun, assuming Miriam was too. She kept waving and smiling, smiling and waving. When Miriam awoke, her muscles were aching and the dream replayed in her mind again and again, leaving her uncomfortable and restless. She got up and rummaged through her desk drawers, leafing through old notebooks, teacher's guides and calendars. Then she opened the one drawer in the desk reserved for Lynne. It was meticulous. Inside were two pens, paper clips, envelopes and a notepad. Blank. As if it was waiting, ready for Miriam to write down her dream.

Lynne always put the comfort of her guests first. The evening before, she had slid a pot roast into the oven in anticipation of their arrival. Miriam had nagged her, "If you are going to offer breakfast and supper, then you bloody well should charge for it." Lynne had endured the reprimand, feeling somewhat guilty, knowing it was Miriam's salary that kept L&M's open, allowing her to be generous towards the guests. She was secretly relieved when they hadn't shown up, and she and Miriam had sat down to a hot and delicious meal. But now Lynne worried that the snow would make the roads treacherous. The guests would be lucky to make it up the mountain, let alone back down in search of a place to eat. So Lynne cut and arranged slices of the leftover pot roast on the only large platter she could find, a beautiful silver salver she had inherited with the house. Looking at the ornate dish, Lynne thought, why not pull out all the stops. So she formally laid the dining room table and brought a couple of bottles of wine up from the basement. Then she tramped outside to clear the driveway and clip branches of holly for the centrepiece. By the time Lynne returned, Miriam had come upstairs, kindled the fire and opened a bottle of red. She sat on the couch clutching a pen and a notepad.

"What are you doing?"

"The place looks great. I thought I'd write a welcome speech to the guests. Something about how things come alive when strangers are in our midst. How we're eternally grateful for . . ."

Lynne picked up the wine bottle. "I was hoping to open this when they arrive."

"Oh yes, and how we are never allowed to drink wine, unless of course there is a reason, a special reason. Like company for instance."

"Okay, I get it," Lynne said, rolling her eyes.

"Oh. I didn't intend that you should get anything. I was speaking mostly for my own amusement, as is the case most of the time."

"So you're lonely? Is that it?"

"Drunk and lonely."

Lynne held up the bottle and examined it.

"You've barely finished one glass of wine."

"I'm an easy drunk," Miriam said, deliberately slurring her words.

Lynne placed candlesticks on the dining table and lit them. Then she poured herself a glass, turned down the lights and sat on the floor in front of the fireplace.

"I thought drinking was against protocol."

"Hang protocol. I'm following your example." Lynne turned her lips in. She was starting to think the guests would not come.

"I didn't realize you were so easily influenced," Miriam responded.

"Anything to make you happy, babe," Lynne offered.

Lynne grabbed Miriam's foot. Miriam pulled it away, causing her loose woollen sock to slip off. "Hey, your feet are cold," said Lynne.

"That's the point of the fire, right." Miriam was icy.

"Right."

Lynne looked into the fire and her jaw stiffened. Miriam, unable to write in the dim light and grateful for an excuse to stop, put aside the notepad. It was a list of things to do. She used to write lists like these when she was in high school to help motivate her. They included such things as audition for the school play, join a sports team, run for student council. Now the list read reckless and pointless: get a lover, take a hike, have another drink. She was working on the last one. Maybe she would work backwards.

Lynne lay on the rug. The two of them remained quiet for a time. Then Miriam spoke, almost inaudibly.

"Why did you have to use the china?

"The china?"

"The china. My mother's china."

"No reason. I mean, if it bothers you . . . ," Lynne said sitting up, alert and ready to scramble into action.

"No, it doesn't. But I want to know why?"

"Miriam, I'll put it back." Lynne got up, moved to the table and started stacking the plates.

"No," Miriam stressed, "I don't mind. I just asked why." Miriam walked towards Lynne and said, "I wish you'd take me at face value instead of guessing what I want."

Lynne continued to put the china back into the hutch. "The guests are coming. It's the first time in a while and I thought we'd celebrate."

"They're not guests." Miriam retrieved the plates off the shelf to reset them. "We don't know them. They are paying customers. They get a bed and breakfast. Nothing more."

"What does that mean?" Lynne gathered the plates.

"Nothing more, not dinner, not entertainment, not . . . Oh forget it."

Miriam clutched the last plate Lynne held in her hand. "Use the china, it just gathers dust otherwise," Miriam insisted.

"It obviously bothers you," Lynne said.

"Use the goddamned china!"

"I said I don't want to use it, I — "

The doorbell rang. The women momentarily stared at each other. Then Lynne turned up the lights and headed towards the door. Miriam reset the table. She held one last plate in her hand and examined the design. There was a white centre surrounded by a detailed rose pattern within a grey border. Why had her mother taken the pains to transport these across three continents? She could not recall any meaningful story, only that they had accompanied their family in every home they had ever lived. And now they had been passed on to her to use when entertaining strangers.

Miriam stood in the centre of the room dressed in a long black evening gown. She was a cross between Cher and Yoko Ono. Glamorous and eccentric, surely, but one was not sure whether it was indulgence or art. Laura, Teri, Monique and Hank were gathered around her, four bodies prone in front of the fire, drinking wine, nibbling on the last of the leftover roast beef, the plates carelessly left on the floor. Lynne's formal dinner had been abandoned by the guests who wanted to warm up by the fire. So Lynne hovered around making sure glasses were topped up, plates were filled with seconds, napkins distributed. She could not give Miriam her full attention, nor did she want to. She suspected Miriam's act was inappropriate and she did not want confirmation.

The guests had finally shown up, showered and sat down to Lynne's cold cuts. During dinner, Miriam had gone into a long rant about how young women had distanced themselves from feminism and, as a result, the movement was unable to renew itself.

"There is little critical analysis about post-feminism," she had explained. "And being lesbian is becoming more of a trend. It seems as if queer culture has lost its political content. There's no left left."

The guests heard her out and tried weakly to respond to her accusations.

"All I'm saying is that most young women, at least in North America, are just self-interested. Looking to build their careers instead of contributing to the betterment of women worldwide."

Miriam was close to pointing fingers at the girls.

"Well," said Laura, her eyes locked on Miriam's, "if changing the world is so important, why are you up here? Running a B&B seems like a pretty indulgent occupation. It's hardly the centre of political agitation unless it's a cover for your underground revolution."

"Laura," Hank cautioned.

"No wait," Miriam interjected, "you're right. I'm rather useless up here. I used to be involved in social justice issues: abortion rights, low-income housing projects, women's shelters."

"Why did you stop?" Teri asked.

"I got tired," Miriam said solemnly. She took a long sip of wine. She could feel Lynne's eyes fixed on her. "It just seemed like I, all of us, were spinning our wheels, never getting anywhere. With every election we worried about losing our funding, women were constantly burning out, there was infighting and — "

"Nah," Lynne broke in. "I took one look at her and dragged her up the mountain to keep her all to myself."

"You mean I chased you up here," Miriam responded setting off a wave of laughter.

"No really," Lynne continued, relieved to see Miriam hadn't slipped into one of her morose moods, "Mir was once a sought-after talent in the women's scene."

"Really?" Monique asked, and then they all demanded that she perform. Miriam, delighted, launched into her act.

"You, you, you and you. You young women are a symbol of our future. You are the breath of the new movement. Like an old mother hen, I'll bring you young chicks in from the cold, nurture you and send you back into the world to carry the torch for womankind." She was drunk, but luckily by that time everyone else was well on her way. Except Lynne.

The four guests were in their early twenties. They were, in fact, escaping Christmas with their families. Miriam tried to size up who was together. She thought Hank, the sensitive butch with dimples sweetly and symmetrically indenting her cheeks, was with Monique, a petite French girl whose blond hair had been reduced to a closely shaven brush cut. But halfway through the evening Monique sat on the lap of Laura — a dark-haired girl with piercings in her nose, eyebrows and tongue — and engaged in some not-so-innocent petting. Teri was harder to read. She was quiet but not shy. Perhaps they were all together. Fuck buddies of sorts! At any rate there was no shortage of chemistry. It was alive in the room, a welcomed guest winking at Miriam, inviting her to join the fun. So Miriam commanded attention, flirted and sang sultry-voiced Edith Piaf songs. When she finished, the women clapped, whistled and yelled out for more. Miriam was elated. More wine was fetched from the basement and generously distributed. This was a raucous gathering of old friends, not strangers paying for room and board.

By 3 a.m. the women had picked out their respective beds. Miriam did not know or care by that time, who was with whom. She polished off the last of the wine and collapsed on the couch, legs apart, her hair tousled and messed.

"They were wonderful."

"You were wonderful," Lynne said. "They loved you."

"And you. What did you think?" Miriam slurred her words and pointed her index finger towards Lynne.

"I think you need to go to bed."

"Carry me." Miriam reached out her arms.

Lynne put an arm around Miriam's waist and another under her thighs. She took a deep breath and then lifted her gallantly up from the couch only to fall backward to the floor. They giggled and held each other.

"Oh my god, I can't move," Lynne grunted under Miriam's weight.

"Well, you're lucky I'm not as heavy as what's-her-name," Miriam blurted out, still laughing.

"What are you talking about?"

"Oh, you know. Someone important or unimportant. See, I've forgotten her name already. Oh well, better try that again," Miriam said turning to face Lynne, but instead of getting up she moved in closer.

"Wait," Lynne began.

But Miriam placed two fingers on Lynne's lips, parting them slightly. Then she kissed her. Lynne returned the kiss, hard and passionately. Her breath quickened as Miriam expertly undid Lynne's belt and slid her hand confidently down the front of her jeans.

"Wait." Lynne clutched Miriam's shoulders and sat up. "Not here." She kissed Miriam's knees before pulling her dress over them. "Go downstairs. I'll be down in a minute."

"Come now." Miriam tugged Lynne's arm.

"I'll clean up a bit. It will only take a second," Lynne added. "Go warm up the bed." Miriam released Lynne.

The thing about basements, Miriam realized, is that you can hear every-thing on the floor above. The first thing Miriam listened for was Lynne's footsteps travelling back and forth from the living room to the kitchen. Then came running water and the clatter of dishes going into the sink. She's handwashing the china, Miriam thought. Gradually, the cleaning-up noises were layered by other sounds drifting in from the nearby bedrooms: the snoring from one room and then, like the slow crescendo from a string section, the soft pleasurable moans from another. Miriam imagined Hank (because she was the cutest) and Teri (she was the nicest), limbs interlocked and tongues exploring. The moaning shifted and became gasps . . . then another round of dishes, this time being stacked in the cupboard. The wine was wearing off. Miriam was too tired to get out of bed but she did not want to fall asleep. The house was vibrant with lovemaking and she was desperate to be part of it.

It was almost noon when Miriam finally awoke with a hangover. She let her arm fall over the bolster. No Lynne. A chorus of chatter, laughter and clinking of dishes rang out gleefully above her. The smell of coffee mingled with familiar breakfast odours coaxed her out of bed and up the stairs.

The breakfast table was dressed up in a white tablecloth and cloth napkins. Freshly squeezed orange juice and coffee had been poured into glasses and mugs. Miriam's china graced the table once again.

When she walked in, she became acutely aware of her own presence. She had not showered but pulled on her robe and fluffy slippers and sauntered in, ready for a cup of coffee, the newspaper or the remote control. Last night's party seemed to deem all formalities unnecessary, but the silence at the table declared this was not the case.

Lynne stared at her. "Please retreat" was the command reflected in her eyes. The others looked up silently. Finally Monique spoke, "Had a hard night, eh?" and she winked at Miriam before heaping another pile of bacon onto her plate. That was the smell.

The sunlight suddenly bolted through the window and cast a film of gold around the room. Even the guests seemed to glow, and standing at the head of the table, directly across from Miriam was Lynne, tall, fresh and poised. In all her glory. She was passing around slices of zucchini loaf on the silver salver. Miriam reached for the last piece and caught her reflection in the platter. The mascara she had put on the night before had smudged dark circles around her eyes. She looked up to see Hank staring at her.

Hank smiled and spoke, "That was a great act last night."

"Oh yeah? All I recall is making a fool of myself."

Hank protested and assured her that she was fabulous.

"Did you girls have a good sleep?" Miriam asked pouring herself some coffee.

"Okay," answered Monique. "But this annoying wind chime kept ringing. I finally had to get up and remove it. Just a little tip, don't hang it over the vent, okay? Every time the heating came on, off went the chimes."

"Jingle bells," Miriam said.

"What?" Monique asked.

"The wind chimes. They're jingle bells, a Christmas decoration," Miriam explained, "to make the house more Christmassy."

"All right, Miriam," Lynne said sharply.

Then Lynne changed the subject. Miriam cast her eyes down as the swell of conversation allowed her some privacy in the midst of strangers.

"Hey Lynne," Teri said, "I don't know if anyone mentioned it yet, but we're going to head towards Tofino to do the rainforest walk. We won't be needing the rooms tonight."

"Oh?" Lynne said, surprised.

"Change of weather, change of plans," Monique explained.

"It's too bad really," Lynne offered. "I was planning to show you one of the trails on the mountain. You know the terrain around here is spectacular. Steep incline but nothing you young city gals can't handle."

"Hey thanks," Monique said, "but we're pretty set."

"You can see the beginning of the trail right outside this window. It's easily a three-hour hike to the top. There's a lookout tower up there. You get a panoramic view, ocean and everything." Lynne was trying to sound casual.

"You won't charge us for showing up late and leaving a day early, will you?" Laura asked.

"Laura," Teri warned.

"No problem. It's a slow period," Lynne said. But as she poured herself another cup of coffee, disappointment weighed heavily, a necklace of jewels turning to stones.

The guests were out of the house within a half hour. Lynne started clearing the table methodically: first the silverware then the plates. She grabbed the coffee pot and Miriam put her hands on it. The heat rose in her palms.

"I'm not finished," Miriam said sternly.

Lynne picked up the jug of orange juice. Miriam picked up a cold, burnt piece of bacon and snapped it between her fingers.

"I thought you didn't eat bacon," Lynne asked.

"And I thought you agreed not to cook it here, in our house, served on my mother's china, for God's sake." Miriam steadied her gaze on Lynne.

Lynne looked back at her. "You look pathetic you know. Undressed, old makeup smeared under your eyes. Look at yourself. No wonder they left. No wonder we don't get any business."

Miriam flung the piece of bacon at Lynne's face. Lynne gasped.

"Christ Miriam, will you . . ."

Then Lynne stormed out of the room, leaving Miriam with a plate of cold bacon and dirty dishes.

The mountain was steep and covered by a fresh layer of snow. Miriam could feel the effort in her calf muscles and the strain in her shoulders. She had hiked it several times with Lynne when they first moved in. Unlike Lynne who had ventured up many times alone, she feared the unsettling rustle of the leaves, the darkness that a forest canopy created. After showering, she had pulled her jeans over her long johns and put on a thick sweater and jacket. The air was still cold and crisp, but the sun was so strong that she had to pull off her scarf and hat and shake out her hair soon after she began the hike.

She wanted to shrug off the evening too. But it followed her, strapped to her back. Nevertheless, she was determined to climb, one foot in front of the other while taking frequent rests with lots of water. She longed to touch the trees. All of them, meld into them, become one. But she chose carefully: a large cedar, ancient and red, drops of moisture dripping off the branches. Extending her arms around the trunk, she pressed her face against it. Her eyes watered. She breathed in the scent.

"Help," she whispered. "Please help me."

Lynne stripped the bed in the last guest room and brought out clean sheets. She was particular about making beds, squaring the corners and folding the top of the sheet over the blanket. She did a thorough job dusting surfaces, vacuuming all the rugs and replacing the toiletries. When the last room was done she made her way downstairs to clean their own room. Lynne began with the bed. One strong tug and the fitted sheet fell onto the floor with the rest of the linen to be laundered. But with it, a sheet of paper fluttered up before floating to the ground. Lynne picked it up recognizing her own handwriting. Two words stared back at her. *Dear Eileen*. She read them out loud, "Dear Eileen." Had she left it there or had Miriam discovered it? "Dear Eileen." There was nothing more. Nothing to feel guilty about.

When Miriam reached the top of the mountain she stumbled and grasped the legs of the lookout tower for support. She had made it. After finishing the last of her water, she started climbing the ladder leading to the wooden platform. She gripped each rung with determination, reminding herself not to look down, just up. One, two, three, all the way to forty-eight. She heaved herself onto the platform and lay on her back, watching the sun inching itself across the sky. When she finally stood up and looked out, she saw it, all of it: the ocean bright blue and rolling towards her, the mountains majestic and proud, the forests, green and expansive, dotted with towns, roads and activity. She could make out ships: tiny cylinders from Russia, Japan, Australia. Yes indeed, the world was still out there and there was still time for Miriam to be part of it. If she awoke early enough the next morning she could catch the ferry to the mainland and make it to her parents' house for dinner. She still had a week before school resumed and she needed a break. Then she remembered tomorrow was Christmas. The ferries would be less frequent but she would eventually make it home.

Lynne sat at the dining room table and applied polish to the silver salver. She glanced out the window noticing the sun nearing the tree line.

Lynne imagined Hank, Teri and the rest of the girls driving along the coastal highway, the sun bouncing off a shimmering sea, giggling and chatting about the antics of the two old dykes at the B&B. Lynne had allowed them to eavesdrop on her and Miriam's most intimate conversations, to appraise their private possessions and finally to measure the bitterness wedged between them. It was brittle and tactile. It could be crushed with minimum effort, releasing a flood of accusations, anger and grief. The guests had witnessed their ugliness and resisted the magnetic force that kept Miriam and her anchored to the hill. The girls had escaped with their secret.

Miriam had been gone for hours. It was getting colder and soon it would be dark. Lynne knew Miriam was a wimp in the winter and would come back full of complaints. I will offer her a massage, Lynne thought, as she vigorously rubbed a cloth against the already shiny surface of the salver.

When she finished, she put on her coat and opened the door — to find Miriam standing in the cold.

"Jesus, I was worried about you. I was just about to go look for you."

"I climbed the mountain."

"And made it back, thank God. Are you okay?"

"Yeah." Miriam walked into the living room. It was spotless.

"Are we expecting more guests?"

"No. It's just us tonight. I was thinking we could drive to town and have dinner out," Lynne offered quietly.

"No. No thanks. I'm tired. I'm going to take a shower and . . ." Then Miriam looked squarely at Lynne. "I'm sleeping upstairs tonight."

"Miriam, come on. Listen, I'm sorry . . . about everything."

"I am too, Lynne."

Then Miriam scrunched up her face, perhaps to keep herself from crying or to stop more words from flowing out. The time for conversation had passed. She turned and walked down the hall, disappearing into one of the guestrooms.

Lynne sat at the table as the sun went down, leaving the room in darkness. Lighting the two candles from the previous evening, she angled the silver salver in her hands to find her reflection. She came from Scottish stock, strong, resilient and proudly unemotional. Yet tears trickled down her face like the rain on the window yesterday morning. There was a pattern to shedding tears and it was clear, systematic and beautiful. In fact she was beautiful. She had not noticed before but she had inherited her aunt's deep green eyes as well as her silver salver and family home. And the one person with whom she had made a home, her only family, was slipping away. Lynne suddenly realized that she, ever considerate, had helped Miriam to the door. She considered following Miriam to the bedroom, waiting patiently in the hall for her cue to go in. And when she did, she would lie down beside Miriam and caress her long into the night. Miriam would drift to sleep to the sound of her voice whispering words of love and reconciliation. But Lynne knew herself to be inarticulate, unable to muster a meaningful apology. She had always been a woman of action. But in this moment, she could do nothing but sit in the quiet and watch as the flames on the candles flickered and died.

The Arrangement

Though they were articulate critics of arranged marriage, both Ravi and Anjali borrowed from the tradition to shape their relationship by focusing on their common characteristics and shared dreams. They were both Indian, middle-class and wanted children without the trappings of marriage. It did not matter that they had differing spiritual beliefs, few common interests and moved in separate circles. Within two weeks of their acquaintance, they had outlined what they wanted from each other in a document, punctuated by bullets, defined by clauses — a pre-nuptial agreement of sorts, except there were no nuptials. None of this head-over-heels, then over-the-falls business for them. Recently divorced, Ravi had no intention of sacrificing his new found freedom for the shackles of marriage and, luckily for him, Anjali agreed with the concept of an open relationship. Anjali, herself, was not ready to compromise her career in contemporary Indian dance, and Ravi, a creature of routine and financially stable, ensured support for child-rearing while she choreographed works around the world. It was an arrangement which, when analyzed, read like a business deal built on bartering, a tit-for-tat exchange, a recipe for success.

So two years later, when they decided to marry, they shocked even themselves by how simple it seemed. They had not counted on or looked for their parents' approval but it was granted. His parents, Rasesh and Lakshmi Advani, liked Anjali. Unlike Ravi's first wife Madeleine, the French-Canadian girl who wore black mini-skirts and ate raw beef, Anjali had simple, modest tastes in clothing, wore no makeup and cooked and ate only vegetarian food. That her vegetarianism was based on her abhorrence of cruelty towards animals and had nothing to do with purity, religion or the demands of caste was unknown to the Advanis. The crucial point was that their grandchildren would be raised vegetarian and their son would be well cared for by a plain and simple girl. With Anjali, they felt their son had made an informed and sensible, if not perfect, choice of mate.

Anjali's parents were also happy with her choice. Chinnan and Pranathi David were used to being introduced to a number of Anjali's "friends," as she called them, and had stopped expecting that one of these relationships would culminate in marriage. For years, Anjali had put off settling down in favour of touring with her dance company. Her involvements, she had told them, were based on her present desires rather than future dreams. So when Anjali and Ravi unexpectedly arrived on the Davids' doorstep with a bottle of champagne in hand and announced their engagement, Chinnan and Pranathi were elated.

After embracing her daughter enthusiastically, Pranathi pulled Anjali into the kitchen to help prepare dinner. Alone with her daughter, she expressed her main concern that Brahmin-born Ravi would force Anjali to convert to Hinduism and their grandchildren would be raised to believe in a pantheon of deities without the guidance of the one true God, Jesus Christ. Anjali had reassured her mother that Ravi believed in the big-bang theory, that gods or goddesses were as fictional to him as Puff the Magic

Dragon. Their children would be raised God-free while being exposed to many religions. They could eventually choose their own spiritual beliefs, if any.

These reassurances provoked a new set of anxieties for Pranathi. There would be not one competing religion but several: Islam, Judaism, Buddhism and perhaps others she did not even know about. Nevertheless, Ravi was a good-looking boy of thirty-six years. He had a high paying job, wore a suit and drove a nice car. He was polite and deferential and, more importantly, seemed to adore their daughter. So Chinnan and Pranathi David gave their blessing with the belief that the couple could be worked on. Now they could finally announce that their forty-year-old Anjali was getting married. They celebrated by uncorking the bottle of champagne.

꒰꒱

Anjali pours oil in her palm and rubs her hands together. "Are you ready? 1–2–3 . . ."

"Cold, cold, cooold," Ravi exclaims tensing his shoulders against her hands kneading his flesh.

"I warned you." Anjali continues massaging his back.

"What is this stuff?"

"An old recipe my mother's great-great-grandmother used. It not only has the power to relax muscles but boosts fertility! You can drink it, rub it on your skin, take it intravenously. Known to be used by whole communities to beget hundreds of little brats who in turn begat thousands of little brats of which one begat me."

"I think it's begot," Ravi suggests.

"Begat, begot, tomato, tomahto. The result is the same."

"It should be, the way that stuff smells," Ravi laughs. "I better be pregnant by the time I get out of bed."

"Very funny." Anjali presses her thumb into a pressure point between his shoulder blades.

"Ouch. Take it easy."

"No pain, no gain," she responds but she releases the pressure and gently rubs the tense area.

"Hey, maybe you should start massaging me somewhere else," Ravi suggests turning over on his back and winking at Anjali.

"Hmm," Anjali smiles, casting her eyes appreciatively over Ravi's long and muscular body. She had once said that he had a perfect dancer's form, but when he demonstrated his skills one night at a club, she couldn't help laughing. He admitted he had no sense of rhythm.

"Why didn't I think of that?" Anjali kneels between Ravi's legs to massage his thighs. "I hope it works this time," she adds.

Ravi pauses and glares at Anjali. His desire, which had risen quickly and urgently, instantly flees. He gets up from the bed.

"Hey, I didn't mean *it*. The massage oil. Come on, don't be so sensitive." Anjali throws a pillow at him.

He deflects it and pulls on his trousers, grabs a shirt, and leaves the room. Anjali listens to his footsteps plodding down the stairs, entering the living room. She sighs, picks up the pillow and buries her head in it. Before long she swings her legs over the bed and stands up. The floor is cold, the room chilly. She puts on her robe and a pair of socks and joins Ravi downstairs.

They sit on the couch facing a wall of photographs. Pictures of their romance stare back. There is a shot of them on top of a pyramid in Mexico, their faces sweaty, their smiles exuberant. Another shows them wine-tasting in France; Anjali is staring past the camera, while Ravi's head is tilted down, fixated on her collar bone. A third shows them swimming in the Indian Ocean. Anjali is extending her hand to Ravi, whose arms are in the air, a panicked look on his face as if he were drowning. Their romance had indeed blossomed and begun far from home.

They were both travelling in India, searching for some R&R — relaxation and their respective roots: he, a north Indian Brahmin and she, a south Indian Christian. Ravi spotted Anjali on a beach in Kerala, her strong legs extended along the length of a towel. Normally, Indians do not don swimsuits and lie on the beach in an effort to tan, but there amongst a sea of white tourists littering the golden strip of sand, lay Anjali.

"Are you Indian?" Ravi asked.

Shielding her eyes, Anjali looked up and studied the stranger.

"No, I'm lesbian," she answered curtly. Then she closed her eyes as if her response would put an end to further inquiries. On the contrary, it cemented Ravi's interest.

"Ah, the Isle of Lesbos," he responded, crouching beside her. He picked up a handful of sand and let it run through his fingers. "I hear your fellow citizens are claiming the name for their exclusive use."

Anjali propped herself up on her elbows and looked at him curiously. "You seem to take a particular interest in the citizens of Lesbos."

"Lesbians in general," he smiled back, "but that is a bit cliché, *n'est-ce pas?*"

"*Et vous parlez français.*"

"*Je suis Canadien,*" he said in an embarrassingly Anglophone accent.

"So am I, as a matter of fact," Anjali confessed. She patted the sand, inviting Ravi to recline beside her. He did and, as they chatted, he explained that he was recently divorced and not interested in relationships, only company that could relate to his sense of alienation. He had been roaming around India searching for some sense of belonging, but instead had felt more and more a stranger. She responded, "Well at least you don't have every Maharajah and fucking descendant of Mountbatten himself hitting on you."

"That bad, huh? So why are you still here then? I mean you're not exactly playing it modest," he said glancing at her bikini then breaking out into a broad smile.

She sat up and drew her knees to her chest and reached for her shirt. "You could say I'm searching for my roots but in a very specific way. I'm researching the *Mudi-attam*, a female fertility dance once practised by my ancestors right here in this region."

"Sounds both intriguing and flaky."

"There's nothing flaky about it," Anjali exclaimed, a bit miffed at his comment. "The dance is practised now for entertainment but it involves about twelve women, hair down, swaying and . . . I guess it does sound a bit flaky the way I'm describing it. But it's quite complex, the ritual and meaning it evoked for the community. I'm studying with Mariamma Chedathy, one of the last living experts in the form. That's why I'm taking a two-week breather. I've been at it for three months now and it's pretty intense."

"But does it work?"

"I don't know; my hair's too short," she laughed.

"Me, I'm all for the old fashioned method. Man, woman, another kind of dance if you like. Hair is optional." Ravi winked playfully. "Say, do you want to go for a drink?" he asked, standing up and dusting the sand from his jeans.

She extended her arm and her small almost childlike hand nearly disappeared in his grasp. Then he pulled her up and led her down the slim margin of beach as the warm waves of the Arabian Sea swallowed their footprints.

That was then. This is now.

"I think I'll go out."

"Fine."

"Look, if you don't want me to go," Ravi offers, taking her hand. She reaches instead for a cigarette in a small wooden box on the coffee table.

"You obviously have to prove something to yourself," Anjali responds.

"What the hell is that supposed to mean?"

"Nothing. Just go." Anjali crosses her legs and lights up a smoke.

"Hey." He brings the cigarette down from her mouth with his index finger.

"Hey," she responds sternly. "You have your habits and I mine."

Ravi acknowledges her with a shrug and gets up from the couch. Leaving, he ushers in a cool current of spring air. Anjali pulls at a shawl folded on the back of the couch and covers herself up to her chin, tucking her feet underneath her. After flicking through the channels, she falls asleep, her face aglow in the TV light.

ॐ

On Sunday morning, the day after Ravi and Anjali announced their engagement, Chinnan and Pranathi David walked solemnly to the front of the church to take part in communion. Pranathi could not help picturing her daughter walking this same aisle, wearing an embroidered ivory silk sari, gold sparkling against her dark skin, a bouquet of roses . . . no, orchids, held in her hands. As Pranathi knelt beside her husband, ready to receive "the blood of Jesus Christ," she whispered a prayer of thanksgiving and solicited a promise from God.

"You must bless and protect Anjali from the cruelty and compromises of married life," she whispered with eyes shut and hands clasped together.

Her own marriage to Chinnan had shunted between silence and resentment, boredom and frustration. They had even exchanged bitter and cruel words not easily forgiven, never forgotten.

"Let it be easy for her, Lord. Make it a blessed life, free from — "

Pranathi felt the sharp jab of an elbow and opened her eyes to see her husband gesturing that the minister was holding the goblet to her lips. She sipped from the cup, confident that her prayer had been heard. But after, as she walked down the aisle to her pew, her mind was focused on one thought: the wedding. She was stumped. After all, in whose tradition would it be? Would they invite the minister from their church or the temple priest? Would the couple walk seven times around a fire, or straight to the altar? Would there be an exchange of rings or garlands? Pranathi sat down and bent her head as the minister began a prayer. His words reverberated in her ears but she could not concentrate. Wedding possibilities kept dancing in her head. She leaned over to her husband and began whispering.

Chinnan opened one eye.

"What?"

"The wedding, we have to plan — "

"Shh," Chinnan responded, looking down to the hymnal in his lap. "You know Anjali and Ravi want it their way. Something informal at city hall."

"Yes, but we cannot accept that. This is our only — "

Chinnan placed two fingers on his wife's lips.

"They were very clear about their wishes," he whispered sternly.

A congregation member in front of them turned disapprovingly. Reluctantly, Pranathi concurred with her husband and bent her head just in time for the final Amen. But throughout the rest of the service she was uneasy.

Back at home, Pranathi served her husband his favourite dish of *njandu* curry, coconut rice and almond *seera* for dessert. After finishing, he sat across from her patting his stomach, fully satisfied. Then she presented him with a guest list of one hundred and fifty people.

"What is this?" Chinnan barked, "I thought I told you — "

"This is not for the wedding, silly man. It is for the engagement ceremony."

"I see," Chinnan responded stiffly. After forty-three years of marriage, he had learned when to accept his wife's ideas, when to resist them and when to put his foot down. Lately, his foot rarely reached the floor.

Pranathi and Chinnan had been contemporaries in university, intellectual equals. But over the years it was she who had sacrificed her career. She had given up her studies and agreed to move to Canada after he won a fellowship at the university. When she enrolled in classes, she found herself pregnant and, after years of taking care of Anjali, could never make her way into the job market — and not from a lack of trying. At one point she jokingly considered joining the ranks of immigrant taxi drivers with MBAs and engineering degrees, if only to be able to tell her story to captive riders. Hoping to discourage his wife from even thinking of such an occupation, Chinnan proclaimed his respect for home economics and deferred to his wife in all domestic matters, mitigating his guilt, trying to make up for all he owed her.

So Chinnan scanned his wife's list in silence. It included both sides of the family, members of the Christian and Hindu communities. As well, there was a smattering of white, black, Asian, Aboriginal, Jewish, Muslim colleagues and friends from all corners of life, beyond the sphere of familial relations.

"I see you've included the full spectrum of Anjali's friends and acquaintances."

"You don't like her friends?" Pranathi asked.

"No, but *they* may not."

The Davids assumed that their future son-in-law's parents were conservative and, like themselves, harboured certain prejudices under a layer of politeness.

"Maybe Anjali won't miss that fellow John, if he is not invited," Pranathi offered, reviewing her list to her husband. "You know, that dancer who wears the blue eye make-up and nail polish."

"He's not a bad fellow, it's just that he — "

"Or that girl who shaved her head . . . she used to be such a pretty girl."

They pondered this for a moment, and then Chinnan turned to his wife. "If we make the engagement party a surprise, then no one can approve or disapprove of the guest list. We can un-invite all the potential undesirables." He intended his comment as a joke, but Pranathi loved the idea. One week before the marriage at city hall, they would invite Ravi and Anjali to a small but formal (wear a sari, Anjali!) dinner for the two families. But there would be a whole array of friends and well-wishers from both sides crouching behind the sofa, positioned strategically behind plants.

"I should have known you would have the perfect solution," Pranathi flattered her husband. "Tonight, you must telephone the Advanis and invite them for tea. Let the festivities begin."

 ॐ

Anjali awakes with a start at 5 a.m. Ravi is still not home. She is cold. The shawl has slipped off, leaving her exposed to the chill air. She gets up and folds the shawl over the couch. Her back is stiff from her awkward sleeping position so she stands and stretches her body, which easily bends and twists in any direction from years of training. As she extends her socked feet forward to stretch her hamstrings, she slips and catches herself.

"Cursed floor," she says as she removes her socks, allowing her bare feet to make contact with the cold, smooth floorboards.

Ravi and Anjali had bought the house one month ago from Ravi's cousin, Arwin, who had married and purchased a larger house with a front lawn and sprawling veranda. Arwin could not stand the fact that some stranger would enjoy the renovations he had perfected on his Cabbagetown house during his bachelor days, so he sold it to Ravi and Anjali far below the market value. They promised to maintain the house in pristine condition, oiling the oak wood floors which Arwin had painstakingly laid by hand. Ravi and Anjali had spent the first two days on their hands and knees keeping to their promise. Until the furniture arrives, they agreed.

"I'm starting to feel like we've entered into a life of bonded labour to that devil cousin of yours."

"I know what you mean," Ravi replied. "I have nightmares that he'll start dropping in every fortnight to check his floors."

"I'm just glad he's stuck in the suburbs. And I hope he gets fat from his wife's oily *parathas*."

"Now, now. You're just jealous."

"Of what?"

"Of their life in the burbs. That's really what you want, isn't it? A life of making *parathas*, rubbing my tired feet when I return from the office."

"Your dreams, baby."

"Maybe," Ravi said as he polishes his way towards her. "In a way I envy Arwin. He owns a big house, drives a luxury car, and married a nice Indian girl."

"Is that what you want? To be married to a *nice* Indian girl?" She turned her face coquettishly up to his.

"Yeah. Do you know any?" Ravi tweaked Anjali's perfect triangular nose.

"You rat," Anjali had replied, swatting him with her rag.

Ravi grabbed the rag and drew her close to him. He brought her hand to his lips.

"So how about it?" he asked softly.

"Are you serious?" Anjali moved away in disbelief.

The next day he got down on one knee and pulled a ring from his pocket.

When they had negotiated their "arrangement," they had been clear it did not involve marriage. But on the day after oiling the floor, it suddenly made sense to them. They joked that they must have been high from the scent of the oil. But neither backed out. After all, for almost two years, ever since they had negotiated their future in a beachside restaurant in Kovalum, Ravi and Anjali had been trying to conceive, racing against the biological clock towards the fulfillment of their shared dream. They had worked out a logical arrangement, and in an impulsive moment they found themselves headed toward irrational matrimony.

After finishing her yoga routine with *surya namaskar*, the salute to the sun, Anjali goes upstairs to the bathroom. She opens the medicine cabinet, withdraws a thermometer and takes her temperature. Normal. She records the number on a chart tacked up between a calendar and the mirror, and traces a line between the dots. She should be ovulating around this time. As she reviews the calendar, she counts the days to confirm her cycle and thinks she may have neglected to mark the week of her last period. She flips through April. March yes, but no April. Puzzled, she sits on the toilet seat to think.

What was I doing at the end of April? she wonders. They had already moved into the house. They were decorating. She had forgotten to mark it down. But that was so unlike her. When did I last buy tampons? There is a fluttering in her stomach as she imagines what could be. March 31st was the beginning of her last period. It is May 10th. She is late. "Oh my God," she says.

She rifles through the medicine cabinet in search of a home pregnancy test, but there are none. Never mind, she will buy another test. No drinking at tonight's dinner. The bitter argument with Ravi is quickly erased from her mind. She goes to the kitchen and drinks a glass of milk and pops a pre-natal pill infused with folic acid, vitamins and minerals, to increase the health of her unborn child. Then she dumps out her emergency cigarettes, resolving never again to touch them no matter how much Ravi infuriates her. Having observed other pregnant women vow off cigarettes, fatty foods and drink, she realizes these are not sacrifices at all but a simple trade-off. Anjali yawns, grateful that it is Saturday. As day breaks, she slips into a negligee and crawls into bed. She drifts off to sleep, buoyant with hope.

ॐ

Drops of water dripped off the perforated spoon into the hot oil, causing it to splatter and set off a series of snapping sounds. Pranathi drew back momentarily before she gathered the batch of *bhajia* from the wok and deposited it into the paper towel-lined bowl. After watching the paper soak up the oil she transferred the savoury snacks into a stainless steel vessel for serving. The doorbell rang and she turned off the burner, washed her hands and started towards the door, when she remembered she was still wearing her apron.

"Chinnan, quickly . . . they are here," she shouted from the kitchen, slipping out of her apron and smoothing down her silvery black hair.

When she entered the living room, Chinnan was hanging up the coats of Rasesh and Lakshmi Advani. Both couples stood in the foyer greeting each other cordially. *"Namascar," "Namascaram,"* they said, palms together and heads bowed. This was the first time they had met, and they had done so without the knowledge of their children. Pranathi did a visual scan of the couple, checking for unsightly skin conditions or deformities in their skeletal structures. She assumed that the Advanis were doing the same, imagining which features would be transmitted through their DNA and reflected in the eyes, ears or noses of their potential grandchildren. Chinnan and Pranathi knew that their dark skin and short stature would be unwelcome characteristics. But the Advanis had already met and accepted Anjali, who carried these traits along with large almond eyes and a straight nose with beautifully flared nostrils, perfect for wearing a *mookuthi*. Pranathi hated that she had to justify dark skin, as if it were not intrinsically beautiful. She took in the Advanis. Yes, they were both quite fair skinned, but his head was rather large and she had hawkish features which overshadowed her pretty smile. Thank goodness, Ravi had inherited the best of both his parents, as Anjali had from them. Together, and with the grace of God, their combined looks and brains would make for beautiful, intelligent and, more importantly, healthy children.

Pranathi welcomed the Advanis into the living room and gestured towards the most comfortable seats in the house. Rasesh Advani sat in a large easy chair. He was tall and imposing, with long legs that stretched out in front of him. Except for a white fringe around his ears and the back of his head, he was completely bald. The baldness is inherited from the genes acquired from the mother's side, Pranathi reminded herself, glancing at her husband's full head of hair.

No one spoke for a time.

"This is a lovely room," Lakshmi said.

"Thank you," replied Pranathi.

Chinnan adjusted his glasses on the bridge of his nose.

Rasesh looked around the tasteful and modestly decorated room. He glanced at a newspaper that was lying open on the side table and read the headline out loud.

"'Nuns Killed by BJP Supporters.' Terrible thing. These fundamentalists are taking things too far," Rasesh said, his eyes scanning the headlines.

"Please go ahead, read the article," Chinnan said. "We are not so formal here."

Chinnan sat opposite his guest, perched on the edge of the sofa, his small hands placed squarely on his knees, as if he were about to jump up any moment.

Rasesh picked up the newspaper and said, "It seems that almost every minority is targeted these days. Muslims, now Christians and all retaliate."

The others nodded as Rasesh continued to read.

Then he suddenly and swiftly put down the paper and said with some conviction, "You know this horrendous issue of communal violence in India — it is not about religion at all but the mob mentality. It is mostly lower castes and uneducated masses that are involved."

Chinnan's eyelids blinked rapidly behind his glasses. "One cannot really say. What is true is that these acts are politically motivated. Wouldn't you agree?"

"Possibly," Rasesh responded. "But no matter who first plants the seed of intolerance, individuals have a choice to participate or not."

"Of course, I could not agree with you more. But look at the power of suggestion and the powerful people inciting the mobs," Chinnan continued. "It is the educated politicians, the fundamentalist leaders and the majority of them, from higher castes."

Neither Rasesh nor Chinnan mentioned aloud what they both were thinking. That the Advanis shared the same name as a prominent politician in the Bharatiya Janata Party, now the Deputy Prime Minister of India.

"No politics please," Pranathi whispered through her teeth, aware of the same thought.

There was a pause.

"So, Ravi tells us you are from Kerala?" Rasesh said.

"Yes. Most of our relations still live in Trivandrum."

"I see," Rasesh reflected. "And your community?"

Ahh, the question. Chinnan had not expected it so soon. The question he had evaded most of his life. But this person, these people, would soon be their relations. The other set of grandparents to their grandchildren.

Chinnan gave his community name, "Pulayar." The room again went quiet. Chinnan was unsure whether his guest would seek further clarification — knowing well just what he was seeking with the question. Chinnan decided to offer the information.

"For those who speak or understand Malayalam, the meaning is clear. Not just the literal meaning of course but the social one. My community is a scheduled caste, the lowest of low on the totem pole one might say. We are untouchables."

"*Harijans* is the term Gandhi Ji used," Rasesh said.

"But the preferred term, at least for us, is Dalits," Chinnan responded.

Pranathi looked at her husband in shock. She had heard his answers to these questions before, and none were so forthright.

"My family converted to Christianity in my generation, so we are very familiar with our community but my wife . . . Pranathi's family is not Dalit," Chinnan clarified.

"Well, language changes to reflect our times and attitudes," Rasesh continued. "We've come some distance from those days of caste discrimination."

Chinnan was not so certain. Certainly caste had been abolished in the constitution of India, but for centuries it had permeated the psyche of its citizens. He had been raised to defer to Brahmins. His childhood was filled with reminders of where his community stood in the pecking order of Indian society. As a child, he had read the signs in front of certain temples forbidding the entrance of dogs, untouchables and Christians. He had been called *viddi* and roughly escorted off a bus when he accidentally brushed up against a woman of a higher caste. He had shrugged off jeers for being a Dalit who gained admission to university on a reservation quota, knowing the ridicule was a consequence of narrow thinking, a small burden he had to bear for an education. And he was lucky compared to what was experienced by others . . .

"Yes, yes," Lakshmi suddenly joined in. "Thank goodness, those days are over. But even here there is an unspoken caste system."

"It is understood as class in this country," Rasesh corrected his wife. He continued to leaf through the paper.

"I am talking about the experience of our children. Throughout school,

Ravi was called Paki-derm by fellow classmates, even his closest friends. For the longest time he didn't know why he was called this or what it meant," Lakshmi continued.

"Well, we can never control the intentions of other people. We can only teach our children to accept difference in others," Chinnan offered.

"Judge not lest ye be judged," Lakshmi interjected.

"Yes, Matthew 7, verse 1. How do you know this?" Pranathi asked, surprised and delighted.

"We cannot escape the Bible in this country. Even Ravi had to say the Lord's Prayer each day at school. At any rate, that is what we all were taught, in one sense or the other. Of course, when I was growing up, my friends were Parsi, Muslim, Christian, Jain . . . ," Lakshmi trailed off.

"And as you know, Hinduism encompasses all religions. All prophets and saints are reincarnations, varied facets of God," Rasesh added.

Yes, Chinnan thought to himself, and the same religion dictates that some castes are so lowly as to be treated worse than oxen, forced to clean the shit of their fellow men.

"And we Christians celebrate *Diwali*, every year," Pranathi added. "How I miss those celebrations in India."

"It is not the same here. Never the same," Lakshmi responded.

"Mr. David, Ravi tells us you are actually Doctor David?" Rasesh interjected.

"PHD," Chinnan replied. He took off his glasses and polished them vigorously. A distinguished scholar, Chinnan often mused about the limitations of science. No matter how much data supported the fact that there was no genetic basis for caste divisions, people still clung to their beliefs that, somehow, Dalits were inferior. Science could prove a fact but not convince people to accept the fact to be true. He had inherited his social standing and the ignorant attitudes that gripped him and so many others.

His wife added, "He has been tenured now at the university since '91. His specialty is in human genetics. I had an interest in biochemistry and began my PHD but could not finish my studies."

"Yes, Ravi told us you are at the university," Rasesh continued, ignoring Pranathi's story. "I am a lowly high school teacher myself."

"I see," Pranathi grunted, affronted by Rasesh's apparent snub.

"There is nothing lowly about that," Chinnan said genuinely. "It is an important profession. You are providing leadership at a crucial time when the child becomes an adult and starts thinking like a responsible human being."

Rasesh spoke gruffly. "Not in my class. They swear and curse. Many are already taking drugs. One student, only fifteen years old, has become pregnant and continues coming to school. She is eight months pregnant. Can you imagine the audacity?" Then Rasesh picked up the newspaper again and folded it squarely in front of him. "Twenty-five years I have taught in that school and suddenly students are complaining about my accent. I've been approached, invited, one might say, to consider early retirement. I will finish my illustrious career at the end of June. I am only fifty-seven. How do you like that?"

Rasesh focused on the paper. Lakshmi averted her eyes. There was an awkward pause. Pranathi re-examined Rasesh. He was quite a bit younger than Chinnan but he appeared much older. She worried that he had some rare disease and suddenly felt embarrassed, sensing an awkward tension of knowing too much about someone with whom you are hardly acquainted.

Pranathi suddenly said, "I think we all need some refreshments. I have *chai, bhajia, chaat* and *bel puri*."

"I will help you," Lakshmi insisted and stood up, elegant in an emerald green sari.

She followed Pranathi down the hall and giggled, "Isn't this naughty of us. We are outsmarting our children, and they thought they were outsmarting us. This city hall nonsense, Mrs. David. Pranathi . . . may I call you Pranathi? Don't you agree?"

Pranathi was taken aback by the open and friendly demeanour of her soon-to-be relation.

"Yes, of course. That is why we telephoned you. Our children deserve some special celebration, even if not the wedding itself. Something to express our love."

As Pranathi dished out the *chaat* into four quarter plates, Lakshmi ladled the *chai* into teacups from a large pot on the stove.

"I have always liked your Anjali," Lakshmi began, provoking a proud smile from Pranathi. "I detest falseness in people."

"Falseness?" Pranathi said, puzzled. "Are you suggesting . . ."

"No, no," Lakshmi explained, "I do like her very much. She seems to be what she appears. We have only one son. And . . . well you must know he is divorced. And my daughters, one is married. Oh, we gave her such a lavish wedding. I will show you the photographs. But my youngest is determined to remain independent. What can we do? We live in such a world where we parents have less and less sway over our children. The problem is we give them everything, try to understand them, accept their decisions — but there is no guarantee. They are adults, after all. Now Ravi's first wife . . . we welcomed her even if she wasn't . . . well she wasn't even Indian. And she came to know us, or so we thought. She touched our feet each time entering the house. She cooked *parathas* and *subzi* perfectly. She wore a *bindi* in our presence. But she turned out to be quite false. Very false. And the jewellery I gave her. You should have seen it. As it is, I will never lay my eyes upon such beautiful treasures again. Oh, that reminds me. I have something for Anjali I wanted to show you."

She pulled a small velvet pouch out of her purse and laid a ruby necklace on the kitchen counter. It sparkled under the light.

"It is beautiful," Pranathi replied, regretting that her daughter did not wear jewellery.

"I thought she would like it. It belonged to my mother," Lakshmi said putting it back into her purse. "Now what I meant to say is that we want to know the girl Ravi is marrying. We don't need to change her. Only to know her. Who she really is."

Pranathi stared at her guest and popped *bhajia* into her mouth, silently chewing on this information. She dared not say anything that would expose her daughter's varied past, her unconventional ideas, her modern and sometimes strange dance moves.

Thank goodness for the necessity of eating, Pranathi thought. And the two women, steadily clutching trays, returned to the living room. By the end of the visit, *chai*, savoury snacks and *mithai* had been consumed and an array of decisions and compromises had been made. A dinner at the Advanis' home was scheduled to finish organizing the party.

As Chinnan closed the door, he spoke with relief, "Well, that seemed to go well."

"With little help from you," Pranathi asserted. "Dalit, indeed. What a time for true confessions." She wiped the sweat from her forehead with the *pallu* of her sari and began to clear away the dishes.

ॐ

Upon leaving his ex-wife Madeleine's house early that Saturday morning, Ravi had taken a drive along the Don Valley Parkway and then through the green-fringed winding roads of Rosedale. A few hours later he found himself in a greasy spoon on Parliament Street, ordering an all-day breakfast special and reviewing his life.

His "outings" were becoming frequent and predictable. He felt uncomfortable leaving Anjali, as he did. But it's her choice, he reminded himself. After all they had agreed that they could both see other people if they wanted. But she chose not to. At least, not at present. When he questioned her about it, Anjali had explained that her mind, body and soul were devoted to having a child, *his* child. Any sexual encounter other than with Ravi seemed a waste of her precious and targeted energy. Ravi was relieved that she wasn't interested in other men. Nevertheless, he felt the pressure of her expectations. Four months ago, he had emerged from the shower to find Anjali sitting on the toilet a look of despair in her eyes.

"What's the matter?" he asked reaching for the towel and wrapping it around his waist. She pointed to her blood-stained underwear stretched between her knees.

"This is what?" she said flatly.

He looked away. It was not that he had an aversion to bodily fluids or was queasy around blood; rather he felt as if he had done something to her. But the problem was he had *not*. He had not impregnated her. He was guilty, her menses was proof of this, and he blamed himself for his "somewhat" low sperm count.

"Somewhat?" he had asked the doctor.

"Well, twenty million sperm per millilitre is considered normal. Anything under that . . . and your last count was under, and since your partner is over forty."

"She's forty this year . . ."

"It's the combination really, a somewhat," he repeated it again, "low sperm count plus the diminishing odds of fertilization with an older woman, *nuli gravida* . . ."

It was as if the doctor were chanting a nursery rhyme to himself, his sing-song voice, rising then falling.

"What?"

"Well your wife — "

"Girlfriend."

The doctor had given Ravi a "whatever" look (the response of choice by insolent teenagers), as if the point were irrelevant. Which Ravi supposed it was. To the doctor, for all primary purposes, Anjali was simply the womb.

"She is obviously not in her prime in terms of childbearing years, and with no pregnancies in her past, from what you say, the conditions for conception are less than ideal."

They were animals, Ravi had thought as he left the clinic. Two animals measured for breeding, reduced to their biology, age and potential. It didn't matter that he was a successful marketing director or that she was a celebrated choreographer and dancer. These were inconsequential in the face of their inability to conceive a child. Ravi hid the diagnosis from Anjali, even though he could see that his deception was causing her grief. She blamed herself: her age, her lack of body fat, her hormones. She took more and more tests, irrationally finding fault with her retroverted uterus, her long fallopian tubes and her irregular cycle.

Anjali flushed the toilet and started rinsing her underwear in the sink.

"Maybe we should go to the fertility clinic," she suggested. "Explore some alternative methods. Intrauterine — "

"I know the methods," Ravi barked.

Anjali hung her underwear on the rack and climbed into the shower. Then Ravi took his place at the sink and began to shave. They were not living together then, but had been spending more and more time at his apartment.

"Well, do you have something against assisted pregnancy? There are many successful cases, and if I stop ovulating . . ." Anjali spoke loudly over the hum of the water.

"That's ridiculous," Ravi said, nicking himself with the razor. "Shit."

"What?"

"Nothing."

"But maybe I have ugly old eggs and your sperm are taking one look and turning back."

"Jesus, there's nothing wrong with your eggs. All *your* tests were fine."

The flow of water stopped. Anjali drew open the shower curtain, soap still slick on her skin.

"What does that mean?"

"It means your tests were fine. You know that; stop going on about it."

"Hang on, buddy." Anjali got out of the shower and Ravi knew the conversation wouldn't be ending soon. "You said, *your* tests were fine. Added emphasis on *your*. What are you . . . ?"

"Okay. I had my sperm count checked," Ravi began.

"You told me it was normal."

Ravi felt claustrophobic. He had shaving cream on his face, and Anjali was drying herself off, blocking the passage to the door. There was no escape. He stared down at the sink, the water disappearing down the drain.

"I had it re-checked." Anjali didn't respond. "I'm sorry, I'm low. I have a low sperm count."

"How long have you known?"

"I went back for another test, a couple of months ago," he lied. It had been closer to six months.

"I can't believe you. I can't fucking believe you," Anjali whispered and stormed down the hall. Ravi heard the bedroom door close and the click of the lock turning.

He gave her time. After shaving, he rinsed his face, applied aftershave and massaged two finger tips of coconut oil into his scalp. Then he took a deep breath before walking down the hall to knock on the door.

"Leave me alone," Anjali shouted through the door.

"But it's my bedroom. I need to get dressed and go to work," he said with his forehead pressed to the door.

She opened it wearing a sweater and pair of slacks. While he dressed, he heard her out: how he should have told her right away, how he had made her suffer, how his lies could ruin their arrangement. He simply listened until she wore herself out and sat on the edge of the bed, silent and thoughtful.

When he finished dressing he stood in front of her and said quietly, "I was embarrassed frankly, very ashamed. I should have told you. I'm sorry, so sorry I caused you pain."

Anjali took his hand lightly. "I am sorry, too, honey. But I'm relieved in a way. I thought there was something wrong with me."

"But there's something wrong with me, so that's okay," he responded, trying to make light of things, feeling guilty for his use of a little lie that eased the telling of the big truth.

"No, it's just that it can be worked on. There are remedies. Didn't the doctor recommend . . . I mean, you still want to, don't you?"

Ravi sat down next to her and she gave his hand a little squeeze. A current of something, electricity perhaps, pulsed in his veins. He smiled and pulled her onto his lap. He loved holding her. She was petite and she fit so perfectly there. He had often pictured their child, also perched on his lap, head wiggling, mouthing delightful, incomprehensible murmurings.

"Of course I do," he said, but even then he feared failing in this most basic, elemental of human functions. The one that promised continuity and hope.

So Ravi began the challenge to produce more and better sperm: he changed his diet and started wearing boxers instead of briefs. He stored his mountain bike in the basement, tucking it under a shelf of cycling trophies. And with Anjali's urging he practised yoga with her to relax and de-stress, sipped a variety of recommended herbal teas and popped "special" vitamins. In fact, their decision to move in together was, in part, an effort to increase their chances. But there always seemed to be some kind of drama associated with sex: post-intercourse headstands and tears at the end of the month. The constant discussion about opportune times and best positions left Ravi with occasional impotence. The flaccid dick syndrome, he joked, when it first occurred. When it happened later and with greater frequency, his smile turned sour. Anjali stopped her comforting caresses and turned away from him. He would stare into the soft down on her back, resenting her seemingly strategic attitude towards sex and him. He was useful to her. That was certain. But did she desire him? Love him? They had avoided the term, not wanting to complicate their understanding. But wasn't that what they were feeling? Even when they argued and hated each other? Wasn't that what *he* was feeling? Where the hell was *her* heart, he wondered? So he sought a familiar home for his.

It is close to 3 p.m. when Ravi finally pulls the car into their driveway. He knows Anjali will be worried, but he was determined not to return until he had resolved a few things. He enters the house and is immediately aware of Anjali's absence. The place feels eerily empty. Perhaps *she* has finally left *me*, he thinks. The dishes from last night's dinner are washed and put away, the living room is tidy and Anjali's ashtray is polished clean: signs that she had waited for him. He pictures her on the couch, her eyebrows knitted together in a stitch of worry. He picks up her sock, hiding near the leg of the coffee table. Even though he feels bad for making her wait, he knows it could not have been helped. He had needed the time.

Plodding upstairs, he enters the bathroom and drops the sock in the hamper. He turns on the shower, then empties his pockets of his keys, wallet and a package of condoms, one of which he used last night with his ex-wife. Madeleine is his back-up, no longer interested in him as a husband, but happy enough to have sex with him when she is between relationships. He sees her like a mother or a prostitute. Someone who gives him comfort with few complications. Madeleine doesn't ask him to leave any trace of himself behind, to plant proof of his virility in her uterus. She is a good lay. No strings attached. No questions asked. Everything a man could want. Oddly dissatisfying.

ॐ

Chinnan twirled around in his swivel chair, closed the journal and smiled with satisfaction. He had authored the featured article in the latest issue of the *Journal of Human Genetics*. Even though he had already presented his hypothesis at several conferences to a positive response, there was nothing like seeing his words in print, endorsed by one of the most accredited journals on scientific research in the world. It was a hefty study. He had mastered a new technique to replace mutated genes responsible for diseases such as autism and bipolar disorder. The trials had resulted in groundbreaking success. At the last conference he attended, Chinnan was questioned as to whether his findings in gene replacement therapy could be applied to genetic determination. He was surprised at the connection to which his methodology was being linked. He answered affirmatively but he had done so uneasily. Genetic determinism was one thing but genetic determination? The term belonged to a different era, indeed a different world. Gene replacement therapy was desired enough when the issue was health-related but would it be used to pick and choose phenotypes to design a child? Would mixed-race couples decide which racially prominent features would appear in their offspring? He had always viewed his work through an ethical lens, considering the social implications as well as the scientific. Research was a double-edged sword, he reflected, and reminded himself that he could not control its future use, only its immediate validity.

Chinnan contemplated all of this as he looked out of the window onto the courtyard outside the faculty office building. The buds on the trees had opened early this year with the warm weather.

The telephone rang. Chinnan picked up the phone to hear Pranathi's voice.

"You are late," she exclaimed. "We are to be at the Advanis' home in a half hour. And the hotel, have you forgotten you were supposed to go to the hotel!"

It was true. He had been distracted, basking in the glow of his success. He had finished teaching class over an hour ago, but had taken the time to read the entire article. Of course Pranathi was upset.

"You are right," Chinnan apologized. "Will you be able to drop by the hotel and write them a cheque? If I go, I will be delayed an extra hour. I can meet you at the Advanis' house."

"Fine. But one day, I promise you, my life will stop revolving around your schedule or lack of one!" She hung up.

Chinnan put the journal in his briefcase and set out towards the subway. He knew his disregard for the time was not completely unconscious. He had dreaded the dinner and the upcoming party preparations. The recent conversations about the guest list, the menu, the ceremony, even auspicious colours for the celebration raised his insecurities like blisters on his skin. It was as if caste distinctions and communal prejudices had been boiled away through time, reduced to a fine gravy and swallowed. It had lost its potency when he and his wife immigrated from India to Canada, but the stigma still lingered, carried from one country to another through the faintest odour on the skin, the angle of a shadow on the road or one's name. It was a mix of shame and anger that propelled his need for vindication. This in turn fed Chinnan's ambition to acquire professional respect and social standing. And even though he had achieved this, his confidence at times would be shaken, triggered by his wife's own need for approval and acceptance.

His only consolation was that his beloved daughter had not inherited any of his own insecurities. She was confident and assertive, assured of her own value and rights. And now she was marrying outside her religion and into a higher caste from her humble "untouchable" origins. But for Chinnan, this was neither a vindication nor a blessing. Instead, it caused him fear. In times of stress, would inherited prejudices surface between Anjali and Ravi? Would this history of difference and status bear down upon them? And if it did, he knew Anjali would feel it acutely. Whether or not Ravi or Anjali knew or cared about such matters, Chinnan could not deny his own heightened awareness of these realities. Suddenly he wished Anjali was marrying one of her own kind.

Pranathi, Lakshmi, and Rasesh were seated around the Advanis' dining room table hunched over a computer.

"And here is the third design for the room layout. As you can see, this is more of a wedding style with a head table in the front of the room," Pranathi explained clicking on the mouse and filling the screen with yet another image of tables and chairs.

"Well perhaps it would be too much, too wedding-like if we had a head table. But you know, I would be very proud to sit there amongst my new family looking out to friends and relations," Rasesh affectionately declared.

Lakshmi and Pranathi nodded, agreeing with his sentiment, secretly wishing that they were planning the wedding itself, and not just an engagement party.

"Well, why not?" Lakshmi suggested. "We are planning this party. We are doing the work."

"I agree," Pranathi said easily. "And if we all agree to it."

"Agree to what?" Chinnan called. He had just arrived, entering through the open patio doors that allowed the warm spring air to circulate widely through the spacious light-filled house.

"David Ji," Rasesh rose from his chair and greeted his guest. He offered him a glass of whiskey and pulled out a chair at the table.

"We've just decided on the room layout and are beginning to organize the seating arrangements," Pranathi said. She had just assigned Rasesh and Lakshmi the tables in the west side of the room. They were to arrange the seating of guests from their community, while she and Chinnan would organize the seating arrangements in the east side.

"Why don't we mix them up?" Lakshmi suggested. "That way people can mingle and get to know the other half."

"That is a great idea," Pranathi agreed, and the two women began trading names and table numbers.

Chinnan sat down and sighed. The whole affair had become bigger and more complicated than anyone had imagined. Immediately after the two couples agreed to the party, Pranathi had picked up the phone and invited a swarm of relatives from India to join them. Almost at once, her niece from Kovalum emailed to say she was coming and his two brothers from the States had booked off vacation time. Lakshmi had also extended the invitation overseas, attracting relatives from Delhi, Dubai and London. RSVPs started coming in, flights were booked and visas secured. The May 10th surprise engagement party had the same pull and promise of a wedding. The original reception room had to be cancelled in view of something larger. Chinnan had crossed his fingers and booked the ballroom with a capacity for five hundred people.

"Are none of you nervous about this?" Chinnan finally said above the chattering voices.

The Advanis looked up from their table plans, and Pranathi shot him a warning look.

"What if the children do not appreciate this?"

"What is there not to appreciate? This is a party. Full of friends and good food," Pranathi exclaimed.

"I am just asking the Advanis their opinion." Chinnan tried to avoid his wife.

She would speak to him later about his rudeness.

"It is a good thing. Weddings are not to be conducted privately in some small room apart from family," Rasesh said firmly. "This was your idea, *bhai*, and we happily concurred."

"Is it not too late to reconsider?" Lakshmi asked.

Chinnan was still uneasy. "Not necessarily, when you consider what we may be risking."

"Of course it is too late," Pranathi began. "Guests have booked their flights. I have already given the deposit for the room, have you forgotten?"

Silence.

"Lakshmi," Rasesh spoke. "Get me my cheque book. I have forgotten to deliver my share."

Pranathi exchanged looks with her husband.

Lakshmi rose from the table and disappeared into the other room.

"This is not about money, Advani Ji," Chinnan tried to backtrack. "I am just thinking out loud. From a young age our Anjali always insisted on doing things her way."

Lakshmi put the cheque book on the table in front of her husband.

"I am tired," she began, her voice tense and revealing, "of young women always doing things their way. My son eloped when he was still in college because his Quebec girlfriend wanted to do things her way. There was no Indian wedding, no priest, no *pooja*. They later explained that they thought neither set of parents would agree to the marriage. Well we accepted it. And look how it turned out. I think we have earned the right to celebrate in our way. We want to show our acceptance of your daughter."

"This will be different. A happy experience," Pranathi said, soothing Lakshmi. "Anjali will be thrilled. It is only my husband who is nervous."

Rasesh handed a cheque to Chinnan as Pranathi looked on, embarrassed and ashamed.

"No, no. I cannot take this. Please accept my apologies. I really — "

"Please do not worry yourself. I had intended to give this to you before. I insist."

Then Rasesh added, "I hope this can be of some help."

Reluctantly, Chinnan folded the piece of paper and slipped it into his pocket. If the amount were too extravagant, he would return it quietly, without the knowledge of the women.

Later on that evening, Pranathi and Lakshmi went into the back garden to prepare the table for their meal. It had turned out to be a beautiful day, more like summer than spring, and the two women happily left their husbands to their own devices.

Rasesh invited Chinnan to take a look at his newly renovated library. As they climbed the stairs, Chinnan noticed the frayed carpet and paint chipping off the baseboards. A grand house that had the air of neglect. At the top of the stairs, double doors opened into a large room.

"I fitted these bookshelves myself, with Ravi's help of course," Rasesh proudly exclaimed.

Chinnan scanned the room. The job was left incomplete, a whole wall had been stripped and pipes were exposed.

"The plan was to renovate the whole house but, well, we invested a fair amount in my eldest daughter's wedding. And I had thought, of course, that I would be working another eight years. This room will come in handy for my retirement. Lots of time to read," Rasesh said, but there was a sadness and resignation in his voice.

At that instant, the phone rang, and Rasesh ducked into the master bedroom to answer it, leaving Chinnan lingering in the hall. Chinnan took advantage of being alone and retrieved the cheque from his pocket. He stared at the number. Perhaps there was a mistake. Chinnan was by no means a greedy or an unfair man, but the amount could not even cover a quarter of the cost for the party. Of course he would not mention it. It may have been intentional. Hearing Rasesh finish the call, Chinnan pushed open a door which was left ajar, hoping to hide for a moment in the bathroom to recover from his shock. Instead, he found himself in a small, sparsely decorated room populated with a *mandir*, a mat and, on the walls, several pictures of lavender-hued gods and goddesses. Amongst them was a painting of Jesus Christ. The pantheon of deities of which ours is one of many, Chinnan said to himself. The thought gave him some comfort.

"Ah, you've found our prayer room," Rasesh exclaimed, patting Chinnan on the shoulder.

Chinnan quickly stuffed the cheque back into his pocket.

"Yes, excuse me. I hope you do not mind, I was looking for the washroom."

"The washroom, of course. The washroom is to the left."

Chinnan started to leave the room. "Wait," Rasesh said. "You can see the full view of the garden from here. That is, if you can hold on for a moment."

"Okay, but only for a moment; you know it gets harder and harder at our age," Chinnan laughed.

"You mean less hard," Rasesh chuckled back.

He drew open the curtains and Chinnan joined his host at the window. The two men surveyed the sprawling garden with yellow and red tulips sprouting amongst lush shrubs. And in the middle of the landscape stood their sari-clad wives, equally colourful, laying the plates and laughing heartily. Chinnan was pleased at their budding friendship. He envied women the ease with which they communicated, the fact that cooking demanded they confer, negotiate and even reveal secrets.

"What do you think they are up to now?" Rasesh asked.

Chinnan turned to his new friend and smiled. "No doubt, they are planning the births of our grandchildren."

ॐ

Anjali orders and pays for a cheese and chutney sandwich at a new veggie café on Church Street. She devours it and considers whether she should be eating spicy food in her condition — now this would be a sacrifice, she thinks. She puts her hands on her stomach. There are no outward signs that she is pregnant. Women her age are known to skip periods, and it still may be too early to tell, but she believes in positive thinking. Concentrating on the centre of her being, she imagines her baby taking root, pulling the walls of her uterus into a cocoon. This can be her secret, a gift she will eventually offer to the world. Please, let me be pregnant, she prays.

After washing the sandwich down with a mixed berry juice, Anjali steps out and walks to the drugstore. She picks up the home pregnancy test, grateful that there is a different pharmaceutical clerk working this Saturday afternoon. The other pharmacist knew her name and always looked on her with pity when she placed yet another blue stick test on the counter. Anxious to know for sure, but fearful of a negative result, Anjali delays returning home and spends the remainder of the day dodging in and out of boutiques trying to balance her contradicting emotions of excitement and dread. She needs to be out of the house. Images of her and Ravi keep popping up in her mind: Anjali complaining, Ravi indifferent, Anjali sulking, Ravi enraged, Anjali smoking, Ravi leaving. She wants to reinvent their relationship, conjure up happy pictures: colour prints, with no edges. The best she can do is change herself. She stumbles into a hair salon and asks for a cut and style, soft and feminine, not too dramatic.

She calms herself on the streetcar ride home by inventing ways to save their relationship. She imagines Ravi's reaction. Would he pamper her, cook her calcium-rich meals, start painting the spare bedroom a sunny yellow? A younger version of herself would have done it alone. But she realizes she is no longer that person. She wishes that she and Ravi were more conventional and had demanded the kind of fidelity and trust which is part and parcel of other relationships. But how can she raise the issue with him; they had both negotiated and agreed to the terms. They were critical of obligatory monogamy, a kind of possessiveness that breeds resentment and hostility between couples. Two years ago neither of them had wanted to compromise their independence.

When Anjali reaches home, the sun is still high in the sky. Spring's promise of new life, she thinks. They have two hours before meeting their parents. Enough time for her to take the test. Or should she? The best diagnosis is with the first urination in the morning. She climbs the stairs and enters their bedroom. She is relieved to see the familiar lump, the tangle of limbs underneath the comforter, the predictability of his sleeping form. Pulling off her jeans, she crawls in beside him. Instinctively, he puts his arm around her waist and she nuzzles her nose into his throat. He smells of himself. That lovely scent, the first hint that told her she was attracted to him. She is happy. They will sleep then shower together. Then they will drive away from their trendy neighborhood, into foreign but familiar territory, distinguished by its uniformity: big modern homes, green mowed lawns, with an equal distance between doorstep and street. The suburbs take on a pattern, like a board game, the green houses in Monopoly. Their lives will also take on a pattern. And so Anjali makes a decision. She will ask Ravi to stop his "outings" and in return she will stop asking him to perform. Even if the result is negative. They will wait and just see what happens. After all, that's the way it's supposed to be. Their marriage alone was making both their families happy. They too could be satisfied.

Lying in bed thinking these thoughts, Anjali feels something akin to love for Ravi. As the room darkens, she kisses him softly on his lips and slides her hand beneath the covers. He sleepily wiggles away from her and turns his back. She stares into the fine hairs on his neck.

"Ravi?" she whispers.

"It's not working," his voice cracks as his body feigns sleep. "We'll tell our parents tonight."

〜

The venue is a five-star hotel in North York, just minutes away from the Davids' home. The Advanis and Davids arrive early to "Indianize" the room. Coverings boasting stylized designs of snakes, mangoes and other organic shapes take the place of the restaurant's crisp white tablecloths. Little brass vases filled with red roses appear on the tables surrounded by circles of *divas*. Oily *samosas*, bursting with potatoes and chickpeas, vegetable *biriyani* and *channa dhal* followed by chicken *korma* and roasted cashew coconut fish curry in silver trays are wheeled in together, then suddenly separated and parked in different areas of the room. All coordinated by servers who work silently and efficiently.

By 6 p.m. the guests start to file in. Pranathi and Lakshmi had abandoned the idea of a mixed seating arrangement after trying to predict who was vegetarian and non-veg, who was married and single, who would get along and who would clash. Instead, the respective mothers invented a game so that people could get to know one another. Upon arrival, each guest is given a tag to wear around his or her neck, naming the party with whom they are associated: David or Advani. Under the name are printed various questions, such as What is the name of the beach where Anjali and Ravi met? In what sport does Ravi compete? What is the name of Anjali's most recent choreographic work?

Lakshmi, wearing a gold embroidered sari, speaks into the microphone at the podium, "Now don't peek at the answers. You may ask for hints from people you meet. The first person to get all three answers correct must shout 'Look out.' The winner will play the role of 'lookout' and warn us when Ravi and Anjali are approaching. You also get a bottle of wine. That was my husband's idea." Everyone laughs. "Now, ready, set, go."

People mingle, giggle and drink the martinis or fruit juice lined up on the bar. The game serves as an ice-breaker, and while some abandoned it in favour of more stimulating conversation, others speed competitively around the room trying to find the clues to their questions. Lakshmi and Pranathi are delighted that there will be a nice buzz of chatter, a diverse mix of curiosity and conversation by the time Anjali and Ravi arrive. Suddenly someone shouts out, "Look out!" and the crowd erupts in cheers.

Chinnan misses the fun. It is his job to escort the couple into the party room. So he sits on the edge of his chair in the hotel lobby wearing his newly dry-cleaned grey suit and maroon tie, his hands nervously folded in his lap and his eyes glued to the revolving doors, anticipating their arrival. He has left a message on their voice mail to remind them of the arrangement. "We'll see you at 7 p.m. Don't be late."

At 6.50 p.m., Pranathi approaches him and kisses his cheek, something she rarely does at home and never in public. He is pleased though. For the last two weeks their relationship has become a warm embrace. Although planning the engagement party was a source of some tension and provoked a number of quarrels, it had forced the two of them to converse, argue, scheme and dream. They laughed together, chided each other and shared a renewed sense of pride, not only in their daughter but also in their own matrimonial success. They could see their old age flow peacefully before them like a serene river, full, wide and reflecting the ever-changing future.

"We are all ready," Pranathi assures her husband smiling broadly. "Everything will be perfect."

"Yes. This will be the first of many things to celebrate," he says. "How they will be surprised."

Then he watches with admiration as his lovely wife walks with purpose and grace down the hall. Hopeful, Chinnan sits back in the plush lobby chair and puts his feet up on the stool.

ॐ

The next hour passes in silence. Anjali shuts herself in the bathroom while Ravi shaves downstairs to give her ample time to get ready. But when she emerges, she is red-eyed, her hair suddenly shorter.

"Your dad left two messages. I gave him a ring back. He refuses to accept an excuse. I couldn't tell him the real reason of course . . ." Anjali does not respond. Ravi continues to rattle on, "Anyway they are expecting us at seven." He glances at his watch. "I think it's better that we show up late rather than not at all."

Anjali slips on an ankle-length jean skirt, a pair of pumps and a blue silk top.

Ravi glances at the sari and blouse folded in plastic at the foot of the bed. A present from his mother to Anjali.

"Do you want me to iron your sari?" he asks.

"No thanks," she answers.

"Look, it would be easier to talk about this."

Anjali's silence unnerves Ravi. Normally she hashes things out until he is dizzy from their circular conversations. Now she seems stunned and saddened by his decision. Somehow he is surprised by this. He cannot believe she has not seen it coming. In fact he had expected her to call it quits before he had. Taking her lead, he dresses down, but not as casually as she, pulling on a pair of dark trousers and a grey shirt. Their parents had expected more formal attire for this first meeting between the families, but he understands her lack of effort, for what is there to celebrate?

The drive to North York is strained. At the wheel, Ravi makes occasional attempts at conversation, commenting on the amount of construction already underway. Anjali nods, staring ahead at the freeway. He too adopts this silence, thinking how he will break the news to his parents. He imagines their disappointed eyes and dreads the onslaught of snide comments they will make, their innuendos at his inability to commit to a relationship, and their repeated regrets at not arranging a match for him when he was young.

As they step out of the car at the hotel parking lot, Ravi says, "Listen, I don't want to make a big fuss. We'll stay for dinner and just tell them that we've changed our minds. No details. No explanations. What do you think?"

"We should have cancelled."

"I can try Ma's cell."

"No. We're here now and I'm starving."

Ravi glances at his watch. "Come on."

As they enter the hotel, Ravi spots Chinnan right away, polishing his glasses. Ravi feels regret, knowing that his breakup with Anjali will likely mean his estrangement from her parents whom he has come to respect and like. He embraces Chinnan. A proud smile spreads across the old man's face as he clasps Anjali's hand and leads the couple down the hallway.

"I thought you weren't going to make it," he tells them, loudly and jovially. "Your mother practically told me to go pick you up and escort you here."

"Dad, I think that's the ballroom . . ." But before Anjali can finish, the dark room they enter bursts into light, and a crowd of exuberant faces greet them. "Surprise!"

Ravi and Anjali stand shell-shocked, moved and shaken. The faces surrounding them are those that have filled their childhoods: relatives from near and far, some who have crossed oceans to be here. Ravi gestures *Namascar* to his Uncle Devraj, from Delhi, who had only to grunt in order for young Ravi to behave at the table. And now hugging him is Anjali's dearest cousin Deepali, who opened her home to them near Kovalum Beach in Kerala. Colleagues and best friends who had shared professional upheavals and personal confidences are scattered through the crowd. Anjali embraces Marie Debassige, her longtime friend and colleague whom she once described as the Karen Kain of Jingle Dress dancing. And here is Ravi's college roommate David Ditor who must have flown in from New York, now shaking his hand and patting him on the back. There are offspring of siblings and cousins from zero to twenty, the next generation looking to them as role models: his cousin's son Nikhil, now sprouting facial hair, and Anjali's god child, Amelia, two years old, darting around in a shiny pink *kameez*. His side and her side, mixing together and wishing them well during a celebration they had not planned, anticipating a wedding they will not have.

There is no time for Ravi to become angry and curse his own parents for agreeing to such a thing, especially when they know him to be crowd shy. The guests keep coming forward to greet them. Then they clear a path towards the head table and podium at the front of the room. Ravi's parents and Anjali's mother stand, waiting for the couple as they walk down an aisle led by the father of the would-be bride. When they reach the front of the room, Ravi notices his mother look Anjali up and down, assessing her appearance. Ravi expects some sign of judgment about her clothing, but instead Lakshmi reaches out and fastens a brilliant ruby necklace around Anjali's neck.

"You are beautiful, my daughter."

Ravi sees the microphone. He knows that words have to be spoken and he fears they must be his. He glances at Anjali, wondering whether she, more comfortable in the limelight, will step up to the podium. But she remains uncharacteristically passive. With what has happened, how can he blame her? She is, after all, the recipient of his decision, forced to accept an unwanted gift. He looks at her face, her large eyes brimming with tears. Most will interpret these to be tears of joy. Maybe they are, he thinks. Perhaps she is relieved to be rid of him. Will she simply get through this, help mop up the mess, and then quietly fade out of his life?

Ravi begins to tremble, thinking maybe he should make a run for it. Head for the hills and never look back. He reminds himself that this is not the ceremony, no vows will be uttered, no public kiss performed to symbolize their union. But suddenly something in him knows he wants just that. And more importantly, he still wants her. There is a moment, which seems to him a lifetime, where no one exists but the two of them. First man, first woman. Or perhaps last man and woman. So he reaches out. His fingers traverse the distance between them and interlock with hers. He feels her smooth skin and the warmth of her palm. And with that one gesture, he bridges the chasm between them and tosses away his reasoning and fear. Anjali squeezes his hand and looks at him directly. There are no questions in her eyes but a knowledge and acceptance of everything they have shared.

Ravi returns her look. "I want to go forward with you. Just you. And them, of course." He glances to the crowd, their expanding family.

"We'll have to work hard," she whispers calmly.

"Yes," he responds. "Anyway, I don't think we have a choice," he adds, glancing nervously at the mircrophone. Then Anjali smiles broadly. "Let's do this together," she says, moving confidently towards the podium.

He moves with her and knows their lives will be entwined, carrying collective and personal histories, wars and arguments, prejudices and resentments, negotiations and compromises. It will be anything but easy. But they are riding a wave now, lifted up by the timeless affirmations of all the lovers who said yes against the odds.

Demure

Demure stands shyly off a main thoroughfare. Tucked into an alley, it is perfect for those who want quick access to its wares and privacy from curious and prudish passersby. At first, the owner worried that people might not find it, but when the Pride Day parade hooted and cheered down Yonge Street, small groups of women (though one couldn't really tell) detoured to its doors. At its peak, Demure was chic, Demure was fusion, Demure was cutting edge! But at its lowest point, it was a shady hole in the wall, at times a curiosity, often ignored and even despised. Whatever the perception, one would not easily guess that Demure was the brainchild of an ambitious mail-order bride from Sri Lanka. Or that the exotic lingerie was stitched piece-by-scanty-piece with the determined fingers of a timid immigrant.

The noise is startling. Sarojini yanks up her pantyhose, the crotch still hanging uncomfortably between her thighs. Letting the flounce of her dress fall, she opens the bathroom door and runs to the kitchen. Eddy is lying flat out on the floor, choking and heaving. Rajani, her sister, crouches over him.

"Don't just stand there. Call an ambulance!" Rajani yells.

"What number?" Sarojini asks, stunned.

"Just get me the phone."

Spilled coffee pools on the table and drips off the edge. Bits of runny yolk are splattered on the overturned chairs and the egg white has slid along the floor to the far corner of the kitchen. Rajani is struggling to support Eddy's weight with her right arm while with her left she repeatedly hits his back.

Sarojini brings the phone to Rajani and watches helplessly as Eddy coughs up a bloody morsel from the surgical opening in his throat. His bulky frame stops convulsing momentarily, and something indistinguishable spurts again from the hole. Sarojini helps her sister prop Eddy against the wall. Rajani telephones 911.

"An emergency! My husband is choking. He cannot breathe," she exclaims, and begins answering a series of questions.

"What can I do?" Sarojini asks, helplessly looking at her sister and brother-in-law.

Eddy heaves and points to the door.

"Go," Rajani commands, the phone still propped between her ear and shoulder. "He wants you to go."

"But you need help," Sarojini insists, now speaking in Tamil.

"Go on. It is better you are not late." Rajani's eyes are fixed on Eddy, who now breathes heavily but slower.

Sarojini steps into her shoes, grabs her purse and leaves the apartment. Alone in the hallway she pauses. The sight of blood, the raspy sound of his breath . . . it is happening again, the after-the-accident feeling. The intense pain in her head coupled with the queasy feeling that her body is turning into liquid. She grasps the doorknob. It is there, fixed and cold. She wants to go back inside, but the door has become a solid rock that does not budge. The dirty grey carpet stretches down the corridor to the elevators in the distance. The stairwell door is closer. Its red exit sign beckons her. She throws herself against the bar and bursts through to the other side. Suddenly and gratefully she feels the strength in her legs return. She clambers down eight flights of stairs to the landing of the main floor. The smell of urine wafts from the corners of the dark stairwell as Sarojini opens the back door and escapes.

༈

The paramedics strap an oxygen cone over Eddy's tracheostomy, hook it up to a canister, and then hoist him onto a stretcher and into the ambulance. Rajani climbs in beside him and clutches his right hand while the paramedic monitors his vital signs.

"He simply choked on his food. Why must he be taken to the hospital?" she asks the paramedic.

"There's something else obstructing his windpipe. I think we got most of it out," he replies, avoiding Rajani's eyes and concentrating instead on the patient.

As the ambulance races to the hospital, Rajani notices that the colour in Eddy's face has completely drained away. He looks whiter than he did in the first photograph he emailed her over ten years ago: his sandy brown hair meticulously combed over a thinning crown, posing in front of an impressive building — the "Eaton Centre" — his place of work, or so he had said. In his emails, he had described his high-rise condominium and his job as a top salesman; what he failed to tell her was that he was a cancer survivor. Rajani learned it only at the Jaffna airport, the first time they saw each other, a week before their planned wedding.

"Twenty years of chain smoking," Eddy had explained. His voice sounded oddly robotic. "The doctors removed a tumour, as round and large as an orange. After my operation, I could breathe again, but I had to learn to speak with this thing." He held out the black box hanging from a chain around his neck. He used it to cover a small hole in his throat, allowing air to pass over his vocal chords and amplify his voice. Rajani was shocked and her parents frightened. But Eddy reassured them that he was cancer-free and had vowed off cigarettes. Rajani understood Eddy's rush to be married, and knew in this regard he was not so different from her.

"It will be all right, Eddy," Rajani whispers as the ambulance sirens wail loudly. Watching him lying still and helpless, Rajani is conscious of both her concern and rising resentment towards Eddy, as if he had some kind of control over what was happening and had chosen the moment for his collapse. He deserves much more from me, Rajani thinks. But still she is torn. Last night Sarojini had woken up shaking, anxious about having to testify in a high-profile murder case. It was to be her first day in court and Rajani had promised to be there. As the first-born of poor farmers and with four younger sisters and no brothers, Rajani is expected to care for her parents in their old age as well as guide and look out for her sisters. Now in Canada, she has only Sarojini under her watch. And she is letting her down.

When they reach the hospital, Eddy is wheeled out into Emergency. The doctor orders a series of tests and Rajani is left to wait. Why hadn't she seen this coming? Eddy had seemed well enough. But then again they had seen little of each other over the last few months. Lately she has been returning home late in the evening from Demure, her lingerie shop, with barely enough time to give him his supper before he is out the door and on his way to his midnight shift at the factory. Even now, with all that is happening, she has no time to spare. If she hurries she will be able to catch Sarojini's testimony in court. Rajani scribbles her cell number on a piece of paper and passes it to the nurse at the reception.

"Call me and let me know if anything changes," she says as she rushes through the door and out.

ॐ

The courtroom is sterile — clean lines with no ornamentation. A clerk with mousy brown hair and a monotonous voice asks Sarojini to raise her right hand and swear to tell the truth. Rajani insisted that Sarojini wear a dress instead of a sari to court. Now Sarojini's skinny legs are shaking uncontrollably in her beige panty hose. Sarojini searches for her sister. Rajani must still be at the hospital. Eddy! What is happening with Eddy? Sarojini rests her eyes on Francis Hargreaves, seated on the other side of the room, and she is jolted into the reality of where she is and what is expected of her. His green eyes, narrow and steady, stare back at her. Sarojini feels her mouth go dry and remembers how he flirted with her when he first appeared at Demure. Even now, surrounded by so many people, he frightens her. She stammers out the oath and is asked to sit down. The Crown attorney steps up.

"Miss Sarojini Sriskandarajah," he asks, "do you know who Francis Hargreaves is?"

Sarojini nods. "Yes."

"Please remember to speak loudly so the members of the jury can hear your every word."

"Yes."

Sarojini points out the man with the green eyes sitting with his lawyer.

"How do you know him? Please tell us where you first saw him."

"He is coming to shop."

Although the Crown suggested using an interpreter, Sarojini declined, overhearing him say that if she could manage in English, she might appear more credible.

"Your Honour." The Crown holds up a plastic bag and with a pair of tongs fishes out the items one by one: a thong, a bra and panty set and a garter and stockings. He holds them out to the jury first, then to Sarojini.

"Do you recognize these items?"

Sarojini drops her eyes as a hot blush spreads across her face.

"Yes . . . they are Demure."

Sarojini can almost feel the silk grazing her skin. It is as if these are her personal things. And in a way, they are of her mind and body. They bear the imprint of her design and craftsmanship, honed over the years. To think that her garments had been mangled and soiled and the women wearing them had been murdered! She feels guilty and ashamed as if she had played a part, consenting to this savagery.

O kadavilae enna kodumai. Oh, what a tragedy, Sarojini thinks.

"Your Honour, I would like to enter these items into evidence as exhibits A, B and C."

"The court will enter exhibits A, B and C into the record," the judge mutters.

A clerk accepts the plastic bag while another types. The Crown turns back to Sarojini.

"Demure is the name of the lingerie shop owned by Mrs. Rajani Robbins. Is that correct?"

"Yes, my sister Rajani."

"What is your association with Demure?"

Sarojini does not respond.

"I will rephrase the question. What do you do at the store? And please speak up," he encourages her.

"I cutting and doing measurements. I working sewing."

Sarojini did more than that. Despite her timid appearance, she was an uncommon inspiration, the engine of the enterprise and foundation to Rajani's towering dreams. In fact it was she who came up with the name.

The idea for Demure was hatched only months after Sarojini arrived in Canada. Sarojini was perched in front of a used Singer sewing machine in Eddy's cramped one-bedroom apartment. Rajani had found Sarojini a job doing piecework, which she could do at home, sewing sleeves onto backs for a sweatshop. Even as a teenager, Sarojini had developed a reputation as a good seamstress and was determined to improve herself in order to earn more money for her sister, who in turn handed it over to her husband. "Yes, it is the whole amount, Eddy!" Sarojini had heard Rajani say.

Rajani, who had been watching Sarojini hard at work, suddenly pulled her into her bedroom.

"Look at this."

Rajani took a small white triangular cloth out of a plastic bag and handed it to Sarojini who peered at the cloth intently, pulling at the small connecting straps.

"Well?" Rajani asked.

"What is it, *Akka*?" Sarojini asked in Tamil.

"What do you think?" Rajani giggled, continuing in her mother tongue.

"I am not sure. A mask for cleaning?"

Rajani laughed and grabbed the cloth, pulling the triangle over her nose and mouth.

"Like this?"

"No. It does not fit properly. Let me try."

Sarojini took the cloth and put it on her own face. Then wrapped the strings behind her ears and repositioned it.

"Silly girl," Rajani laughed, grabbing the cloth from Sarojini. Then she reached underneath her skirt and took off her cotton briefs, stepped into the cloth contraption and pulled it up. She hiked up her skirt to reveal the tiny piece of fabric between her legs. A small white tag hung from the left strap.

"What are you doing?" Sarojini exclaimed, averting her eyes from the sight of her sister's near nakedness.

"Oh dear, I forgot you are not used to all this. But this is the way it is here. This is what women are wearing. Even to the seaside in front of so many people. Now, try not to be too shocked."

Rajani turned around to show her sister the full view of her black bottom, the white string disappearing between the globes.

"*Vekkakedu!*" Sarojini exclaimed. "It is not covering anything."

"That's the point!" Rajani explained. "It's supposed to be revealing, sexy."

"Oh my god, I put that on my nose! *Chee chee*!" Sarojini began wiping her face violently with the sleeve of her shirt.

"Never mind. This is a brand new thong. The first time it has been worn."

Rajani slipped out of the thong then pulled on her panties, allowing her skirt to fall, recovering her modesty. She sat down.

"Sorry to upset you, sister. You can see it on television or in movies like the one we saw last weekend with Demi Moore, *Striptease*," Rajani said.

"What is demimore?"

"Not what, but who. My favourite actress. Now what do you say? Can you sew these?"

Sarojini looked down at her hands. What was her sister asking of her?

"What would *Amma* say?" Sarojini asked upset, her fingers nervously stitching the air.

"*Amma* is not here. And I am trying to teach you something." Rajani drew closer to her sister and pointed out the price tag on the thong. "Look at this. $14.99. And that is *before* tax."

Sarojini finally looked up. "So costly."

"And so many are willing to buy this and pay more."

Sarojini carefully took the thong by the straps. "This is about eight inches across, feels like cotton jersey but stretchy. Simple stitching. Very little work."

"Exactly." Rajani's eyes were gleaming. "If you can sew them, I can sell them."

The next day, while Rajani researched how to set up a small business, Sarojini searched the Webster's College Dictionary for Rajani's favourite actress. While Sarojini could not find Demi Moore, she did discover the meaning of *demure*: "Characterized by shyness or modesty; reserved, or affectedly or coyly decorous . . ."

When Sarojini told Rajani, her sister jumped. "That's it. Demure: Lingerie for Ladies. I like it. It's sexy *and* it has class."

Sarojini beamed, happy to have pleased her sister. Then she sat down at her sewing machine and after she finished sewing twenty pieces for the sweatshop, she gathered the leftover scraps of white cotton and cut them into triangles. Then she sewed on some straps. They were functional but not at all pretty. Sarojini opened her sewing basket and fished out a handful of sequins. She slipped gold thread through the needle and began lining the cloth with a decorative edge. The result was amateurish but showed promise. Sarojini kept experimenting and, by midnight, had created a Demure original.

From where she sits in the witness box, Sarojini has a perfect view of the top of the Crown attorney's head. His hair is parted neatly on the right and sprinkled with dandruff, as if covered by a light layer of snow. The Crown points to a black thong, with threads escaping like loose strands from a tightly woven plait.

"On August 7, 2003, the defendant walked into Demure and bought these garments."

"Yes."

"How can you be sure? That was almost three years ago."

"The date Eddy first went hospital." Sarojini can still see the despair on Rajani's face as she leaned over the counter at Demure, gripping the telephone, hearing that Eddy had fainted at work. Then Rajani left Sarojini to mind the store, for the first time.

"I offer the court the hospital record of the admittance of Edward Robbins at the Eastern General Hospital, dated August 7, 2003." He hands the paper to the clerk.

"And how many customers did you see on August 7th?" the Crown continues.

"Three. I remember I talking English and I talking to three peoples. I am very proud."

"Do you remember what the defendant bought?"

"He is buying many things. For his wife he says."

"For his wife? So you remember the conversation?"

"Yes. He says wife . . . " She pauses and looks down at her hands as they make small stitching motions.

"Please go ahead."

Sarojini feels her legs quiver. She brings her hand up to her mouth. "He says wife my size." Sarojini glances at the defendant and can feel his eyes on her, running over her, through her.

"Please, Miss Sriskandarajah, could you speak a little louder."

"He buying several items," Sarojini continues, a sudden heat rising in her body.

The Crown points once again to the lingerie.

"Were these the items that he bought?"

Sarojini looks at the items displayed in front of her: the black thong with the red embroidered cobra uncoiling towards the crotch, the indigo silk bra and panty set with the silver sequins, the purple stockings with beaded garters. She stares at her handiwork, admiring the intricacy of the stitching, wondering where they had been, what they had experienced.

"Could the witness please answer the question," the judge interrupts.

"Yes," she says sadly.

"Thank you, Miss Sriskandarajah."

As Sarojini walks back to her seat, she feels ashamed. All these strangers are watching her. Three women had been murdered and some were saying that Demure was partly to blame. And although Sarojini does not want to admit it, she has to agree. She never felt comfortable with what they were doing. She only wanted to please her sister.

﹏

Eddy feels the tension in his arms from the jabs of needles and a pulling sensation where the intravenous feed is strapped securely to his skin. They had moved him from emergency to the intensive care unit. All morning he was questioned, examined, prodded and tested. A very different experience from the time three years ago when he had been taken to hospital after fainting while finishing his midnight shift. This time he is drowsy from painkillers and wakes up for brief moments, remembering where he is before drifting elsewhere in a dreamlike state. Images fleet through his mind and carry him from the hospital bed to a lush plantain field in east Sri Lanka.

He had been so happy there, those early weeks of his marriage. On the bus ride from the airport to their village, Eddy sat next to her father and spoke to Rajani who sat across the aisle, still under her mother's protective watch. He played with the black box, moving it back and forth in front of the hole and angling it in different directions, demonstrating the various sounds he could make. Passengers in the bus turned and stared, but Rajani watched curiously, giggling like a child entertained by a clown.

Walking with Rajani through her village, he must have appeared a giant. The villagers' eyes locked on him while children followed behind hoping to collect candies and pennies that seemed to sprout from his pockets. Rajani showed him the market stalls and the community information centre where she had taken computer classes and sent him surreptitious emails. She led him through the plantain fields where she used to work with her sisters every morning before school. He came to know her father, a lean and illiterate farmer only five years older than Eddy. And her mother, who had learned how to read and write at missionary school and was quietly determined to ensure her daughters would lead a better life.

Her younger sisters were shy and deferential with him, except the youngest, Sarojini. Only eleven years old, she pulled him victoriously into her games and coveted small objects that were of no value but rare and precious to her: a key chain, colourful foil candy wrappers, packages of travel wipes from the plane. Eddy envied the warmth and touch of their family life and the dark, dense, wet green Sri Lankan countryside. But he also observed what was happening around them: military vehicles patrolling the roads, stirring up dust and dread. Villages just like these, he was quietly told, were being bombed in neighbouring states. He pitied the villagers' abject poverty and their suffering at the hands of their political masters and he felt heroic knowing he would soon airlift his precious Rajani to safety. Deeper still, he felt cared for and special. "Eddy, would you like more tea?" "No, sit down Eddy, I will fetch that . . ." "I will press your legs if you are tired." Rajani served him, listened to him and, to his relief, didn't seem repulsed by his disfigurement.

Eddy smiles at the memory and opens his eyes to the walls of the hospital room. He looks for Rajani by his bedside. Instead he sees a nurse positioning a tube near his throat. She has a sour look on her face as she begins to drain his trachea.

༄

Leaving Eddy at the hospital, Rajani catches the streetcar westbound. It is crowded but she determinedly squeezes past the standing passengers and finds a seat in the back beside a teenager. The girl looks out the window, the delicate wires of an iPod trailing from her ears. Rajani thinks she must be the same age as Francis Hargreaves' youngest victim. But this girl is very much alive, tapping her toes, snippets of lyrics tumbling from her mouth. Rajani notices her faraway gaze and reminisces about what it is like to be innocent and trusting, with nothing but the hope of a fun-filled future promised by the melodic strains of a pop song. Rajani recognizes the tune and strains to hear the voice leaking from the girl's earpiece.

Rajani taps the girl on her shoulder.

The girl turns. "What?" she says loudly over the music.

"I was wondering who you are listening to?"

"Ayline Wheatley." The girl is irritated but still polite.

"I thought so. I'm a big fan. And Ayline Wheatley is a big fan of Demure."

The girl removes her earpiece as Rajani hands her a lilac business card.

"You know Ayline Wheatley wore one of our pieces on a late night talk show."

"Oh yeah?"

"It was three years ago but she still shops at Demure regularly," Rajani exaggerates.

Rajani does not actually remember Ayline Wheatley coming into the store, but she remembers every detail of her performance on the talk show. It was during Demure's first year of business. Eddy was at work, Sarojini sat on the couch embroidering a pair of panties and Rajani was surfing the channels.

"Sarojini! She's wearing our bra."

Indeed, a tall, willowy redhead was swaying and singing into a microphone, wearing jeans and a Demure original: a gold bra with small square mirrors patterned on the cups. After her performance, the singer plopped down onto the couch beside the talk show host. Perched on the edge of their own couch, Rajani and Sarojini watched with anticipation.

"You look super-duper sen-sa-tion-al!" the talk show host said, making humorous googly eyes at Ayline Wheatley's breasts.

"Oh this?" She laughed flashing her large white teeth between painted lips. "Nice huh? I bought this right after my performance at Toronto Pride." Ayline Wheatley fingered the bra straps as she spoke. "My guitarist Stacey showed up in this cool bra with sequins all over it, like mermaid scales."

"But yours has, what are those . . . ?" The host leaned in. "Hey, can we get a close up here," he called to the camera. "You don't mind, do you?"

"Close ups? Bring 'em on!" she laughed, making love to the audience.

"So, do people ever, you know, come up to you to check their makeup in the mirrors? Oops, I can see a bit of lint on my lapel." The host mimed the action of picking off the speck, pretending to check his appearance in her left breast.

"I know, I know. It's unique. The pattern is actually Rajasthani or something. I found it at this teeny, tiny hole in the wall, called Demure. Run by these sweet but nervous little Indian women making all these gorgeous, sexy bits. I snatched up half the store. Check it out!"

Ayline Wheatley stood up and faced the audience. She cupped her breasts, causing the mirrors to reflect the light. As more cheers and wolf-whistles were heard from the TV audience, Sarojini queried softly in Tamil, "She said we are from India? But we are Sri Lankan."

Rajani shouted joyfully, "And who is she calling nervous!"

"Excuse me," the girl says loudly over her music. "This is my stop."

Rajani looks up, startled out of her reverie. She notices the street corner, only three blocks to Demure.

"I am getting off here myself," Rajani says, suddenly changing her mind about attending court. She jumps out of her seat, leading the girl down the crowded aisle. "Why don't you come with me, I'll give you a fifty percent discount on anything in the store."

But the girl gives her a wary look. "Not today, but thanks for the card," she says. After they step off the streetcar, Rajani watches the potential customer walk in the opposite direction of Demure.

"Too much," Rajani says out loud.

Rajani glances at her wrist. In all the hurry, she has forgotten to put on her watch. She reaches into her handbag and pulls out a gold watch that bears the name, Dior. The only gift she has bought herself since Demure's modest success. A small reward for all her efforts, something she puts on when she goes to work, and takes off before returning home to Eddy. Rajani slides it onto her wrist. It is 11 a.m. Sarojini has probably finished testifying by now. Anyway, how can she keep the store closed during business hours?

It is a sunny morning and already very warm. Rajani will have to put the air conditioner on again. She has tried to cut down on electricity, one of many efforts to save money. Over the past year, sales had plummeted. Eddy had reassured her, "It is just a slump. All businesses have peaks and valleys." But Rajani cannot help thinking the decline in customers is directly linked to the Demure lingerie found on Francis Hargreaves' victims.

The two sisters had worked so hard that they were close to having enough money to bring their parents to Canada. Rajani has no intention of giving up her dreams because of bad publicity from a murder case. But if the saying is true that "there is no such thing as *bad* publicity," Rajani will find a way to capitalize on the trial. As she turns into the alley, Demure's gleaming windows seem to say, I knew you would come. She feels the swell of pride, unlocks the door and flips the sign to "Open."

After leaving the courthouse, Sarojini makes her way through town; her heart begins to race as she approaches Demure. A black van is parked outside and television cameras are filming something. Someone clearing a space for the cameraman bumps against her rudely. Sarojini squeezes through the crowd and enters the store. Rajani is at the counter speaking to a woman who writes furiously on a notepad.

"Yes," the woman says, "the piece on Demure will be on the 6 p.m. news. Thank you for your time, Mrs. Robbins." The woman shakes Rajani's hand, turns to her crew and waves them off. The voices of the crowd outside rise and fade as the door opens and swings shut behind her.

Sarojini touches Rajani on the arm. "*Akka?* What is happening? I thought you were at the hospital." Sarojini speaks rapidly. Tired of speaking English all day, she is relieved to see Rajani and speak her mother tongue.

"Oh Sarojini! You are here. I am sorry I couldn't come to court. How was it? Did you do well?"

"Yes, everything was okay. The lawyer said it was fine. Tomorrow the other one will question me. How is Eddy? What is happening here?"

"Oh, a wonderful thing! NRT News interviewed me as part of their coverage on the trial. I hope it will bring more customers. But look at those people." Rajani points towards the window. "They were so curious a moment ago, but now that the TV cameras have gone, they are disappearing too."

Rajani picks up her handbag. "Sarojini, you have to mind the shop until closing. I am sorry to leave you like this, but I have to go to the hospital for visiting hours."

"Eddy, how is Eddy?" Sarojini calls out in English. "Tell him get better."

"I will," Rajani promises stepping out to the tinkle of the bells.

The street is now empty and the sun blinks hotly between the gaps in the opposite buildings. Sarojini goes behind the counter and bows her head to a framed and signed photograph of Ayline Wheatley, wearing the mirror-covered bra. Demure's Goddess. Rajani had pestered the singer's agent for months to secure the photo, and for months afterwards, the sisters humorously but gratefully adorned it with flowers and chanted before it every morning as sales doubled and tripled. Not long before Ayline Wheatley had worn a Demure bra on TV, Pride Day participants and spectators had discovered the spot. Customers came, and then left swinging discreet Demure lilac paper bags. Some of the women even walked out into the street wearing silky camisoles, stuffing their old tops into their knapsacks.

For the first time, Sarojini entertained the thought that being sexy could be normal, healthy and fun. In Sri Lanka, she had been taught to cover her body, shielding it from the eyes of men. As she grew older, the restrictions on her dress and body grew greater. The countryside was overrun with soldiers and rebels, lost, hungry men who craved power and acted without restraint. Here, though, the customers welcomed the looks, cheers and innuendo. Even those women modestly outfitted in T-shirts and jeans glowed with sensual confidence. Sarojini took particular notice of dark-skinned girls who, unlike her, moved with ease and openness. What was taboo back home was acceptable here, something she still could not describe in her own language but was beginning to appreciate.

Slowly, Sarojini started to experiment with her own clothes, wearing tank tops and fitted jeans, and occasionally underneath was her own hand-stitched lace panties or a slippery thong. Not long after that, Francis Hargreaves had walked in, and Demure and everything in it started to feel dirty and depraved. Sarojini reverted to wearing high collared shirts over baggy trousers.

She glances at the dressing room. The curtain is closed. Fear ripples through her body. I'm just being silly, she thinks, and walks purposefully towards it, drawing the curtain open. Empty. No surprises. Then she switches off the air conditioning. She wants to feel the heat, missing the dense humid air of Sri Lanka, the wet, green foliage in the fields. The dirt . . .

What to do next? Sarojini busies herself, rearranging clothes on the sales rack. She straightens the sign, "Half Price on Everything." Still, there are no customers. Even with Pride Week lately over. Some regulars pop in once in a while to offer support as much as to shop but, as Rajani suggested, the murders and now the trial of Francis Hargreaves seemed to have damaged the store's reputation. A student, a bank clerk and a waitress all had been raped and murdered, with nothing in common except being found dead in lingerie from Demure. When the women were first reported missing, neither Sarojini nor Rajani paid much attention. After all, news like this seemed commonplace. Then Rajani received a call, and together the sisters went to the police station to identify the lingerie.

The bells tinkle, Sarojini straightens her back and turns around. A woman strides purposefully to the centre of the store, stops and announces, "So this is it. This is where he shopped."

Sarojini squints at the woman. "May I help you?"

She had practised this phrase and others repeatedly on the day Francis Hargreaves came in.

The woman shakes her head. "No, just looking." She gives the shop a second once-over and abruptly leaves. These kinds of visits were becoming more frequent. People came to gape, comment and move on.

Once the woman is out of earshot, Sarojini calls out angrily, "Thank you for shopping at Demure."

☞

Rajani sits down in the chair beside Eddy's hospital bed. He is grateful for a private room and for Rajani, there beside him. She has brought him his toothbrush, his housecoat and slippers. Small personal things to keep him comfortable. He does not tell her that he cannot lift himself from his bed. And that she looks beautiful. Even with a sterile mask covering half her face, her eyes sparkle and her hair shines. He likes it that the hospital staff recognize this young vivacious creature to be his wife.

Rajani fusses over him. She props up his pillow, wipes his forehead with a cold, damp cloth, but when she hands him his voice box, he declines with the wave of his hand. It hurts to speak.

"That's all right, my love," she says gently, turning on the TV. "We have to watch the news anyway. I have a surprise for you. There is a small feature on Demure tonight." A few minutes later, they watch as the camera pans across Demure's storefront window, zooming in on the costumed mannequins. The door opens, the wind chimes tinkle — the gift he had given Rajani on the day of Demure's opening.

Demure's opening three years ago had been marked only by a banner hung on the storefront and a small advertisement in a local community newspaper. Eddy had sauntered in following his midnight shift and a long subway ride downtown, a gift tucked under his arm. Leaning against the counter, he watched his wife at work on her first customer.

"Let me show you our special line of bras. This design is exquisite, don't you think? Can I help you find your size?" Rajani asked eagerly.

The woman moved away warily in the direction of the door. Rajani followed her trying to convince her that there must be something she would like. When she left, Rajani stood crestfallen, staring out the window.

"You need a bell," Eddy offered. "Something to hang on the door, so you know when a customer enters or exits. Give them time to look around, approach them slowly and let them leave without a fuss. The experience will be relaxed, and even if they don't buy now, they will later. Believe me, it works selling shoes. Underwear is no different."

"Hmm," Rajani responded.

Then Eddy handed her the gift. Beautiful silver wind chimes, red-ribboned from China. She hadn't seemed to appreciate his advice or his gift. Instead she kept her eyes anxiously on the door, indifferent to him. On his way home he picked up a movie and a carton of cigarettes. He spent the morning staring at the TV screen. In the moments when he tore himself away, he opened kitchen cabinets, broom closets and bureau drawers. He wasn't sure what he was looking for but he kept searching. The only thing he found was a growing collection of lingerie in Rajani's top drawer. She hadn't worn them for him, and he wondered whether she might be having an affair. But he didn't dare ask. If she said yes, he would have to do something about it. He preferred to shut the drawer, slide another videocassette into the slot and inhale smoke through the hole in his throat.

Now as they sit together in the hospital room, Eddy turns up the volume on the TV and listens to the reporter providing background on the murder trial. Rajani takes his hand excitedly as they watch the camera pan across the racks of lingerie and zoom in on a red lace bustier, caressing it with its lens. Slowly the camera moves to a close-up of the long, slender fingers of a woman, a gold watch glistening on her wrist. I didn't give that to her, Eddy ponders. He wonders who did. He feels the smart of rejection. On the TV, Rajani gestures passionately as she speaks. Rajani in the hospital room squeezes his hand. He notices she isn't wearing the watch.

"Lingerie makes a woman feel beautiful and in control. When she wears beautiful clothes, she's not an object but the star of her own show."

Eddy is surprised by his wife's ability to express herself. He is even more surprised at her ease in front of the camera. The reporter asks another question.

"Some detractors, even feminist groups, are saying that lingerie contributes to the objectification of women and leads to their degradation. Do you think this is true?"

Clearly irritated, Rajani snaps, "I am disgusted people would think that." Then catching herself, she continues in a calmer voice. "It all depends on how you look at things. If one looks with love and curiosity, one sees the potential for beauty, desire and connection. If one looks with hate and depravity, then even the most innocent object is defiled and made ugly."

"Are you saying beauty is in the eye of the beholder?"

"Absolutely, and if anyone has doubts about where we stand with regard to respect for women, we have been fundraising for a woman's shelter. Five percent of our sales will be donated towards this cause."

The camera pans back to the red bustier.

Rajani quickly adds, "We are also having a sale to promote our new Canada Day specials."

When the interview is over, Eddy turns off the TV and opens his arms for Rajani. She hugs him awkwardly over the tubing connected to his body. He brings her hand to his mouth. Then he looks down to her bare wrist and gestures for his black box. Rajani puts the chain around his neck.

"You forgot your gold watch," he says with much effort.

"Oh that," she says hesitantly. She knows Eddy likes to control the finances, keeping a strict account of all spending. "The journalist gave it to me to wear. I had to return it after the interview. She thought it would look nice, make me look like a successful business woman."

"You are," he says and winks at her.

"Oh Eddy," she replies bashfully.

He likes her play at modesty, but he understands exactly what it is. Each continues to act out their early marriage roles: Eddy the provider and Rajani the provided for, even though things have changed dramatically between them.

Rajani had stepped into his life and into his shoes and was now the main provider for their home. Before his surgery and before meeting Rajani, Eddy had worked at Shoe Horn, selling designer brands and exotic styles: pointed-toe python boots, calf-leather brogues and horse-bit loafers. Eddy learned the art of precisely measuring even the most unusual male foot, the subtle nuances of design and the salesman's guiding principle — the customer is always right. It did not take him long to become the top salesperson. So after the surgery, while he was still adjusting to his new way of speaking, he was shocked when his manager took him aside and told him they were letting him go. "Falling sales." Weeks later, and after several beers, the manager had confided to Eddy: "Customers don't want to be talked to through your . . ." And then he added, "Sorry Ed, but it's better coming from me than them."

Eddy had thought about suing, citing discrimination. But then he genuinely believed the customer was right and his former manager was expressing not his personal view but theirs. Eddy was lost. Shoe Horn represented not just prestige and a paycheque. It was his life. His new job working at a factory was humiliating, so he poured all his diligence and attention to detail into finding a wife. After some harsh and painful encounters with women he met through online dating, he discovered the overseas matrimonial sites.

There were blond bombshells from Eastern Europe but he kept straying to the websites featuring delicate ladies from Asia or dark beauties from

Africa. When he stumbled upon a photo of a pretty girl from tiny, war-torn and insignificant Sri Lanka, he emailed Rajani immediately. He wasn't really lying, he told himself as he sent her his photo in front of the Eaton Centre. It was just that the future hadn't caught up with the past. Pre-surgery Eddy courted pre-Demure Rajani in cyberspace. And they accepted each other for better or worse from their distant corners of disappointment and hope.

Rajani is still sitting on the edge of his hospital bed when the nurse enters.

"Time to drain your trachea, Mr. Robbins," she says. "And I'm afraid visiting hours are over."

"But I only just got here," Rajani exclaims. She stands up, her back to Eddy. Reaching into her handbag she withdraws the gold watch momentarily and puts it back. Eddy can make out the metallic links, the shine against her dark fingers. "It's only seven o'clock."

"Well, visiting hours start at four and end at seven. You'll have to come earlier tomorrow. The patient has to rest."

"Well, I will. And I want to speak to the doctor and find out Eddy's diagnosis. Will he be in?"

"Yes. He would like to speak with you. Can you come first thing in the morning?"

"Umm."

"Okay. I'll tell him you will be here at four in the afternoon."

Eddy closes his eyes. He can feel Rajani's lips on his cheek as he feigns sleep. She lied to him.

ॐ

The defence lawyer smells of cologne. He is tall, with dark curly brown hair, and moves with an air of casual confidence. In fact, the defence is the complete opposite of the Crown from the day before with his dandruff-specked hair and clownish manner.

"Miss Sri-skan-da-ra-jah." He enunciates each syllable of her name. "Did I get it right?"

"Yes." Sarojini feels stronger today, knowing Rajani is in the court, watching and praying for her.

"Or should I say *Ms*. Sriskandarajah."

"Sorry?" Sarojini responds.

"Do you prefer Miss or Ms?"

"I am not understanding."

"Objection," the Crown protests. "He is confusing the witness."

"Get on with your questioning," the judge says indifferently.

"Excuse me, I was just determining whether the witness pays attention to details," the defence explains. "You see, many career women prefer Ms. And given that you and your sister are successful business women, I just assumed you would prefer that title. You are a successful business woman, correct?"

The Crown stands up to speak. "Objection, Your Honour. The witness' relationship to the store has been made clear to the court."

"Make your point, counsellor," the judge says wearily.

"I'll proceed. Ms. Sriskandarajah, on August 7, 2003, you were the only person minding the store. Now, as you confirmed in your testimony yesterday, this was the first time you dealt with customers, the first time you had to work the cash and ring in sales. That is a lot of responsibility. You must have been under a certain amount of stress. Yet you seem to remember every single customer that came in that day, what they bought and who they were buying for?"

"Yes."

"Remarkable memory. I wish I had a memory like yours." He grins at Sarojini and then turns to the courtroom, inviting all to share in his self-effacing remark.

"Thank you," Sarojini replies softly.

"Now, you are sure that the three people who came into the store were buying lingerie for themselves."

"Yes."

"Yes. So you are saying that the defendant, Mr. Francis Hargreaves, was buying lingerie for himself." The defence lawyer chuckles again.

"No. I mean . . . he, himself do buying but he buying for wife."

"And the others, the two other people? For whom were they buying lingerie?"

"They are ladies. They buy for own self."

"Did they tell you this?"

"Well . . . I thought."

"So, the others didn't explicitly tell you for whom they were buying lingerie. But you claim that Francis Hargreaves told you that he was buying something for his wife."

"Yes."

"Ms. Sriskandarajah? Did you notice the defendant wearing a wedding ring?"

"I . . . no, I don't know."

"So you claim he was buying something for his wife, yet you cannot remember whether he wore a ring. This detail escaped you. Tell me, did you remember to ring in the sale?"

Sarojini looks blankly past the defence lawyer. She catches a glimpse of Francis Hargreaves.

"A bill of sale, a receipt? Was there anything to prove these items were actually sold?"

"No," Sarojini begins. "He took lingerie but not pay."

"Oh. So now you are saying you gave him the lingerie for free. Do you do this often? Please answer the question."

She tries to form her answer but in the back of her mind she hears a voice. *Please, we have some questions . . .*

Sarojini tries to recall the question, the heat suddenly unbearable.

"Please answer the question," the defence repeats.

Then she feels cold and hears, *It is just routine, for your protection, the protection of the village . . .*

Ripple of fear . . .

"Ms. Sriskandarajah."

"No."

"So the accused happened to go into the store and tell you he was buying lingerie for his wife. But you have no recollection of a wedding band. And you let him have some lingerie for free. Is this correct?"

Sarojini remains silent. It is happening. The accident. She needs to hold on.

The judge intervenes. "The witness will answer the question."

The defence moves towards her. She glances over his shoulder. The defendant smiles at her.

"Will you answer my question, Ms. Sriskandarajah? Answer the question."

Sarojini can feel the sweat trickle down her face, her skin grows cold and her body turns to liquid. She rises weightlessly above the stand, above his curly hair, above the box-like room, above the dirt road and plantain fields, above the soldiers, above her own body.

"*Yariandom*," she whispers. "*Yariandom, yariandom.*"

She had murmured that word over and over, but neither the soldiers nor her friends seemed to hear. She glimpsed her friends' trailing *dupattas*, as they disappeared down the road. Just moments ago they had been laughing, having left school early in an act of teenage defiance. They had all seen the jeep coming, stirring up the dirt, four men waving their rifles and smiling broadly. One in each seat. Four in the jeep. The four girls counted them and giggled, teasing each other about who would be paired with whom. But when the soldiers stopped — "Please, we have some questions" — her friends were frightened and ran. One soldier grabbed hold of Sarojini's arm while the other soldiers began chasing her friends. They soon abandoned that idea and returned to Sarojini. They asked her, "Will you answer some questions?" She was willing. After all, they needed her help. Perhaps she could help them. Also she was terrified that if she didn't help, her teachers and then her parents would find out. The soldiers said they were searching for rebels in the area. They said the rebels were using the villagers, hiding behind them for cover, even using innocent girls like her. They had questions. Of course she would help them. They crowded around her.

"We have to do a search to see if you are carrying any weapons. It is a matter of routine, a regulation."

Fifteen-year-old Sarojini complied. She was pushed from the road into the plantain field, a beautiful clear blue sky hung above her. It was mid-May, the full heat of summer was upon them, and although she could feel the sweat trickling down her face, she was getting colder and colder. Her limbs grew stiff. Her bare skin prickled with goose bumps. The earth froze under her. The ground was hard as the soldiers started to search for weapons. Some tool was soundlessly banging and banging against a rock that would not budge. Harder, they tried to shift it. One soldier after another took his turn. The earth kept churning up mud and filth and blood. But where were the weapons they were so convinced she had? She could see them digging, bodies hunched over her until nothing was left but a void, a dark and empty hole. Sarojini suddenly felt the mud on her fingers, under her nails, the aching muscles in her legs spread open, her raw parts wounded and exposed. She blinked up to the sun, surprised she was still alive. A soldier, standing above her tucked something into his pants. His dark, ghoulish thing. She could not even say the word in her language. *They* were the ones hiding the weapons, she thought as the jeep roared off. Then she dragged her ravaged body from the earth. The earth that had yielded such sustenance, such beauty, had turned in on itself. The sky too had betrayed her, turning grey, then black, crushing everything underneath. A monsoon in the middle of May. And all she could hear was the voice in her head repeating over and over, *"Yariandom."* Dirty.

౨

PAKI SLUTS.

The words were sprayed in huge, white block letters across the storefront window. A brick had been thrown through the glass door, shattering it and scattering shards on the ground. The alarm screams. It must have happened only moments ago, in broad daylight in an alley off a main thoroughfare.

This scene greets Rajani and Sarojini like a slap in the face when they return from court. The judge had seemed displeased. He had adjourned the cross examination to the next day and ordered a court translator. As the trial continues, the sisters are becoming more and more notorious. The vandalism is proof of this.

"Oh my God. *Aiyo, aiyo*. What next will happen?" Rajani exclaims, taking in the catastrophe. Sarojini stands in shock staring at the writing on the window. She reads the words out loud.

"What is Paki?" she asks.

Rajani answers with irritation. "For God's sake, Sarojini. Short for Pakistani, it's a derogatory word for —"

"What are sluts?" she asks.

Rajani rolls her eyes.

"Why they write this?" Sarojini asks in a dull faraway tone.

Rajani faces her sister directly, now addressing her in Tamil. "Not they, just one silly insignificant person, probably on drugs, desperate and stupid. Just forget about it. Come on, we need to clean this up."

Rajani steps carefully over the glass pieces and unlocks the door. Inside, she sees the wind chimes sprawled and tangled on the floor. She picks it up hurriedly and hangs it on the battered door. The phone is ringing. She glances at her cell. Off. She had forgotten to turn it on after court. She answers the phone on the counter. The police are on their way. Then she goes outside to see Sarojini, standing stone-still in front of the window.

"Sarojini! What are you doing? Come inside," Rajani says, approaching her sister.

"*Akka,* he didn't kill me," Sarojini says in Tamil.

"What?" Rajani asks irritably.

"He did not kill me."

"What are you talking about?"

"Those three women . . . he killed them all," Sarojini says.

"Yes. We know that. It is a tragedy." Rajani looks expectantly at her sister, urging her to continue. "What is it?"

"He could have killed me but he didn't," Sarojini explains. "Lots of times I could have been killed but I was spared."

Earlier, Rajani had been annoyed at Sarojini for stammering and erupting into Tamil in court. Now she looks at her sister with sympathy. It is true, what she just said. Sarojini had escaped death several times, in Sri Lanka and here. Death had swept her up in a wave and cast her aside, wounded, altered, but still alive. And here in their beloved Demure, her sister had been alone with a murderer.

Rajani speaks gently. "You're safe now, Sarojini."

"But why? Why did he do it? Why did he kill them?"

Rajani is uncomfortable. How should she know? Why do men fight, rape and kill? It was like asking why it rained. Why do we breathe? "Maybe he was angry. Maybe he hated them. Maybe he just could."

Sarojini continues to stare at the words on the window. "Those poor women. What they must have felt during their last moments. What were they thinking?"

"It must have been horrific."

"It was," Sarojini whispers softly.

Rajani studies her sister. Sarojini's eyes do not glaze over, nor do her legs start to shift. She continues speaking. Rajani finds this simple act remarkable.

"He could have killed me. There was no one else in the store. It would have been easy. He liked me, not really liked, but he . . . I mean he was attracted to me . . . but I didn't die. Others were killed, but not me?"

"Well, no one can really say why, but . . . maybe he was scared someone would come in and find —"

"No," Sarojini interrupts. "What am I supposed to do? What am I supposed to do with all this? These things in my head."

Rajani has never heard her sister speak with such urgency.

"Tell me. You can tell me."

Sarojini turns from the window to face Rajani but looks down to her hands.

"I know what they did to me, back home. Now I understand the accident. I never had a name for it. But it was the same, wasn't it? What he did to those three women, four soldiers did to me."

Rajani is terrified and relieved. For the first time, Sarojini has referred to the accident. What had happened to her in Sri Lanka. Rajani had asked her about it, but Sarojini had been silent. Rajani suddenly feels so much younger than her baby sister.

Rajani embraces Sarojini on the street, in front of Demure. But Sarojini's body feels stiff.

"What is it, *Thangachi?*" Rajani addresses her younger sister affectionately.

"I think I know why they did that to me." Now there are tears welling up in Sarojini's eyes. "You see, I was willing to help, I was friendly, I answered them, I stayed . . . even with the murderer, Francis Hargreaves, I smiled at him, I . . ."

"No. What he did, what any of them did . . . Francis Hargreaves, the soldiers. It was not you. You think you influenced it, could have changed it. Maybe it's easier to think there was a reason, and if we acted differently, we could have prevented it . . . but sometimes, there's nothing. Simply nothing you could have done. No, Sarojini. It was not your fault. None of it."

Occasionally people pass by glancing at them, then looking away. A lovers' quarrel, a sisterly row, the rage and tears of storeowners facing ruin. There is no separation between public and private in that moment. Rajani wipes the tears off her sister's face with a handkerchief.

Sarojini looks up to the window. "Paki sluts! Are we Paki sluts?"

"I think many would see us that way."

"But we are from Sri Lanka, not Pakistan."

"Then I guess we are Sri Lankan sluts!" Rajani asserts with a sad but defiant laugh.

Hand in hand, they go inside the store and wait for the police.

It is Sarojini, not Rajani standing in the doorway of Eddy's hospital room. A nurse enters behind her.

"Mr. Robbins, you have a visitor," the nurse says.

"Hello Eddy," Sarojini says, speaking through the mask on her face. "Rajani not come. There trouble at store. She talking police, she tells me come here. She very, very, very sorry. She coming later."

Eddy closes his eyes and then waves her in. Rajani has sent her sister in her place.

"Mr. Robbins," the nurse says, "Dr. Schultz will be in shortly to explain the diagnosis. Please take a seat, Miss . . ."

"Sriskandarajah," Sarojini offers.

The nurse smiles and leaves. Sarojini sits down in the chair. Eddy glances at Sarojini and then to the table: his black box, a pad and pencil and the remote control. They sit together in silence and wait.

He wonders whether he had made the right decision by agreeing to take Sarojini in six years ago. Had it been six or seven years?

He remembers how he and Rajani were sitting on the couch. She had settled inside the crook of his arm and turned her tear-filled eyes to him, clutching a letter from her mother. She translated the Tamil script, "*Amma* says, 'Sarojini no longer speaks. After the accident it seems no one can pry a word from her mouth. For a whole year she sat in a corner day and night, sewing and darning until her fingers bled.'"

When Eddy did not respond, for the first time Rajani raised her voice to him. "You do not understand, Eddy! The accident has ruined her. She was in hospital and everyone knows her condition. She will never find a husband there. You have to help her! Please help her."

Rajani didn't give details and Eddy never asked. He assumed his wife's sister had been disfigured, perhaps worse than his own throat, and he felt sympathetic, a kind of solidarity with her predicament. Finally he agreed to sponsor Sarojini. Her parents sold some land for the price of a plane ticket and entrusted their youngest daughter to her oldest sister in Toronto. Sarojini, sixteen years old and wearing a sari, arrived silent and seemingly aloof. She had become the complete opposite of the little girl whom he had met in Sri Lanka. The girl who, full of joy, coveted candy wrappers and proudly pulled him into her games.

Dr. Schultz enters and picks up the chart at the end of Eddy's bed and introduces himself to Sarojini. She says, "Hello, I am Eddy's . . ." She forgets the word for sister-in-law. "Wife sister."

"Are you comfortable, Mr. Robbins?"

Eddy nods.

"Well, I'm glad you are here." He looks at Sarojini, then back at Eddy. "The prognosis does not look good. The cancer has metastasized or spread into different areas, having started locally in the throat. There is the re-occurrence of the tumour, but the results from the CAT scan — that is the computerized axial tomography — shows cancer in the lungs, liver and spleen. Almost everywhere except your brain. That is in top condition. We could operate on the tumour but it would not help the other areas. I am afraid it is terminal. I am sorry. Do you have any questions?"

Eddy points to the paper and pen. Sarojini passes it to him. He writes, "Time left?"

The doctor shakes his head. "I really don't know how much time you have left. An hour or a month. Somewhere in between. The nurse will bring you some reading material that you can look through. There is a number to call for counselling if you want." He begins to turn. "Mrs. Robbins, you can stay the night if you wish."

Sarojini then corrects him, "I am not wife. I sister."

"Oh," the doctor says. "Right." Then he disappears as suddenly as he had appeared.

Sarojini turns to Eddy. "I sorry, Eddy. I sorry for this. For everything." But Eddy is silent, as silent as Sarojini had been the day she arrived. "Are you okay, Eddy?"

Eddy shakes his head, no. Then he lifts the pen.

His once robotic voice is now replaced by shaky handwriting, "What was your accident?"

Sarojini slowly takes the paper and writes — "4 men raped me. I was 15." Sarojini shows him the note.

Eddy looks at Sarojini and nods. Their eyes meet, momentarily.

⌒

As Rajani rides the bus to the hospital, her heart is heavy with what she has experienced in the space of one evening. She cannot believe what Sarojini has told her. Perhaps her sister's English is worse than she thought. Maybe that explained her stammering on the stand and then reverting to Tamil earlier in the day. How can she possibly think Eddy is dying? She remembers how three years ago Eddy had experienced a fainting spell at work and was admitted for tests, and then sent home from outpatients that very day. Eddy never complained. At least not about his health. And the cancer? He had assured her it was gone. And if it ever came back? They could cut it out again. The health care here is superior, Eddy remarked. Sarojini must have misunderstood the doctor.

The elevator doors open and Rajani steps into the quiet of the hospital floor. She notices a surgeon pass by in her operating greens. She thinks momentarily of the life her mother wanted for her: to be the first in their extended family to obtain a university education, to train and practise medicine in their village. Oh, if only she had achieved the thirty percent higher grade average required for Tamil students applying to universities in Jaffna. If only her intelligence held more value than her looks. If only the power in her country and the world could shift . . . What might have been? But then she would never have posted her photograph on the website. She would never have met Eddy. She would not be here.

Rajani approaches the registration desk and informs the nurse that she is there to visit Edward Robbins. The nurse looks at her book. "He is not in this ward. Please, take a seat and I'll try to locate him."

The nurse starts typing into the computer. Rajani has heard of this scenario. Where patients simply disappear off the records and hospital floors, their names and bodies transferred unceremoniously to the morgue.

Rajani cannot accept that ten years of life with Eddy must end like this. It must be a test, she thinks. After all, hadn't their married life begun as a series of endurance tests? Beginning on their wedding day, Rajani had turned her eyes to the ground and followed Eddy seven times around the nuptial fire, placing her trust in a man she had known for just a week. And after the wedding ceremony, she was duty bound to open herself night after night and comply with Eddy's desires. Daily, she had to smell his sweat, meet his gaze, listen to his voice and engage her mind within the limited sphere of *his* interests. Survival dictated that she speak softly, giggle in response to Eddy's jokes, anticipate his needs and keep her critical thinking in check. Conscious of all the hairpin turns she was making and would continue to make, she boarded a plane with Eddy to Canada.

In Canada, she faced another test as she stepped into his cramped and musty apartment. So this was the high-rise condominium he had described as luxurious. She swallowed her anger and silently vowed to make their situation better. She learned when to spend and when to save, how to budget and invest. And when she dreamed up Demure and made it a reality, she handed her earnings, well most of them, to Eddy. Hadn't she been a good wife? Hadn't she passed all the tests? She had thought so.

But after ten years, their marriage had gradually become a salve, something to heal wounds and soothe disappointments. It became a simple friendship built upon sharing a meal and anticipating a new video. And after Demure, it seemed they had more in common than she thought. Eddy gave her advice and was a sure support. She came to respect him, even enjoy him. Thinking of Eddy, Rajani does not regret any of her decisions. She realizes now there is nothing she can do. No decision of hers can reverse what is happening to Eddy. "One hour or one month." She must see her husband.

The nurse taps Rajani on the shoulder. "Edward Robbins has been moved to palliative care." She points the way, still calling out directions, as Rajani hurries down the hall.

⁓

Time is only meaningful if it is used as a container where actions are deposited. But Eddy has no actions to deposit, nothing to fill it with. Instead, time is consuming him, devouring him silently, a toothless mouth masticating and dissolving every inch of his body. Each day the pain intensifies, his strength weakens and he feels closer to his end. And he wants it to come. So he stops glancing at the clock, keeping track of the date and noticing whether the sky is light or dark. Hospital staff wander in and out of his room. Some stand by his bedside and fiddle with tubes, insert needles, clean him. He hears their voices as if he is not there. He could be floating. They could be floating. Ghosts. Goblins. Night terrors from childhood merge with adult fantasies. Everything, a dream.

When the woman with the dark face enters and sits on his bed, he remembers he is in a new room and she must be a new nurse. He doesn't care if it is day or night, or whether she has come to save him or perform a mercy killing. He accepts whatever she does as the next thing to happen to him.

"Eddy. Eddy, can you hear me?"

He knows her voice but has forgotten how to speak.

"Oh Eddy, I have been thinking of you all day. You are getting better, aren't you?"

The nurse touches his face and it is not a bad feeling. Her hands have been there before. He remembers them, a soft and sure touch.

"Even in this darkness, you look so pale. You know, Eddy, that was the first thing I noticed about you. Even at home under the sun, your skin hardly coloured. Of course you wore that wide-brimmed ridiculous hat and spoke loudly through your black box. All the villagers thought you were so strange. But you had a sense of humour. I almost wanted to cry when I saw you, but you made me laugh. Eddy, are you listening?"

Eddy can feel the slant of the mattress where it sinks under her weight.

The nurse continues talking. "Sarojini was questioned by the defence lawyer today. She's being called in again tomorrow. The judge wants a translator for her. She is nervous, poor thing. I was there. And . . . oh, Eddy, Demure is going under. It was vandalized today, a brick thrown through the door, nasty graffiti on the window. The police came. I had the glass replaced and . . . It's slipping away, Eddy, and I can't stop it. I keep thinking what can I do, how can I stop . . ."

The nurse's wrist is cold and hard. Then Eddy realizes he is touching her watch. Gold and glistening against her dark skin. He notices her glance down at it.

"I have a confession, Eddy. I bought this for myself. I've been squirreling away money, mostly for the airfares for *Amma* and *Appa* but . . . some of it I spent on me. This was a present for me. My reward. I hope you don't mind," she says tentatively looking up to him.

He recognizes her eyes and smiles. Rajani. And although he knows she deserves better, he realizes without a doubt that she is his. Then he feels for her hand and holds it. He realizes she is trembling.

"Eddy, what am I going to do?" she appeals to him. He can tell she is frightened.

Eddy pushes back the covers and opens the crook of his arm. Rajani slips in beside him and covers herself with the sheet. He feels warm now, feeling her breath on his chest. She is just the right size, the perfect fit.

༄

Early the next morning, Sarojini is back in the witness stand. Next to her is a court-appointed interpreter. The cross-examination continues, and Sarojini fears the questions from the defence lawyer. But Rajani has encouraged her to speak out. So Sarojini commits to tell all she knows. She searches now for Rajani, as she had done on the first day of court, hoping she has come. She focuses instead on her fingers, which mime the in-and-out motion of a needle and thread. It helps to anchor her in this world and in this moment, as she speaks Tamil, telling the court what happened on August 7, 2003.

"No, I did not give him the lingerie."

"But neither can you prove that he paid for it. In fact, Ms. Sriskandara-jah, you cannot prove that he was in the store. There is no evidence, only some vague memory of the actions of a man you claim to have remembered three years ago. Your testimony is inconsistent. No further questions."

"No!" Sarojini shouts in English. "I am scared."

"Your Honour, I am finished with the witness."

"I would like to hear what the witness has to say," the judge says. "Please continue." The interpreter resumes and Sarojini returns to Tamil, her hands sewing methodically, stitching the words together carefully.

"He left the store with the bag, and I was too frightened after what he had done."

Sarojini allows her mind to travel back to the day. "I was nervous at first, being alone at the store. So I practised the lines 'May I help you,' 'That will be $49.99 please,' and 'Thank you for shopping at Demure.' After I sold some lingerie to the first customer, a woman, I felt more confident.

"Two hours passed before he came in. Earlier I was asked how I re-membered what he looked like. Well . . . I remember because I watched him. It was the first time I thought a man looked nice. He was a nice look-ing man with green eyes."

The defence lawyer interrupts her. "So now you tell us you were flirt-ing with the defendant?"

And strangely, the defendant, Francis Hargreaves, interrupts the de-fence. "Let her talk." A slow and strange smile crosses the defendant's face. He stares at Sarojini and she looks away.

"Counsellor?" the judge intervenes. Then he nods to Sarojini to continue.

Sarojini starts to feel the heat again but breathes deeply and continues the stitching motion with her hands.

"In my culture, we do not look at men, but this day, well I . . . looked. I remembered the advice Rajani had given me. 'Mostly we will have wo-men customers, but once in a while a man may shop for presents for his wife or girlfriend. You must convince them of what a woman would like.'

"So finally I spoke to the man, 'May I help you?' 'I'll just look around if you don't mind,' he said, and turned away.

"I stayed behind the counter and watched him run his fingers through the racks of panties, checking the labels, feeling the textures. Then he moved to the bras and made a fist that he fitted into a cup: A, B, C. As I watched him, I became aware that he was watching me, too. I looked away feeling uncomfortable. Then I finally asked, 'Do you want to buy something for your wife?'

"'Yes,' he nodded, 'my wife is about your size.' He smiled at me, innocently, almost like a little boy. I felt funny, flattered and something else I can't describe . . .

"Some time passed and I started to feel restless. I wanted to finish the embroidery I had started that morning. I finally asked again, 'Do you want to see something?'

"The man held up a bra and panty set, and said, 'Would you model this for me? It would help me decide.'

"I felt his eyes move up and down my body. I was surprised and confused.

"'Why? I mean . . . what?' I asked. I thought I must have misunderstood his request. He repeated the question, this time ending with a broad smile. It was not innocent.

"I didn't know what to do, so I went back to my sewing machine behind the curtain. I knew I should not leave a customer alone in the store. But my head started pounding, and my legs felt weak. I had to sit down. I pressed the pedal and listened to the whir of the needle. I wasn't sewing anything but I wanted to sound busy. Too busy to model the lingerie, or do anything else.

"After some time I stopped the machine. Everything was quiet. I peeked out and saw the room was empty. I hadn't heard the bells ring as he left, but then how could I have over the sewing machine. So I picked up a stack of yellow silk and a pair of scissors, and went back to the counter to begin cutting a new pattern. I saw a slight fluttering from behind the dressing-room curtain. Why was the curtain drawn? And then, a sound. Was someone there? I went to the dressing room, still clutching the scissors. It was as if someone was struggling to breathe. Maybe someone had walked in, tried on some clothing and fainted. Perhaps she was having a heart attack. Whoever was in there was weak or ill and needed help. I drew the curtain slightly back with my free hand and saw him. Him."

Sarojini pointed to the defendant. He smiled back. She did not look away.

"It was him. He was . . . he had no clothes on. He was naked and sitting on the stool. In his lap was indigo silk and something else, bouncing. Then I saw what *it* was." Sarojini feels the hot blush rise in her face. It is still so difficult to say the word in her language. "He lunged towards me but I hit his wrist with the scissors, dropped them and . . . I wanted to run but could not. My legs could hardly carry me away. This thing happens to me, I get weak. I needed the counter for support. I stayed there.

"Then the man came out fully clothed and set the lingerie on the counter and said, 'I'll take these.' Then with his other hand, he pointed the scissors towards me, at my mouth. 'I believe these are yours,' he said.

"I couldn't move. Then I heard the bells. I wasn't sure whether someone else entered. I just watched the man lay the pair of scissors on the counter. I picked up the scissors and cut tissue paper to wrap the lingerie in before putting them into the paper bag. He grabbed the bag and walked away. He did not pay. Then before I could stop him, another customer was in front of me laying a small heap of white and blue underwear from the discount bin on the counter. The bells tinkled as the man left the store. And I asked the new customer, 'Will that be all?'"

The interpreter has a calm and steady voice. Sarojini feels exhausted. It is as if she has transferred all her strength and energy to this woman who stands beside her, communicating her experience so clearly and easily.

The judge asks the defence, "Are there further questions for this witness?"

"No, Your Honour."

The judge turns to Sarojini, "Miss Sriskandarajah, you understand that you are under oath. Is this the complete truth?"

Sarojini understands the judge but waits for the interpreter to finish the question before she answers. "Yes, Your Honour."

"Thank you for your testimony. You are dismissed."

Sarojini leaves the stand. She does not need to worry about her shaking legs, for her body is fully covered in her white *kurta pyjama*. But her cover is not from a sense of shame. It gives her comfort and confidence. As she walks to the back of the court she glances at Francis Hargreaves. He looks less threatening with the jury sitting opposite him, grave and committed.

Sarojini walks past members of the victims' families. A woman, a mother perhaps, looks at her and says, "Thank you." Sarojini whispers, "I am sorry for your loss." And Sarojini realizes something has changed within her. Then she opens the door and walks out of the courtroom.

༄

Rajani can sense the sunlight filter into the hospital room through the sheets over her head. She hears the orderly enter the room. He rolls the table up to the bed and sets down the breakfast tray, and then leaves without waking Eddy or noticing her.

Rajani feels happy. In a strange unexpected way she feels fulfilled, almost powerful. Maybe it comes from just having spent a night with Eddy. Or perhaps it is the realization that neither wifely duty nor gratitude brought her here. Simply the desire to be with her loved one. A choice. She pulls the sheet down and props herself up on her elbow.

She glances at her watch. "I've been here much of the night. Can you believe it?" She stares at Eddy for some time as he sleeps. His eyes are closed. His skin, ashen white. His breath, ghostlike. Through the plastic oxygen cone, she can see the hole in his throat. Something that once shocked her suddenly fills her with a sad fondness. Like a scar triggering a memory of a childhood tumble, a mixture of pain and pride. She wakes Eddy gently, knowing she will have to leave him behind.

༄

The next day is Canada Day. Edward Robbins dies peacefully in his sleep, with his wife close by. When Sarojini hears the news, she joins Rajani at the hospital, but the sisters cannot bear to return to their lonely apartment. Even though it is a holiday, they take the streetcar downtown to Demure. Rajani clutches a plastic bag containing Eddy's housecoat, slippers, his toothbrush and his black box. There are celebrations throughout the city. People wave flags or wear them, like capes floating from their shoulders. Some even have maple leafs painted on their faces. Although the revellers are all around them, they seem far away, on another planet that has somehow fused overnight with theirs.

Rajani and Sarojini approach Demure. The storefront window is still scarred with graffiti. The glass on the door has been replaced but everything feels precarious as if any loud sound or swift movement will topple the store. Sarojini opens the door but instead of going to her sewing machine, she sits behind the counter with Rajani. Ayline Wheatley's photo is still there, a reminder of a more hopeful time.

The sisters quietly plan Eddy's funeral. Then they do some accounting, reviewing the books and making grim calculations for the next few months.

Sarojini prepares some tea. Finally, she picks up the newspaper and begins reading — slowly, with determination — the account of the trial. Francis Hargreaves has been sentenced to life imprisonment. There was much evidence against the accused. Sarojini's testimony was only a part. A connecting piece. She looks up from the article, proud of her small but necessary contribution.

Rajani stands near the window. She stares through the graffiti, meaningless now beside her heartache and grief. Sarojini opens the door to let the breeze in. The bells tinkle gently. Then she brings Rajani a cup of tea.

"Do you remember how it started?" Rajani asks, speaking Tamil.

Sarojini shakes her head.

"We were all on the couch. I was tucked under Eddy's arm. It was Saturday night, his night off. A time for us to relax, make love and fall asleep in complete darkness. He had brought home the video *Striptease* with Demi Moore."

"Your favourite actress."

"Yes. We all watched together, this dancing woman. Our thoughts must have been so different."

"I remember," Sarojini says. "The next day I looked up Demi Moore in the dictionary and learned the meaning of 'demure.'"

"And Eddy went out and bought me a thong."

As the two sisters stare out the window, through the angry white words, they recall the events that came before. They think about those who survived and those who died, those who were silenced and those who learned to speak. In the end, what has come of this? It is hard to tell, but one thing is certain. They are here. Still.

Girlfriends

Sarita is driving east in a red Pontiac. It is the same car her parents bought her when she left home to pursue a career in the music business. Fifteen years later she maps her route back to her hometown, visiting the familiar landscape of her childhood, which ironically makes her feel more foreign with every kilometre she travels. She has embarked on a mission of madness propelled by her own insane desire to live a life of honesty.

Vikram Acharya, Sarita's father, turns seventy in October. He requires a nurse to assist him through his daily tasks: getting up, bathing, dressing, shopping, cooking and lying back down. Otherwise his mind is as lucid as ever. He reads the *Chronicle Herald* and the *Globe and Mail* every morning and occasionally visits the library to read the *New York Times*, the *Times of London* and *India Today*. He sleeps only to rest his body, which he complains has let him down despite a lifetime of vegetarianism and yoga. The last time Sarita saw him was two years ago when she flew home for the death anniversary of her mother, Madhuri. Sarita worries about the steady decline of her father's health since her mother's passing.

I will invite my father to come live with us, Sarita thinks. I will tell my father who "us" is.

The landscape reels in a repetitive pattern of crops, fences, telephone poles. Rural New Brunswick, although picturesque for a while, becomes tedious. It echoes the boredom Sarita experienced during her high school years, a boredom that stirred a panic inside her, urging her to leave home as soon as possible. She reaches for her cellphone, sitting on the empty seat beside her, and checks to see if Ling called. No messages. Sarita tosses the phone back onto the seat, rolls down the window and frees her long hair from the clasp fastened at her neck. Her hair flies but her thoughts are fixated on Ling.

They had an argument the morning she left Toronto. It began with Ling badgering her about scratching the surface of the new non-stick frying pan while preparing their Saturday morning pancakes. Sarita responded coldly by dishing out the pancakes and abandoning the frying pan in the kitchen sink. It was a silent fight. Simple really. Ling felt she should be accompanying Sarita. Sarita thought Ling's presence would complicate matters. They parted with a terse goodbye and skipped their usual kiss.

Sarita tries to counter these bitter thoughts by imagining her lover in a gentler scenario. She sees Ling sweetly cajoling one of her young patients to stick out his tongue. Ling never persuades children with promises of candy or presents. She simply asks, "What tastes worse, broccoli or tuna?" Then when the tongue of disgust juts out for a second, in goes the tongue depressor, swab or whatever apparatus is needed for diagnosis, and the job is done with little or no protest from the unsuspecting participant. The children trust her, even the ones with bandaged torsos or hairless heads, having gone through chemotherapy.

She's a saint, Sarita thinks. How can I argue with a saint?

Sarita feels guilty about leaving the frying pan. Now she is too far away to turn back and clean up her mess.

Highway signs mark the progress of Sarita's journey: "Welcome to Nova

Scotia." The small towns of Springhill, Amherst and Oxford suddenly bloom into existence. After one and a half days on the road Sarita should roll into East Hants early this evening.

She turns the dial of the radio and tunes in to the familiar voice of Willie Nelson. *You were always on my mind* . . . She grew up on Willie, Hank Snow and Glen Campbell, music so culturally contrary to the *raags* her father would play on his sitar and the beautiful *bhajans* her mother sang. Sarita sat outside these songs like a deaf audience member, endured them like the lame relative brought to an outing only because she could not be left alone. Her preference was to tune into CKCL and listen to Tammy Wynette, and crossover country homegrowns like Anne Murray and John Allan Cameron. This music inspired her dreams, a future on stage as a singing minstrel, equipped with cowboy boots, a fringed leather jacket and big hair.

She puts on her radio voice, "And now, next up on the Grand Ole Opry, the world famous Sareeda Acharya, with her hit single 'I'm an Indian Cowboy.'"

She smiles thinking how oblivious she had been to herself, her dark hair and skin, her family history, even her favourite foods. Now her self-awareness is an antenna, picking up signals of discomfort, risk and danger.

The scenery changes: a sprinkle of houses on the hillside, a funnel of smoke from the mouth of a factory in the distance, the trembling lip of the sea lapping the red clay banks. Southeast. Direction home.

In a short while, Sarita will see her father. They had maintained consistent and punctual telephone calls on Sunday afternoons. She adopted a non-committal, conciliatory tone. "Are you well? How is your health?" And he would respond in the affirmative adding, "I saw on the news, Toronto had that terrible storm. Is it true they had to call in the army to clear the roads?" So all traces of warmth and familial connection hung between inquiries of health and updates on the weather. With her mother gone, there was no soft buffer between father and daughter. No easy communication. Nothing in common.

Sarita remembers little of the days after her mother's death. She had donned an unreadable face and graciously nodded when friends and acquaintances expressed condolences and wishes for her to settle down and raise a family. Afterwards, she turned her attention to sorting out her mother's things and hired a nurse to care for her father, whose health had slipped from bad to worse. She paid bills, sent boxes of clothes to the Salvation Army and closed the ashram that her parents had operated since she was a child. After this series of tasks put a distance between her and her mother's death, she flew back to Toronto, walked into her one-bedroom apartment, collapsed on the sofa and wept. She fell into a deep depression, nurtured by self-imposed isolation and hours of television.

On a rare occasion, a couple of Sarita's friends had been successful in dragging her out of her apartment. They took her to an International Women's Day dance. While her friends joined others on a crowded dance floor, Sarita quietly nursed a beer at a corner table. Halfway through the evening, she was approached by a dynamic woman who introduced herself, announced that it was her birthday, and that she was born in the year of the Dragon — the only mythological creature in the lunar calendar. Sarita was so taken aback by the sudden and original offer to dance that she could not muster up an excuse to remain in her seat. Ling confessed that she had accepted a birthday dare to ask every wallflower in the room to dance. She also made it clear that she had no intention of forfeiting such intriguing company for the sake of carrying out the dare.

Sexy, smart and single, Ling had stomped into Sarita's life and dragged her out of her state of grief. She took Sarita camping, bought season tickets to a comedy club and taught her how to drive a motorcycle. Six months later, Sarita hired a U-Haul truck and had her mail redirected to Ling's address.

As she turns off the main highway, Sarita remembers the familiar strip of road her father drove every summer when he took the family camping or travelling out of province. The area is full of landmarks that spark nostalgic yearnings: the Wentworth Valley ski lodge, the Campers Villa with the red wagon wheel at its entrance, the mouth of a cave which faces the highway and conceals a river between its walls. Sarita's father would often pull the car over and get out just to search for a rare wild flower. Then he would quiz Sarita on the common ones they could spot. Such a game made it easy to laugh and share. But she was a child then. Now she tries to imagine a different conversation.

She will walk into the house, offer him a cup of tea and announce proudly, *Dad, I've found my life partner, the woman of my dreams . . . and she is a she. Her name is Ling. And yes, she's Chinese. No, I haven't forgotten that China invaded India in the year of my birth, but you can't . . . Yes, I know you love Chinese food, but I'm afraid she can't cook that well, although she does have great taste in cookware. Guess what, she's a doctor. I remember you said that if I didn't become a doctor, I should at least marry one. No, marrying a man is out of the question but . . . happy? Yes, I am happy, so very happy and well, we own a lovely house, in a great neighbourhood, and the reason I — well, we'd like you to come live with us. Yes? Oh Dad, thank you, and you won't regret . . .*

The lines are too pat. Her father would never ask if she was happy, let alone accept her relationship with Ling. The only time he ever mentioned the *L* word was when he was doing a crossword puzzle, searching for seven letters to describe a native of Sappho's home. And the only time Sarita was aware that he witnessed lesbians (at least thespians who acted like lesbians) was in a film about Vita Sackville West. When a love scene began, he cleared his throat and left the room muttering, "This country has no morals." Sarita recalls her mother's response, "The film is set in England, Vik, not Canada." Sarita reconsiders the conversation she will have with her father. Perhaps she should turn back. She decides to stop for fuel.

Irving Oil still controls this territory. Sarita remembers singing the jingle on the radio, "When you see the Diamond, Irving Red White and Blue, lalalala, it's waiting for you." She signals, slows down and turns into the station. It is a familiar friend, beckoning her home, a lighthouse guiding safe passage to shore.

Sarita belongs to a generation of children who grew up singing advertising jingles, attaching themselves to big oil companies like teddy bears. No matter how she tries, she can't resist the diamond in favour of the more politically correct Petro-Can she just passed. She continues to make Irving rich, because its logo reads home to her.

The gas station offers both full and self service. After being alone for hours, Sarita desires human contact. She steps out of the car and waits for the attendant. A heavy-set man with a scowl on his face stares at her as he approaches. If she were a cat, her tail would thicken, her back would arch, her claws extend. Instead, her inner voice rehearses the possible responses, *What's the matter, never seen a real Indian before? Or is it because I'm so drop dead gorgeous that you can't keep your eyes off me?*

"Sareeda," he says, "that you?"

His voice precedes his outstretched hand. The familiar east coast accent opens their lines of communication, the one that slides Ts into Ds and lingers long on Es and As.

"Yes?" she answers perturbed.

"I'm Greg. Greg McKenna. East Hants High."

"Greg McKenna?" She stares back at him, decoding his features now dulled and layered by years of eating, washing, working, living. Indeed, it is Greg McKenna. Greg was one of those guys with whom Sarita had been too shy to speak.

"Wow. I didn't recognize you."

"It would be the extra poundage," he offers. "You look the same . . . really good, actually." He compliments her with confidence.

She smiles, remembering Greg as a boy out of her league: athletic, handsome and popular. There was always a contingent of girls vying for his attention as he strode down the school corridors. He even had two or three boys shadowing him, hanging on his words, mimicking his gestures. Now Sarita notices his double chin, receding hairline and thick waist. There were pleasant features somewhere tucked away, blue eyes and broad shoulders, but time humbles or perhaps betrays.

"Guess ya want some gas?" He shoves the pump into the side of the car.

"Fill her up." She slips into a pattern of colloquial sayings she used before she learned how to deconstruct language. Her east coast accent soon slides out under her articulate, professional voice. She can almost taste it, salty and rough.

"Home for a visit?" Greg asks.

"A week's vacation." She leans against the side of the car, craving a cigarette. Then she remembers the safety rule about never lighting matches near fuel tanks and the fact that she hasn't smoked for years. She looks around.

"Do you own this place?"

"Matter a fact I do. It's a franchise. I guess it would be pretty pathetic if I was a hired hand," he chuckles. "But things are kinda slow. Had to lay off some workers recently."

He clears his throat and continues, "So where do you call home these days?" He dips the windshield sponge into the filmy, soapy water. The handle seems to disappear into his large, fleshy but capable hands. Like a wand, he slides it over the dirty window. All clean.

"I live in Toronto."

"And this baby brought you all the way here?" He pats the rear end of the Pontiac.

"Believe it or not, I got this car soon after I left high school." She pats the roof, mimicking his action.

"Hey, we've got a twenty-year reunion coming up in 2000. Gonna make it back?"

"I doubt it. Work, you know . . ."

"So what do you do there?"

"I'm a DJ for an FM station."

Sarita can hear her radio voice emerging. The voice that separates her lives, maintains order, protects her privacy. She stifles the voice, trying to act normal.

"I had a brief career as a singer/songwriter. I got sidetracked. Was better playing hits on the radio than making them up myself."

"Right. You were one of the band types." He smiles. "So, does your dad still have that yoga centre?"

"No. We closed it down when my mother died."

"Oh yeah. I heard about the accident. Sorry."

"Thanks. It's been several years but it feels like . . ." Sarita exhales a long breath. "Well, you never get over something like that. Anyway, Dad couldn't keep the ashram going without her."

"Too bad. My ex-wife, Sandra Fleming, you remember Sandy? She was really into it. I couldn't sit still for very long. Too fidgety. I kept wanting to shift positions." He laughs. "I think that's why she divorced me. How 'bout you? Got any divorces in your past?"

"No divorces as such, a few ex's. But then," she pauses and continues, "I guess you need to get married before getting a divorce."

"Never made it legal, eh?" He pulls out the nozzle, tightens the cap on the fuel tank and hinges the hose onto the pump.

"No," she responds flatly. Sarita hands him her credit card. He moves sluggishly into the office to do the transaction. She contemplates her monosyllabic answer, her habit of capping off a conversation when things get a bit too personal. Close down. Subtext: ask no questions, hear no lies. She is a pro at self-protection or possibly self-censorship, practised on her parents for some twenty years.

Greg comes back out with a six-pack of cola and a big bag of potato chips.

"Here. Take this for the road. And say hello to your dad. He'll remember me as the guy whose feet kept falling asleep in the lotus position."

"Thanks." She puts the cans and chips through the open window and places them on the passenger seat. Greg smiles and looks at Sarita. Not staring, just looking.

Sarita gazes out over the highway to the closed-down trailer park. Most drivers choose the new toll highway instead of Route 4, avoiding the up and down dizzy feeling of the hills. Sarita is cheap and sentimental; she prefers the original road. She wonders how long Greg will have to wait before the next old world traveller stops by.

"It's real nice to see ya, Sareeda." Her antenna picks up down home, easy listening, not too hard, not too soft. Then he diverts his eyes. "Listen, if you're around, maybe I could pick you up, go for lobster or somethin'?"

She straightens up, surprised, "Oh. Like a date?"

"I was hopin'," he says, his voice a bit uncertain.

"Wow. Another time, I would have jumped at the chance to eat lobster with you, even though I'm . . . vegetarian actually."

"We could have vegetables." He grins.

"But . . . ," Sarita interrupts then slows down. "The thing is I'm in a relationship."

"Serious is it?" he probes with a sweet smile.

Sarita relaxes. "Well, if I could, I'd make it legal."

"Uh oh. You got a guy with a commitment problem?"

"Oh no. No guy. The problem is women can't marry women in this country. Not yet anyway. But we're working on it." She waits for his response wondering whether she has to clarify things by saying the *L* word.

"Her name's Ling," she offers, "my partner."

Greg gazes out to the highway. "It's odd, eh?" he says.

Sarita regrets being so open. It's lovely, not odd, she thinks. It's pronounced by tossing your tongue from the roof of your mouth and letting the sound resonate in the back. Ling.

Then Greg says, "You can drive when you're sixteen, vote when you're eighteen and drink when you're nineteen, but you can be pushing forty and still not be able to marry the person you want. Strange world."

"I'll say," Sarita responds, now smiling broadly. "Oh, should I give those back?" She indicates the chips and the cola.

"Nah." He laughs and waves her away. She gets into her car and catches a glimpse of Greg's retreating figure in her rear-view mirror. Then it hits her. She just came out to the captain of the football team. She chuckles as she steps on the gas.

The road is uneven, erupting into small bumps and crevices. Her favourite part of the drive is coming up: the area where the mountains shadow the highway and you can see the river cut its way through the ravine. She remembers waiting for this section whenever her family drove northwest. Sarita would open the window and lean her head out as far as she could, letting the wind whip her hair about, ignoring the worried commands of her mother. Moving vehicles never did provide a good enough view. She pulls over. The wind is warm. The sun christens the gold and green leaves of the maples. The river sparkles below. On the other side of the highway she sees now the entrance of the cave that cuts into the side of the mountain. Dark, reddish clay walls hide a river: cool, refreshing, deep. Still, it must travel far to emerge on the other side where it can be seen and appreciated for what it is.

As she stands on the shoulder of the road and gazes down the steep ravine, she wonders why she stayed away so long.

ॐ

As he looks out the window, Vikram Acharya ignores the Shubenacadie River for the first time in his life. Instead, he reviews the changes he made to the front yard: the new mailbox is metal and lockable, the gravel road is now smoothly paved and the fence has been freshly painted. The property looks well cared for. Sarita should be pleased.

It was the summer sun reflecting on the river and the pristine ice coating it in winter that held Vikram captive in this part of the world.

"Such fragile and impermanent beauty!" he had exclaimed to his wife, Madhuri. He could never leave, so he and Madhuri accepted jobs as teachers at a rural high school, bought a farmhouse and opened an ashram. Vikram had the windows in the front room widened and lengthened so that anyone attending his Saturday morning yoga sessions could, while even in a headstand, enjoy the view: the intense colours in summer and the subtle ones in winter.

Vikram glances at his watch apprehensively. Then he sighs and makes his way over to a capacious couch, a hand-sewn quilt draped over its back. The room had changed. Some years ago it was minimally furnished with a pattern of exercise mats on the floor and a sandalwood shrine, display-ing representations of Brahma, Vishnu and Shiva. The shrine had been shifted to a remote corner of the room, making space for a large TV and stereo system. Vikram settles himself in front of it and clutches the remote control when he hears the car ascend the driveway.

"Deidre," he shouts, "she's come. Sarita is here."

"How do I look?" Deidre Jordan enters the room wearing a red print cotton dress, hugging her voluptuous figure.

"Change it."

"What?"

"It's too . . . mmm."

Deidre glares at him. "Okay, I'm out of here if you're going to go and get weird on me."

"I am simply commenting that you don't look very professional."

"I stopped being professional a year ago."

"The nurse's uniform might be a more appropriate choice," he offers seriously. Then breaking into a wide grin he says, "No, you look sexy in that too."

"Dirty old man." Deidre moves over to him and places a kiss on the top of his shiny, bald head. "She won't even notice me."

"I somehow doubt that," he says smiling. Then he rises from the couch. Vikram still maintains a dignified and elegantly lean figure.

Deidre extends her arm towards him, lending support. She hands him his cane and he adjusts his body by leaning his weight upon it.

"I'm infinitely better at everything when I'm horizontal," he says rub-bing his hip.

"That's what you think." Deidre gives him one of her warning looks. "Okay, today you introduce me as the nurse, but your daughter is going to be mighty suspicious when the nurse goes to tuck the patient in and doesn't come out until the next morning."

"Sarita's a late riser. She'll never notice. The one thing I could never teach my daughter was how to rise and shine at 6 a.m." Vikram opens the door, "Sarita, Sarita. Come in."

Sarita stands in the doorway; the weight of her shoulder bag distorts her strong but slender frame. Vikram takes her in. She is lovely but she seems tired, less vital. Sarita drops her bag with a thud and bends to touch her father's feet. Vikram gives her his blessing. He tries to lift her bag.

"Dad, wait, you don't have to."

"I have to. My daughter has travelled thousands of miles, alone, to visit me. Come. Sarita meet Deidre."

Sarita extends her hand. "Pleased to meet you, and thanks for everything. It was wonderful of you to jump in for Mrs. Munroe. Do you know how she is?"

"Oh she's fine. She loves her new position at the hospital. She won't be doing private care anymore. For your father or anyone else."

"Well I'm thrilled she recommended you. I don't know how Dad could have managed these two years without you. You will stay on, won't you?"

"Deidre is a fixture here," Vikram cuts in. "As you can see, she keeps me in top form."

"Above and beyond the call of duty," Deidre adds.

"No. I hope he gives you time off. I'm a firm believer in overtime pay." Sarita looks disapprovingly at her father.

"Come, Sarita. We'll eat and then you can tell us your news and update us on workers' rights."

Vikram directs everyone into the kitchen where the wide window overlooks the river. Sarita washes her hands and sits down at the table set for three, as Deidre bustles about serving dollops of *dhal* and *subzi* on heaps of rice.

"Oh. So you cook Indian food?" Sarita says, scooping the food up with her fingers.

"Actually your father made this. I've tried cooking Indian but . . . well, I'm on supper duty tomorrow so you'll get a taste of my cooking then." Deidre flashes her beautiful smile at Sarita. She is sixty-two-years old but has that smooth glowing complexion that defies the tug and pull of age.

"Oh, you don't have to cook while I'm here. I can take over the household things."

"Actually I'd prefer — " Vikram responds.

"In fact, Deidre," Sarita interrupts, "if you show me the routine, I'm sure I could take care of Dad for a few days. I mean if it doesn't require too much skill."

Deidre smiles. "Your father's like an old tomcat. He fends for himself."

"Really? His health has improved that much."

"Yes, Sarita. My health has improved greatly, due to the dedicated care of Deidre here."

"Well in that case, Deidre, why don't you take the week off? I'm sure we can manage. And if we need your help — "

"I don't think that's a good idea," Vikram interjects.

Deidre's face opens into a slow, wide smile. "I think Sarita's got something there. I've been meaning to visit my mother. You know, she's much older than you, Vik, and she has nobody cleaning up after her. Thanks, Sarita. I'll leave you my number just in case." Deidre gets up from the table.

"Oh I didn't mean this second," Sarita appeals to Deidre who scribbles her number on a note and hands it to Sarita.

"Oh, I know, dear. But why wait. There's not much daylight left. I'll just finish up, pack some things and be at Mama's before sundown. How's that for spontaneity?"

"Deidre, stop this. What if . . . ?" Vikram speaks sternly.

"What if what?" Deidre responds, sitting down at the table across from Vikram.

Vikram has no answer.

"Fine. That settles it," Deidre says.

She finishes the food on her plate then disappears into one of the bedrooms. Moments later, she reappears, clutching a tartan cloth suitcase and a sweater.

"Now don't forget my number, though you probably won't need it unless you want to know where the mop is. And by the way," she turns to Vikram, "the dishes are all yours. Bye all, and have fun."

Deidre, her red dress and tartan bag leave the house. Sarita shrugs. Vikram reaches for his cane, hoists himself up and walks to the window. Sarita follows him. They watch Deidre throw her case onto the back seat of the car. The river is rose-tinted with the evening sun unabashedly throwing its gaze upon it.

"Hey. Isn't that your car?" Sarita looks quizzically at her father.

"Yes. But it's practically hers. My legs you see . . ."

Sarita makes her way back to the table and spoons some lime pickle onto her plate.

"Deidre seems friendly. I have to hand it to you, Dad. There was a time when you seemed quite intolerant of blacks, Muslims, Chinese . . . I'm surprised you hired her."

"Yes. Me too. By the way, she calls herself African Canadian."

"Good for her. I'm glad someone is teaching you identity politics."

Vikram nods in agreement and looks down at his plate. The food is suddenly unappetizing.

After dinner and dishes, Vikram and Sarita sit down in front of the television to watch a handsome young brown man read the evening news. They resume an old habit of keeping silent through the program and chatting during the commercials.

"Remember, when he first started on CBC, Mum used to hope I'd marry him."

"Well it made sense to her; he is Indian and grew up here. In New Brunswick, I think. She had big dreams for you. Marrying the news anchor was just one of many."

"Dear Ma."

"He is married and has children, so I've heard," Vikram says.

A toothpaste ad begins, featuring a slim woman in a t-shirt and underwear. Sarita and Vikram fall silent, noticing the model's shapely legs. Neither pays attention to her shiny, white teeth. Then the news anchor returns and Sarita breaks the silence rule.

"Dad, I wanted to talk — "

"One moment," he stops her.

The screen flickers with faraway images of a war — a green tinted city, periodically lit up by explosions. So far away from this quiet house on a hill overlooking a river. Glancing out the window, Sarita can see the strip of water become gloomy under a darkening sky. Soon it will all be black. Country nights.

Before the news program finishes, Vikram rises. Sarita asks her father if he needs her help.

"I am fine. Your room is all made up."

"Thank you."

"Don't thank me. Good night." He hobbles out of the room.

Sarita turns off the handsome Indian man and lies on the couch, staring at the ceiling. She is home, sort of. Every time Sarita has returned since her mother's death, she has felt her mother's presence: the flutter of the curtains pushing into the room by a warm wind or the familiar and humorous creaks of the floorboards. This time things feel different. Although Madhuri's memory is evoked in the very contour of each room, the place has changed. The furniture is rearranged, there is less space, and the only physical trace of Madhuri is a framed picture hanging in the hall. Perhaps there are more photos in her father's bedroom, Sarita thinks. Maybe it is hard for him to see her day after day. As Sarita rises to go to her room, she can hear the faint sound of her father's voice. Is he on the telephone? Maybe he talks to himself. There is no mother, only a daughter, a wobbly old man and a conversation that must occur. Sarita lies down on her old bed and uses her cellphone to call Ling. Ling patiently listens to Sarita's anxiety, then gradually becomes annoyed.

"I don't know why you've put this off for so long. There's never a good time and he's never going to like it . . . you don't expect him to say — oh thank god, I always hoped you'd turn out a lesbian. You'll just have to trust yourself and relax. He's a grown-up. Now you have to be one."

At 3 a.m. Sarita climbs out of bed. The phone conversation keeps replaying in her head. She is hungry. She is angry with Ling for telling her off.

For speaking the truth. She walks into the kitchen and stumbles around in the dark. Opening the refrigerator, she rummages around for some left-overs. There is some *dhal*, rice, fruit salad and something wrapped in foil. She reaches for it and unwraps a half-eaten roast chicken. Surprised at her find, she gasps as the chicken slides out of her hand and drops with a thud onto the floor. Bits of congealed fat and oil splatter from the carcass onto nearby surfaces. Her fingers feel slimy. She rushes to the sink to wash her hands before surveying the mess. The overhead light goes on.

"Sarita, what are you doing?" Vikram stands in the doorway in his housecoat, his trusty cane by his side.

"There's a chicken in your fridge."

"I know." Vikram hobbles to the closet and returns with a broom, a dustpan and a rag. "Deidre made it," he says.

Sarita continues, "You let her cook meat? Here?"

Vikram starts to sweep away the mess.

"Dad, I'll do that." Sarita wrestles the broom and rag away from her father and begins wiping the grease off the floor.

"She doesn't like vegetarian food very much."

"Oh," Sarita says.

"Well . . ."

Sarita rinses the rag.

". . . can you manage?"

"Of course, no problem."

"I'll go back to bed then." Vikram turns and heads into his bedroom. For the first time Sarita notices that this is the same room Deidre had popped into, to retrieve her suitcase.

Vikram rises at 6 a.m., two hours later than was his habit before his wife died and he had to close the ashram after developing rheumatoid arthritis. In the past he would begin the day with devotional meditation. Now he sits on the edge of the bed, prepares a needle and injects his thigh with cortisone. "Who would have thought I would need steroids to get out of bed," he laughed when the doctor first prescribed the drugs. But it worked. Now he is able to self-administer his medication, fix his own breakfast and take an Indian-style bath. All this accomplished before Deidre awakes. He enjoys the fact that at this early hour, he is sprightlier than his live-in nurse. Hell, he didn't need her anymore. Well, not as a nurse anyway. But this morning she was gone, as was the morning tranquility. Sarita knocks on his door.

"Dad. Can I get you anything? Do you want some breakfast? Do you need help with the bath?"

"I'm fine. I'm coming." Vikram is starting to feel uncomfortable with Sarita's presence. Or maybe it is Deidre's absence. He putters around the room like a lost dog. When he finally emerges, Sarita has a meal laid out: toast, fruit salad, cereal, tea.

"Good morning, Dad. I made breakfast."

"Yes. I see that." He glances at the spread. "I usually have half a grapefruit . . ."

"But your health — "

"Sarita, if you want me to become ill, talk about my health. If you want me to live long, hand me the newspaper or tell me something interesting about your big city."

"I'm just concerned."

"Don't be concerned. Everything is under control."

"Is it?" Sarita asks. Vikram chooses not to answer.

"How do you like your room?"

"It's the only room that hasn't changed. One would never know this place was once an ashram," Sarita says. Then she studies her father. She remembers his morning *pooja* at the shrine.

"Can you manage to meditate now, with your health?"

"I can no longer sit without extreme pain."

"I'm sorry." Sarita frowns, thinking of her father's once agile limbs, his ability to remain still for hours in *Dhyana*, focused and in complete oneness with God.

"It's okay. There is a lot to be said for upright meditation. I spend hours standing in front of that window," he says, picking at his food. She watches him steadily.

"All Mum's things are gone."

Vikram looks up from his bowl. "Not all."

"It's different. Being here."

Vikram doesn't know how to respond. Nor does he know how to inquire about Sarita's life. In the end, he is grateful for the abundance of food. It gives them both something to do.

On the third day of the visit, Sarita and Vikram decide to drive to a spot that Madhuri was fond of. They take the old Halifax highway past the Mi'kmaq trading post into Maitland. There is a lookout point over the Bay of Fundy where Sarita, as a child, had scrambled down the bank, to a chorus of "be carefuls" shouted by her mother and echoed by her father. Now it is Vikram insisting on climbing down the slope to walk along the muddy riverbed and Sarita voicing her concern. With his cane in his right hand and the other firmly gripping Sarita's forearm, he negotiates the rocks and weeds.

"Do you remember this flower, Sarita?"

"Mmm. It's a mallow, I think." She reaches for the stem.

"No, no." He stops her.

"I forgot. It's illegal to pick them, right?"

"It's a bindweed. And yes, better leave it in its own territory."

"No forced migration for this little thing," Sarita adds, steadying herself and her father.

"And those?" Vikram points towards a cascade of small white flowers on the slope.

"That, of course, is the beautiful, famous, but poisonous Queen Anne's lace. Originally from Europe."

"They're immigrants, like us," Vikram suggests.

"No. Not like us. Europeans were colonists, much like those dandelions, taking root everywhere, invading gardens, dominating lawns," she says facetiously.

"But remember, they are not altogether bad. Dandelions are pretty to some and edible to others."

"That's true. They have their place."

They laugh as they reach the bottom of the slope. The tide is out and the bay is reduced to a film of still water. On either side of the muddy banks, grass and cattails grow tall and straight while wild flowers bob their heads shyly towards them.

"Ah," Vikram exclaims, pointing out a purple-fringed orchid. "Your mother was so delighted with these and surprised they could even grow here."

"She was such an avid gardener. Growing so many beautiful flowers, orchids, roses, clematis . . ."

"And you," he reminds her.

Sarita smiles. "That's a nice way of putting it. All a kid needs is a little sun and water."

"Your mother was very practical."

"I know," Sarita says. "I miss her." Then after a moment she adds, "Those words sound so simple."

"Yes. They are simple but they contain the fullness of our hearts."

Sarita watches her father bend carefully and run his closed palm around the stem of the orchid, freeing the little petals from their stalk. He throws them into the quiet water and watches them float on the surface, sprinkling it with spots of colour.

After a moment Sarita whispers, "I thought that was illegal."

"Well, I can break the law once in a while for your mother."

Sarita's gaze follows the drifting petals.

"That's lovely. Breaking the law for someone you love."

A wind picks up, causing ripples to interrupt the calm surface of the water. They begin walking again. Sarita is content and confident. This is a good time to begin their talk.

Then Vikram says tentatively, "Sarita, I've asked Deidre to come back home."

"What?"

"Deidre. I asked her to come back so that you may get to know her."

Sarita stops as Vikram continues walking. He notices and turns to face her now several feet away. "Did you hear me?"

"Yes," Sarita barks louder than necessary. He waits for her. She does not move.

The wind begins to moan. He raises his voice above it. "I just think you both should get acquainted."

"Why are you talking about your nurse?" Sarita asks accusingly.

"I am just — "

"We were talking about Mum. Why are you suddenly talking about your nurse?"

Vikram is confounded. "Deidre is not my nurse, she's — "

"I don't care!" Sarita suddenly shouts.

Sarita and Vikram notice a couple walking nearby within earshot.

"I'm going back to the car. I forgot my camera."

Before Vikram can respond, Sarita walks past him towards the hill. He takes a seat on a large rock and watches the tide roll in. Scrambling up the slope, Sarita climbs into her car and locks the doors as if barricading herself against certain knowledge from which she cannot escape. She feels safe here in this old and familiar space. It is her refuge, her only consistent home. She turns on the radio, bypassing the rock and hip-hop stations. There is no authentic country music station anymore, she thinks. It is a little bit of everything: pop, country, folk, rock. Years ago a music producer advised her to do crossover music, some kind of eastern and western fusion, to capitalize on her background, her ethnicity. She looks at herself in the rear-view mirror, black circles around red eyes. Con-fusion is more like it, she thinks. I must call Ling. Sarita dials her cell and is greeted by both of their voices alternating phrases of the message.

Ling: Hello, you've reached Ling and Sarita —

Sarita: Sarita and Ling —

Together: Leave us a message. Thank you.

Sarita disconnects and sets the cell on the dashboard. She drums her fingers on the steering wheel, angry and upset. Unsure of how to face her father, she closes her eyes and falls into a troubled sleep. When she awakes, the sky is turning mauve with the onset of clouds. She can see the river from the car but there is no sign of Vikram. Sarita gets out and walks to the edge of the slope. After scanning both directions, she slips hurriedly down and curses herself for being so reactive. She walks along the river, retracing their path. This is open space, how could he disappear? Yet he has. Now she clears her throat and summons her loudest voice to command his response.

"Dad, Dad, where are you?"

The grass is now waving its blades, signalling a warning as the river swells with the incoming tide. As she walks, she feels the pull of clay underfoot and the splatter of rain on her face. Always listen to your fears, she reminds herself. Thank goodness, she has her cell. She reaches for the front pocket of her jeans. "Damn it," she says out loud. She left the phone in the car. Now she turns and runs in the downpour, chased by a river and regret. Back along the bank and carefully up an extremely slippery slope. When she reaches the top she nearly collapses against the car. She hears the beep of the horn.

In the car, dry and munching on potato chips, is Vikram. He rolls down his window.

"Where were you?" Sarita demands. Vikram holds out the package of chips. She waves it away and catches her breath. "How did you get here?"

"A gentleman in a Jeep drove me back to your car. Four-wheel-drive vehicles travel all over the riverbed and up the banks, as if it were pavement. Astounding really," he says enthusiastically. Then he slows down, noticing Sarita blinking away tears. "I was tired. It was getting cold. He offered me a lift, drove along the river and back onto the highway. Nice fellow."

"Thank goodness you're safe."

Sarita steps into the car and wipes her face with the sleeve of her sweat-shirt. Vikram stretches his arm in front of her, holding open the bag of potato chips.

"I hope you don't mind," he asks referring to the chips. "I found these here."

Sarita reaches her fingers inside and then suddenly, clasps her two hands together, scrunching up the bag.

"Jesus," she exclaims, "I can't . . ." She realizes she has just used profanity in front of her father. She stutters on, "I was so worried about you. I can't believe you would accept a ride with a stranger. Anything could have happened."

"But nothing . . ."

"It could have," she says. "It's careless, thoughtless, so . . ."

Suddenly, Sarita realizes she is shouting at her father. Someone she has never shown her anger to. Not even as a child. Someone she was taught to respect no matter what. She stops.

They sit quietly for a while, both looking out beyond the confines of the car.

After a moment Vikram says, "It was you who left me, Sarita."

Sarita glances at her father for a moment and then away. Was he trying to make her feel guilty?

Then he offers softly, "It was difficult."

"The slope?" Sarita responds, putting on her seatbelt.

"When your mother died. It's been . . . well, it was quite a challenge. I faced a crisis in faith, as they say. So much of my devotion to God was linked intrinsically to my relationship with your mother. When she died, I just wanted to go with her. Traditionally, the Hindu widow is expected to follow her husband to death. Even if she is living, all pleasure, desire, participation ceases. Her life stops, so to speak. That is exactly what happened to me. The world ceased to exist and my body began to fail me. Then about three years ago, I woke early one winter morning and stepped outside wearing only my slippers and housecoat. There had been a terrible storm the night before. Ice was laden on the tree branches, thick on the roads. There was nothing in the air but silence and death, incredible stillness and infinite beauty. In that moment I felt everything: cold, pain, sorrow, elation. I realized I no longer wanted to pass out of this life. I simply wanted your mother back. Here. Physically beside me." Vikram pauses and continues, "That proved impossible even with devotion. But even with that knowledge, I chose to remain part of this world."

Sarita looks at her father's profile, his strong chin, long straight nose, the high cheekbones and smooth skin. He never wears his suffering on his face. Hers, in contrast, betrays her emotions through teary eyes, a runny nose and skin that breaks out under stress. She admires his stoicism, his ability to reveal his emotions with dignity and control.

"I'm sorry, Dad."

"Don't worry, Sarita," Vikram says, turning to his daughter. "I have not given up and become an atheist. I have just learned to relax a little."

Sarita smiles. She starts the engine and reverses down the hill, away from the wild flowers, the rocks, the river.

Sarita wakes up before the sun rises. Deidre will be coming back tomorrow and Sarita has not had the conversation. She knows Ling will be sleeping, but she must speak with her. She is awake, completely, and she needs Ling to be awake with her. Ling picks up.

"What's wrong?"

"I can't tell him."

"Have you changed your mind?"

"He's having an affair." Sarita pauses and then says, "With his nurse."

"Well, I guess he's not that much of an invalid."

"Ling!"

"I'm sorry, honey, but affairs usually mean companionship, fun, sex."

"Please don't mention sex. I've been trying to avoid that scenario."

"All right, all right. Well, is he happy?"

"I don't know. He's just so cagey about it."

"Listen, Sarita, maybe he just doesn't know how to talk to you. He might be scared of your reaction."

"My reaction. What does he care about my reaction? He hasn't said anything, but I can feel it. His resentment. He resents me for suggesting Deidre take the week off. He resents me for being here."

"That makes two of us."

Silence.

"You're still angry with me," Sarita states. Then she pleads, "Can't you understand, it would have been harder with you here?"

"Sarita," Ling speaks firmly but kindly, "I'm approaching middle-age. I've lived most of my adult life alone. Now I'm opening our home, willing to welcome your father, whom I've never met, into my life. Is that not hard? I'm not doing this for my own amusement?"

Sarita asks hesitantly, "Why *are* you doing it?"

Ling replies softy, "Oh Sarita."

Sarita senses the deep tingly feeling that usually precedes a caress. But there is no one there to touch, only the cold phone in her hand.

After Sarita puts down the phone, she vows to have the talk with her father. Overcome by relief and hunger she goes to the kitchen to get a snack. Vikram is sitting at the table, carving a loaf of bread.

"Dad, I'm glad you're up. There's something I've been meaning to ask you."

Vikram beckons her to sit down with a wave of his hand.

"I came home for a reason. Well, two reasons actually. I wanted to see how you were getting along."

"And?"

"And you seem to be quite fine. And the second, well we're so far apart . . ."

"Please say what you need to say," Vikram says quietly.

Sarita sees that he is tired and most likely in pain as he periodically massages his leg.

"I think you should come live with us," Sarita blurts out.

"Us?" Vikram asks calmly.

"I've been meaning to tell you . . ."

"Yes, yes," Vikram responds impatiently as if these explanations are interfering with the purpose of the conversation.

"I think it would be better if we took care of you? My partner, Ling and I."

"I see."

"You don't seem surprised?"

"Chinese is it. Her name?"

"I mean the fact that I'm living with a woman."

"Your mother told me many years ago about you — your nature is how she put it."

"She knew?" Sarita is amazed.

"She often reminded me that this nature of yours is evident in our history, carved into temples and often mentioned in poetry. Anyway, why do you think we did not arrange your marriage with the newsman?"

"But why didn't she say something, or you?"

"What was there to say? You didn't say anything."

Sarita smiles. "So you're okay with it? You, you don't mind."

"I wouldn't say that. No." Vikram's voice was unreadable, his answer final.

Sarita feels a hot flush all over her body. She did not expect her father's rejection to have a physical effect. No. He is not okay. He is not okay with it. He is not okay with her. She rises from the table, turns her back to him, pressing her hands against the counter as if the closer she gets to it, the smaller she will become. So small that she can finally melt into the surface and disappear. But it does not happen. She is still here. He is still there. She pours coffee grains into the coffee filter.

"Sarita," Vikram addresses his daughter's back, "I have a confession of my own."

"I know," she mutters.

Vikram gets up and opens the fridge bringing out some cheese, mustard and something wrapped in wax paper.

"Good. Then you won't mind if I help myself."

Sarita turns around. "What!"

"This." He unwraps the wax paper to reveal slices of turkey.

"So she feeds you meat."

"I don't need to be fed, yet."

Sarita stiffens.

"But you're having an affair with your maid." Sarita spells it out, as if explaining the severity of his crime.

"My maid? I expected more from you, Sarita."

"I'm sorry. It's just . . . you don't expect me to take it seriously. What about Mum?"

"Your mother was here. Now she is not. I am old, I was lonely and . . ."

"You don't expect this to last?"

Vikram chuckles, "*I* don't expect to last." Then more seriously, he says, "I only want the present and I want to spend it with Deidre."

He continues, "No matter how comfortable you and Lee — "

"Ling."

"Ling make me, I will never be as comfortable as I am with the woman I love."

"Love?"

"Yes. Do you know it?"

Sarita drops her eyes. All of a sudden she feels shy, vulnerable. Love. Her father is so confident. But she? Does she love Ling?

"Yes," she whispers.

"Good. It's a gift." Vikram spreads the mustard. Then he reaches for the turkey slices and meticulously layers them together with the cheese on the bread. Sarita stares at him.

"Sorry, I've shocked you."

"I should have known, with chickens falling from the sky and all."

"It's very good." Vikram gestures toward the turkey. Sarita gingerly picks up a slice and dangles it from the tips of her fingers then drops it back onto the cutting board as if shaking off an insect.

"Why?" she asks, trying to hide her distaste.

"You see, Deidre has these vast family gatherings with grandparents, nieces, nephews, and they have celebratory meals. Chicken, lobster . . . I simply wanted to partake in the festivities. Be part of her life. And I guess I was curious."

"And tomorrow?"

"Tomorrow Deidre will come back home, meet my only child and be fully recognized as part of my life. And . . ." He slaps together the sandwich and says, "Soon, if you invite us, I will bring Deidre to Toronto to meet Ling. Then we will become part of yours?"

"I see. I have my girlfriend and you have yours. Is that it?"

"If you like." He takes a big bite out of his sandwich. "Are you sure you don't want some," he teases her. "It's delicious with Dijon mustard."

"No thanks. I'll stick with cheese." Sarita helps herself.

Beyond them, the river turns from deep grey to yellow as the sun yawns and stretches its rays across the eastern horizon, embracing everything within its sight. Sarita pours coffee into two mugs and hands one to Vikram. They drink in relative peace.

"Do you think your mother would like her?" Vikram asks.

"Deidre?" Sarita asks hesitantly.

"Ling," he answers.

"I don't know." Sarita's brow deepens as she ponders this for the first time.

"Well," Vikram asks, "what does she do for a living?"

"She's a pediatrician."

"Ah. A medical doctor. Good. Very good."

ABOUT THE AUTHOR

Sheila James was born in England and raised in Nova Scotia. Trained in music, she has performed and composed for stage and various media. She has released a recording of original children's songs, *Radio K.I.D.S.* Her performance art character and alter ego, Jimmy Susheel, has graced the stage of many festivals from Desh Pardesh (Toronto) to Women in View (Vancouver). Inspired by art and social justice, she has facilitated numerous "theatre of the oppressed" workshops. She also founded two community arts theatre groups: The Rice Girls and *Stree* Theatre. She has written several stage plays, including *All Whispers / No Words* and *A Canadian Monsoon*, which were produced by Company of Sirens, the latter in association with Theatre Passe Muraille. She has created and collaborated on four videos: *She's a Diva, Unmapping Desire, Lakme Takes Flight* and *Orphan Dyke,* and authored one screenplay, *Erased*, which have all been screened internationally to acclaim. The award-winning *Unmapping Desire* has been translated into French and German and broadcast by ZDF in Europe. Her poetry and short fiction have been published in various anthologies and journals. Sheila holds a BA (Honours) in Music from York University and an MFA in Creative Writing and Theatre from the University of British Columbia. She currently lives in Ottawa.